NO WAITING TO DIE

Alan Neibauer

Belayne Publishing

This book is a work of fiction. Names, characters, places, and incidents either are products of the author's imagination or are used fictitiously, and any resemblance to actual persons, living or dead, business establishments, events, or locales is entirely coincidental.

No Waiting To Die

A Belayne Book

First Printing
2002
Second Printing
2002
All rights reserved.
Copyright © 2002 by Alan Neibauer

This book, or parts thereof, may not be reproduced in any form without permission.
For information, contact Belayne Publishing at
www.belayne.com
Longport, NJ 08403

For more information on Alan Neibauer, please visit
www.neibauer.net

ISBN: 0-9718989-0-1
Library of Congress Control Number:
2002090732

Belayne Publishing and the "B" design
are trademarks belonging to Belayne Publishing

10 9 8 7 6 5 4 3 2

Right or wrong, I wanted to take care of this myself, to get the satisfaction of hurting Green and the others, as they had hurt Heather. One part of my mind knew that the police should be called; that we had enough evidence to warrant an investigation; that this was getting too dangerous for me to handle with a couple of amateurs. But none of that mattered. I wanted to see Green writhe in pain as Heather did, to see Cartmonde feel his arm being broken, slowly and deliberately.

That's all I could think about. This compelling hatred boiled in my head, intensifying with each painful breath, with each glance at the woman I loved.

Reynold London

She was killed by a karate blow to the neck.

One chop, no waiting to die.

Dedicated to
The Incomparable Barbara

Chapter 1

Did you ever feel like a real idiot, just out of place and totally out of whack? No matter what you did, you just wanted to crawl into a hole somewhere? If not, you're either the luckiest son-of-a-gun on the planet or you're just plain lying. Well, that's exactly how I felt that morning; the morning that started with two murders, and that kicked off events that would spiral way out of control and change my life forever.

It was one of those hot Philadelphia days that just soaked you with sweat no matter how little you wore. I had on a white linen suit and cotton shirt, a tropical outfit the tailor told me, but the sweat still made rings on the jacket under my arms. I looked like a jerk wearing a suit on a day like this, with everyone around me in short sleeve shirts and shorts, but I needed the jacket to hide the 38 under my left arm and the middle age spread under my belt.

It isn't easy being a detective these days, especially an older one. Younger women weren't impressed enough with the fabricated glamour of the job. I guess they never saw the reruns of Peter Gun or Mike Hammer; they just looked at me and saw a 48-year-old playing cop.

The older women weren't impressed much either. By this time in their lives, all they wanted was to spend money and entertain friends while their husbands worked 60 hours a week, staying out of their way.

I suppose I thought so much about women because I had no time for them, or no opportunity of finding the right one. I spent most of my time tailing wayward husbands or lesbian wives, knocking on doors for background checks, or collecting cars the owners couldn't pay for. Now that I think of it, I wasn't very impressed with myself either.

After all, the best I could show for 25 years was a marginal business doing the sort of work most detectives turned down. I had no big accounts, was never in the spotlight, and only once dealt with a murder case, when a 75-year-old lady hired me to find out who killed her cat.

Of course, I never got shot at or hassled by the police. But I was the court's best customer, spending more time in small claims trying to pry my fee from clients than I spent on their jobs. The only reason I carried the 38, I'll admit, was to prove to myself that I was really a detective after all.

This particular day I was on Fourth Street, standing next to my 1992 Toyota Tercel, watching the front of the Bourse Building. I was following a husband whose wife just didn't want him anymore. The poor sap didn't mess around, never drank or gambled. His only vice, it seemed, was being a devoted and boring husband who could no longer put up with his wife's personality and spending habits. She hired me to see if he did anything she could hold against him. It seemed like a waste of money; but it was her money not mine and I came cheap enough. This was the fourth day that I followed him on his business rounds.

Warren Trendle was a greeting card salesman (good lord, what have I been reduced to!) that went to any shop that sold cards, and many that didn't, trying to talk them into carrying his line. No one ever heard of his company so few stores wanted to bump out their better selling brands or make room for something new, but old Warren wouldn't give up. He'd drive to one part of town, park his car, and spend the day walking in and out of stores carrying a case full of samples that seemed too large even for King Kong.

Warren was making his first stop of the day at the Bourse, a reconditioned office building now with a basement and three lower floors full of trendy shops and restaurants. You know, the kind of stores that visitors looked at but are too pricey for the locals. The top two floors of shops were around a balcony, so the ground floor looked up three flights. The five upper floors were offices, with mostly lawyers, advertising firms, a doctor or two.

I gave up following Trendle into every store, and with large buildings and malls, I usually waited outside to give him a head start. I knew the Bourse had several stores that might carry cards so I figured I'd give the jerk twenty minutes or so before going in. I knew it wasn't the best detective work, but you get what you pay for.

At about 10:30 I wandered into the building and went to the first store on the ground floor, but no Warren there or in any stores on that level. The old boy was making pretty good time, I thought.

I couldn't find him on the second level either, and that was strange because there were two stores that sold cards of some sort. Maybe he started on top for a change.

I hustled up the escalator to the top floor before I remembered that it contained only food shops. Hoping that Warren stopped for a coffee I took a quick look around but didn't see him anywhere.

What an asshole, I really screwed this one up. Warren's probably up in some office plugging the hell out of some nympho secretary or 12-year old boy, and I'm down here picking my nose. Goddamn it.

The Bourse has two main exists so I decided to go downstairs and stand in the center of the ground floor where I could see both at the same time. From the third floor there were two ways downstairs. The down escalators were at opposite ends of the building so I'd have to run from east to west, go down one level, then run west to east for the next escalator. At the north end of the balcony, near the center, was an open staircase that folded back and forth on itself, going all the way down. It seemed the most direct route so I ran down the stairs, taking two steps at a time, holding onto the handrail, excusing myself when bumping into the tourists at each landing.

Jesus, I thought I was sweating outside. The building was cool but my self-hatred turned up the sweat glands to maximum so it rolled into my eyes and down my sleeves. I could feel my shirt sticking to my back and my shorts ridding up into my crotch.

What a sight. Here was a dripping wet madman standing in the center of a posh mall spinning his head from left to right, leaving pools of body fluid on the ground. Talk about being unobtrusive. People were staring at me, shopkeepers were standing at their doorways glaring, even the little convict schoolchildren cutting class for the day were walking 20 feet out of their way to avoid me. My goddamn gun was probably a ball of rust by now and every lunatic in the building was thanking God they weren't me.

And goddamn Warren. Probably having the immoral time of his life while his wife spends his hard earned money paying for this tub of whale flab to stink up the Bourse Building.

Warren. I saw him at the Fifth Street exit. I started to run but slipped on the sweat into a flower stand about 15 feet from me. I careened head first into the containers of cut flowers, like a ballplayer sliding onto base, just barely missing the old woman wrapping up a rose. Bowling for flowers. I tried to get up but my feet were tangled in the plants and the flower lady was yelling at me in some obscure foreign language. But I finally made it to my feet and ran toward the exit, or rather walked fast trying to look as normal as a parade of clowns in a cemetery.

I didn't see him at first. Fifth Street was pretty busy that time of the day; there were trucks making deliveries, and large news vans from the television station housed in the corner building were parked along the side. He was a pretty average sized guy, and there were a lot of Warrens walking around, salesmen on their daily rounds carrying briefcases and sample boxes.

Finally, I spotted Warren crossing the street. He walked over to a car I didn't recognize and sort of leaned against it. Then the old guy slipped to the street face down, his legs just going out from under him. That's when I noticed the trail of blood running across the street.

I was the first one over to him and I turned him around to see if he was still conscious. As he came around, his jacket opened up and I could see his shirt bloodstained and his right hand holding the end of a butterfly knife, like you see in those karate movies, that someone stuck right into his gut. Warren's dead, laying there in the street bleeding, and I'm worrying about collecting from his old lady. How the hell can I explain this one, not that she would care that much?

"You see lady, I was following your husband like you paid me to do. Only I was too lazy to really follow him every minute, so I stood in the center of the Bourse dripping wet while someone made a pin cushion out of the old man. Who did it? How the hell should I know? Can I have my money now?"

Worse than that, Warren's blood was running all over my tropical suit and onto my shoes, some Japanese tourist was taking my picture, and a meter maid was ticketing the car we're next to like Warren and me were invisible. Christ, I hate this job.

What would Mike Hammer do?

I grabbed Warren's case and figured there may be something in there, like an appointment book or something. My hands were full of blood now so I had trouble opening the case, but when I finally got both latches undone I found there weren't any cards inside; just stacks of hundred dollar bills and a 44 magnum. Jesus, get me out of there.

"Hold it right there."

Cops were standing on either side, their guns drawn, staring down at this idiot full of blood with his hands inside a dead guy's briefcase full of money.

I closed my eyes.

"The whole story, one more time."

Detective Bennite was about my age, a little thinner, but with more hair. I had already told him the whole story, showed him my license and notebook, gave him my client's name and phone number. He gave a little snicker when I explained how I lost Warren, and he said something nasty about private detectives. I don't think Bennite had much love for detectives, probably thinking all of us were incompetent slobs praying on the misfortunes of little old ladies. I certainly didn't do anything to change his mind.

For the second time I told the same embarrassing story.

"So you stood outside waiting. That's what you call following someone?"

"Like I said, for three days Trendle followed the same pattern. I figured why take a chance of being spotted when he went into the first couple of stores."

"Did you ever think that just today he might do something different?"

"The guy's a card salesman. I figured what could happen? Someone knock him off because they didn't like his Labor Day cards?"

"Well, someone did knock him off. And why was a card salesman walking around with close to a quarter of a million dollars."

"Jesus, a quarter of million. Maybe he had a good Mother's Day."

"Don't be a wise guy, asshole. Maybe you're no killer, just a two-bite slob of a detective that can't even tail right. But if you want to keep that worthless license you better start giving everything right now."

"I told you everything. The guy goes into the Bourse and comes out like a side of beef at the butcher. I don't know why he had so much cash. I don't know where he went. I don't know who killed him. But if I were you, I'd ask his old lady."

"Thanks for the advice, shithead. By the way, Mrs. Trendle confirmed your story. She did hire you to tail her husband. She said you were the cheapest detective she called, and she wanted me to tell you not to expect the last payment. Now get out of here. Just be ready to answer a few more questions."

Christ, the woman doesn't want to pay. Not another one. She paid me to get dirt on her husband, not be his bodyguard. This time I had it. No small claims court. I'd go right to the lady and demand she pay me. I was out three days of pay, her husband ruined my new suit, and now the cops were up my ass.

I walked back to the Bourse and found a parking ticket on

the Toyota. Add fifty bucks to the bill.

Mrs. Trendle lived about 15 miles away in the northeast section of the city. I went down Race Street and up Route 95 to the Academy Road exit. Her house was about five minutes from there off of Frankford Avenue.

Plain houses, middle class, neat but nothing special. Row houses they're called in Philadelphia. If Warren carried a quarter of million with him every day wouldn't they live a little fancier? What was a greeting card salesman doing with that much money? And why would anyone want to kill a guy who sold valentines?

I pulled up to the Trendle house. There was a black Lincoln parked outside and the front house door was open, just the screen door was closed. As I got closer up the walk, I could here yelling coming from inside. A woman was yelling something about capes, I couldn't tell for sure because my ears aren't like they use to be, and some guy was just screaming back.

Okay. I figured she's probably already spending Warren's insurance money on a mink cape and she's fighting with the salesman over the price. Hell, if she could afford mink she could damn well pay my bill.

"Mrs. Trendle," I called. "It's London. Reynold London. I know you're distraught but we have to talk."

Silence. The woman stopped yelling. The man stopped yelling. No noise from inside, nothing at all.

"Mrs. Trendle. We have to talk. I'm not leaving here until I get my money."

Still nothing.

Well, I'm not taking it any more. I saw the door was unlocked.

"Mrs. Trendle. I'm coming in. If you won't come out here I'm coming in. Don't give me any grief. I just want the money you owe me."

The house was a mess. Junk was scattered all over, the stuffing falling from pillows, and drawers were overturned on the floor.

"Good housekeeping, Mrs. Trendle. Where are you?"

I walked through the living room and dining room and into the kitchen. She certainly didn't clean, so maybe she cooked.

As I turned the corner I saw her standing there. Not Mrs. Trendle, but an oriental woman, with straight dark hair to the shoulders, high cheek bones and deep set eyes. She wore a simple white silk blouse open low, no jewelry or makeup, and dark loose-fitting slacks. Braless, her nipples pushed against the inside of the blouse so I could see their outlines clearly.

What a beauty.

As I started to speak, she lashed out with a blow to my midsection, and as I fell backwards I heard a man laugh.

"Okay, I'll take half off. Tell Mrs. Trendle I'll take half off."

The beauty took a step toward me and I could see she would cream me again. I scampered on all fours out to the living room and just had enough time to stand up and turn around when she kicked me on my right shoulder. I fell against the wall.

"Jesus lady, what's this shit all about?"

"The tapes. Where are the tapes?"

"Lady, all I want is my pay. I don't know anything about no tapes."

Zap. I took a hard one right into the stomach. But this time I got her; I threw up on her shoes.

"The tapes. Where are they?"

"Lady, like I said, I don't have any tapes."

She drew back slowly into some sort of karate stance, thinking I was so fat and scared that time didn't matter. But no matter how well my mother raised me this was enough. Like I'm supposed to take this Bruce Lee crap and not hit her because she's a lady.

I reached out with my left hand and grabbed a lamp standing on the nearby table. Maybe this broad knew how to dish it out but could she take it? I swung the lamp with all my might right into her head. The shade fell off and I saw the bulb break against her forehead. I supposed it stunned her because she staggered back a few feet then looked right at me, puzzled.

While she was dazed, I started to the door. I should have moved faster because I made it only a few feet before I heard this scream, turned around, and saw her leap into the air directly at me.

In my own panic I slipped on some paper onto the floor, but as she flew over me I just lifted up my foot as far as it could reach and caught her right in her beautiful ass. She went down hard, but just then this guy came running out of the kitchen, screaming, straight at me. Well, I put the old foot into action again and jammed it right between his legs as hard as I could. He bent over and I jammed it up one more time, just in case I missed one the last time, then I pushed him back with both hands.

Meanwhile, the lady started to get, up so I ran out the front door, got to my car, and drove to a phone booth down the street.

Detective Bennite got there in about 25 minutes. I met him at the phone booth and followed him to the Trendle house. By the time we got there the Lincoln was gone. The two who attacked me probably survived, but I wouldn't want to be that guy's lover after my foot got done with him.

Bennite called for Mrs. Trendle a couple of times, and when there was no answer, he went in slowly. I could tell he wasn't too pleased with me so I waited outside on the steps until I heard him scream "London get in here" from the basement.

All I ever wanted was my money, but in the basement I found Bennite standing over Mrs. Trendle. The lady was laying face down with a butterfly knife sticking straight out of her neck.

"You didn't say anything about this on the phone, London."

"I didn't know anything about it. Like I said, Miss Karate kept me pretty occupied upstairs. Is she dead?"

"She ain't dancing, genius. There's enough blood on the floor to float the Queen Mary and she's got a knife almost clear across her neck. You guess if she's dead."

I'll never get paid now.

"Is this the woman who hired you?"

"That's Mrs. Trendle alright. Last time I saw her was about a week ago, upstairs in the living room. It looks like they killed her and were searching the house when I came in."

"Any other conclusions, Sherlock?"

"They were trying to find some tapes. Maybe Trendle was blackmailing somebody. That's why he had all that money. But they got tired of paying him off and killed him. They didn't find the tapes on him so they came here looking. Only Mrs. Trendle didn't know anything about it, so they killed her then tried to find the tapes in the house."

Bennite just looked at me for a minute. "Brilliant. They pay this guy a quarter of a million bucks then search him. When they don't find the tapes they kill him with this karate knife then let him walk out of the building with their money."

He walked upstairs, took a look around the living room then continued, "Did you ever learn how to search a room in detective school, genius?"

"I can do a pretty good job."

"Well, the people that did this sure can't. Some pillows are slashed, some aren't. Most of the drawers have been emptied but the bookshelves weren't touched. Nothing's been done in the dining room or kitchen. So the living room is the only room they searched."

"So they weren't professionals."

"Bingo."

"But they kill like professionals."

"I don't think so. A professional wouldn't have killed Trendle and let him take all of the money with him. They certainly wouldn't have killed both him and Mrs. Trendle without first getting what they were looking for."

"Well, maybe they did find it," I said. "Maybe they found it somewhere in the living room. That's why they stopped searching."

"Sure. Then they waited around and started yelling at each other in the kitchen, with the nearly decapitated Mrs. Trendle lying downstairs, and they never closed the front door. I'll call this in and then let's go downtown so I can get a description of the karate kid. And let's talk about your license."

Shit.

Chapter 2

Bennite questioned me for about two hours then let me go. He called some clients of mine for reference, and told me to return the next day with anything I had on file about Trendle or his wife. I didn't like giving up my files like that but both the Trendles were dead now and I couldn't see the profit in detective-client confidentiality. I thought that the more I cooperated the easier I'll get out of this thing with my license.

It was about 8 p.m. when I got back to the office, which was about the only thing that I took pride in. Most of what I made went straight into rent. I had this two-room office in a high rise in Society Hill. It wasn't cheap but sort of made up for everything else I lacked in life.

The outer room was set up to look like a reception room, so every time a client came in I carefully explained that my "secretary" had just stepped out, or was on vacation, or just broke a leg. I made sure the place looked like I had a secretary, even picking out these picture frames in Woolworth's that came with photos of a nice average family. You know, the pictures that everyone else throws away when they put their own pictures in the frame. The group on my picture became the Brace family: Herb, Sandra, and little Ronald. The three of them were smiling with the sea and setting sun in the background. Sandra Brace was my second secretary. I had to fire the first, buy another frame and picture in Woolworth's, when a client recognized the woman in the picture as a porno star.

Sandra was one hell of a secretary and office manager. She kept pretty plants and always had a neat desk, but she could never quite pick up the phone before the answering service. I guess everyone has their faults.

My own office was just as nice, except I kept my pictures in a desk drawer. One was a nice shot of an attractive woman about 40 with two older children standing behind her. I pulled that out when I wanted to look respectable. The other was of this blond knockout in a string bikini, lying on the beach with her lips and legs spread just enough to tease the pants off a monk. That was when I wanted to look younger.

Behind my desk, to the left and right of the window, were shelves full of books. Most were 50-year-old law books that I inherited from a dead uncle, along with reams of his legal stationary that really came in handy when I had to threaten clients to pay. Of course, once or twice their lawyer tried to call Uncle Paul, that is if they didn't notice his building was torn down in 1965 for a parking lot.

Separating the two rooms was one of those partitions with wood on the bottom and frosted glass on top. This way I could see when some one entered the outer office. As soon as they closed the door I'd ring the intercom.

"Sandra, can you come in and take a memo to the DA. Sandra are you out there?"

Of course, when she didn't answer I'd open the door pretending to be annoyed.

"Oh, I'm terribly sorry. My secretary seems to have popped out. How can I help you?"

It actually worked pretty well.

I was at my desk, thumbing through Trendle's case file when I heard the outer door open and I saw the outline of a man enter the outer office. I rang for Sandra.

"Sandra, bring in the organized crime file please and get the Paris office on the phone. Sandra?"

I waited about ten seconds then walked over to the door. Four, three, two, one, open the door and look annoyed.

"Sandra, where are..."

It was the guy from Mrs. Trendle's, the one that wore my shoe for an athletic supporter. He was holding a short barrel chrome-plated Smith and Wesson 38, pointed straight at me. Thank God Sandra didn't get caught in the middle of this.

"Just walk out slowly, turn around and sit on the floor," he said. It might have been my imagination but his voice seemed a bit higher pitched.

"Listen, the DA will be walking in any second now to discuss the organized crime case. If I were you I'd just put that water pistol away and get out as fast as I could."

"Reynold London, detective for 25 years. Makes about 40 grand a year, if he's lucky, and spends most of it on his office. Specializes in shit jobs for anyone with a buck. Not married, no family, no friends. Four years in the marines."

"Don't tell me. You read that in Who's Who."

"Sit down, with your back facing me. Put your hands over your head and bend your head between your legs."

"You didn't say Simon says."

I was still walking toward him very slowly. For a minute I thought that if I got close enough I could knock the gun out of his hand and jam my fist down his throat, but he seemed a little itchy. He put his hand between his legs then said, "I'd listen to me if I were you. I've got a personal reason to blow little London right into the next room."

The thought of peeing out of a plastic tube the rest of my life was argument enough. I turned around slowly then sat down, lowering my head as far forward as it could go.

"Put your hands over your head."

"Okay. Now what's up?" I asked.

"I've got someone here who wants to talk to you. Keep your head down and don't look around. One peek, even a small one, and you'll have two 38 slugs for nuts. I'll bet it would be an improvement."

"You're the one wearing my shoe leather for shorts."

I went a little too far that time because he gave out a groan and started for me. Just as he got to my back, I heard, "That's enough Sim. Just calm down." I didn't recognize the voice.

"London, I'm going to ask you a few questions," the new voice said. "Like Sim told you, if you try to look up just once I'll make Sim a very happy boy and let him have you for dinner. You know he wasn't very happy when he left Mrs. Trendle's today."

"I guess Sim and the Karate Lady work for you."

"They and many others," the voice said. "They were there to collect my property. Property that Mr. Trendle got hold of and never returned."

"So Karate Lady or one of your other faithful employees played shish kabob with Warren's gut and his old lady's neck."

"None of my employees had anything to do with, or have any knowledge of, the death of Mr. or Mrs. Trendle. In fact, they were totally unaware that Mrs. Trendle was in the basement when you encountered them. If they had, they would have telephoned the authorities."

"Well, how nice. Good law abiding citizens wouldn't have tried to beat the crap out of me without at least asking my name."

He didn't say anything for a few seconds as if he was

carefully planning his next move.

"I'm afraid Sim and his associate became too enthusiastic in their work. You see, I generate a great deal of energy in my employees and provide them with excellent rewards when they achieve their goals. In this case, their reward would have been quite substantial."

"So that means they didn't find what they were looking for," I guessed.

"Quite right."

The blood was starting to rush to my head and I was getting nauseous from keeping my head down. I kept staring at this little ant on the carpet under me. At first the little critter just stood very still wondering, I suppose, what this behemoth was doing in his space. In between sentences I would blow a little air or spit on him trying to get him to move, but the more uncomfortable I became the more I wanted to take it out on the little ant. He (or is it she, how do you tell with ants) didn't have anything to do with my predicament, but here's this little ant as free as a bird while I'm crouched on the ground like some kind of guru with a gun at my head. Instead of being angry, however, I began to feel sorry for the ant.

After all, how would you like it if everything else in the world were bigger than you? In some ways, the little thing was just as helpless as I was. He could be stepped on at any time, eaten by some other bug, or even drown in my saliva, I suppose. And if he lived he was only one infinitesimal ant among millions that all looked exactly alike. How could they tell whom they were making love to? I couldn't always tell which end of the thing I was even looking at.

Thinking about the stupid ant made me miss what the boss

was saying but I regained concentration in half sentence.

"... so as you can see, we are in a predicament. We did not mean to harm you and only have to resort to this treatment so you cannot identify me and link us with the killings."

What goddamn predicament? That little fart of an ant made me miss the most important part. My legs are killing me, I got mixed up in two murders, and now some ant makes me miss something important. So I pretended to stretch a little and banged my forehead right into the little sucker.

"Don't turn around London", said Sim as he came behind me and pushed his foot onto my back.

"That's alright," the boss said. "Mr. London must be quite uncomfortable."

"Thanks for the concern," I sneered.

"Mr. London. Evidently you are a rather mediocre detective. You seem to have questionable experience and credentials. You are as insignificant as that ant you killed in such a charming manner."

How did he see that?

"But you are unfortunately tied up in an affair that can be very costly to me and my company. Believe me, Mr. London, under ordinary circumstances I would not even consider hiring you to take out our trash."

Thanks for the endorsement.

"However, I am proposing a very limited partnership. You will retrieve the missing property. You will be highly paid for the service and you will be left out of any other potentially violent situation."

Sim started pacing a little now. It seemed he wasn't very

happy with the thought of letting me live and I wasn't sure how far I could trust either one these guys.

"What happens if I don't find your stuff, or if I go straight to the police with this whole story?"

"Well, let's start backwards," the boss said. "You have not seen my face, so you will be unable to identify me. Sim here, and that is not his real name, will be transferred to a different part of the country by this afternoon so you will not be able to locate him. As for his associate, you called her the Karate Lady; she has an excellent alibi for her whereabouts when you said she was at Mrs. Trendle's. You will look like a fool, if not a raving lunatic, if you identify her and claim she is involved.

"Now, what occurs if you do not retrieve the property? You appear almost too stupid, Mr. London, to have anything to do with the missing property. From all appearances, it seems that you have stumbled onto this situation like that ant happened to find itself under your head.

"But perhaps no one could really be as incompetent as you and still be in business. So like that ant, if we find you too annoying or too useless, an associate of Sim's who you have not yet met will kill you. That is not the way we like to do business but we may have no other option available."

Okay, it seemed like an offer I couldn't refuse.

"How highly paid will I be when and if I return your property?" I asked.

"You will be paid one percent of the value of the property to my company."

Sim really didn't like that. He started to say "But Mr. Gr..." but was cut off with when the boss said, "Your reward would be a quarter of a million dollars."

The amount certainly sounded familiar since I just saw that much in cash in Warren's case. There were too many zeros for me to really be accurate but I figured that must mean that the total value of the property must be something like 25 million dollars. Sweet Jesus!

I took a guess and said, "Is that the same quarter of million you paid to Trendle?"

"From this moment on London, Mr. and Mrs. Trendle have nothing to do with our conversations."

"Okay, let's go into my office and you can fill me in on all of the details." I started to get up but Sim came back again with his foot.

"You have all of the details we can give you, London."

"Come on! I can't do much with this little. What was the property? How was it stolen? How can I get in touch with you?"

Sim kept up the pressure on my back.

"London," the boss said, "I strongly believe that you couldn't do much even if you were in our innermost confidence. We will tell you nothing more for now, and we will contact you when we want a report on your progress.

"Just keep in mind that we are talking about a very costly piece of property and one that has already cost several lives, those of Mr. and Mrs. Trendle and several more of which you are unaware. Not including your pet ant."

At that Sim made a movement behind me, pressed hard on my back and came down with what must have been the barrel of his gun on my head.

I woke up staring right into Bennite's ugly mug. I was lying on my office couch with a pain in the head that I thought only a wife could cause. It felt like the Statue of Liberty just beaned me with her torch.

Bennite had that "you're such a jerk" look and was talking to someone. I was still a little foggy and couldn't make out the words, so I scanned the room and saw a woman standing about five feet behind Bennite. I never saw the broad before but she looked really worried, like she cared if I lived or died. She was tall and thin, but not so skinny to be ugly, with medium length brown hair. She was wearing a red and black dress that hugged her waist, showing off a pretty nice front porch.

But Bennite's voice was starting to make contact with my brain.

"London, London," he was yelling, now shaking me.

"Don't wear it out," I said. "What the hell happened?"

"That's what I'd like to know. I got a call from Miss Brace, your secretary here, that she found you laying on the floor out cold."

"Miss Brace?" Maybe I was dead.

"When we got here, she had you on the couch and you were just starting to come to. Who did this?"

I lied. "No one. I tripped as I was walking out and must have hit my head on the desk or something."

"This bruise didn't come from any desk, London."

"I don't know. Maybe Trendle's ghost came back for revenge. I just remember that one minute I was fine, the next I was staring at this ogre standing over me screaming my name. Like I died and went straight to hell."

I looked over to the lady.

"As for Miss Brace ..."

"I just found him on the ground like I said, Detective. I saw that nothing seemed broken, so I got the janitor to carry him to the couch. I put some damp paper towels on his face and called the police."

"Well, I'm glad you did. If this jerk died I certainly want to be around for the pleasure. Listen, London, when your empty head clears a little come down to the station. Maybe you'll remember if you were hit by a desk or a ghost."

I could tell he didn't believe me but probably thought I was too stupid or small time to be hiding anything important. He nodded goodbye to the lady and walked out. I tried to sit up but my head hurt too much to rise.

"Okay, Miss Brace. Just who the hell are you?"

She came close to me and kneeled down by the couch. When she did her dress hiked up a few inches above her knees. God, what legs.

"If you could stop looking up my skirt, I'll explain what happened."

It took me a few seconds to give up the view.

"Okay, let's hear it."

"I'm sorry to have used your secretary's name to call the police. I found you lying so still I thought you might have been dead. You needed help but I didn't want to get involved with the police."

Our faces were about a foot apart and I was glad I traded views. She had flawless skin and bright intelligent eyes, a deep almost pastel blue, but I was transfixed on her mouth. As she talked her lips moved sensually and her tongue would just appear between rows of straight perfect teeth. I never knew lips could be so sexy before, and I just wanted her to go on talking forever.

"I noticed your secretary's nameplate on the desk so I used her name to notify the police. Mr. London, can you hear me?"

I knew what she said all right but not from my ears. Somehow her words went directly from her lips, through my eyes, and to my brain. She just knelt there, silent, her lips just slightly apart. Slowly they went into a broad brilliant smile and she took my hand in hers.

"Mr. London, are you alright?"

"I sure am, Miss?" Lord let her be a Miss.

"Oh, I'm sorry. My name is Heather Goldwyn."

"I've got a lot to thank you for Miss Goldwyn, but also a few questions." I was able to sit up on the couch but kept onto her hand. "Like what brought you up here in the first place."

"I need to hire a private detective. I live a few floors up and remembered seeing your nameplate down in the lobby. When I got down here, the door was open and I found you in the strangest position on the floor. I could tell something was wrong, so I rang Fred and he helped me carry you to the couch."

Her eyes looked up slightly and she started laughing. Not a "you're a fool" laugh but a "what a funny joke" one.

"I'm sorry," she said. "But there seems to be a dead ant in the center of your forehead."

Goddamn ant!

"That must have gotten there when I fell." I stood up and started to wipe my forehead with my sleeve when I figured that's no way to impress a babe like this. So I reached into my pocket for a tissue and turned around while I scrapped the creature off of my head. Turning back around I said, "Now how can I help you, Miss Goldwyn?"

Her eyes moved quickly from my forehead to my eyes.

"I want to hire you to find my brother. He came for a visit from Long Island, that's where he lives, two weeks ago. He stayed with me for about a week then one day he was gone."

"Maybe he went back home?"

"I tried calling him there but mom hasn't seen or heard from him. She's really worried. And he left all of his clothes, everything he brought down with him, at my place. He just left one morning to go to the store and never came back."

In all these years I only had one other missing person case, a wealthy woman disappeared from her estate in the middle of the night. That was real detective work: tracking down clues, interviewing friends and relatives, living on an expense account. It was just like the movies, trying to tell the liars from the rest of the pack. After two weeks of investigation, of using all of the tricks I knew, nothing had paid off. Then one day I went out to the estate to take one more look around for clues. The house was supposed to be empty so I figured I could look around without being disturbed. Anyway I used the key the old man gave me to get in and was down on all fours behind a sofa in the den looking under the furniture when the doorbell rings.

I didn't want to be bothered so I just kept on looking. The bell rang two more times then after about a minute, when I thought they'd given up, I heard a key go into the door. Meanwhile I'm still crawling around under the furniture, real quiet like. Through the sofa legs I saw two people enter, a man and a woman. Legs like those just had to be a woman's.

It turned out that it was the missing broad and some John she ran away with coming back to collect some clothing and jewels, maybe rifle the safe or something.

They started talking about how exciting it was to be sneaking around in the old lady's house and I guess they got a little too overheated because all of a sudden I saw clothes dropping on the floor, then these two dropped right down, the guy landing on top, just on the other side of the sofa I was hiding behind. Now picture this. All I could see was this naked woman, and she was some lady, and certain parts of the guy on top of her, if you know what I mean. He started rubbing and pushing, she started moaning and grabbing, both of them talking dirty. Now he's finally ready for the big time. I saw his hands slide up her thighs and under her rear end, her legs go off the ground, and he's getting ready for the launching when she swung her head to the right, opened her eyes real wide as he made contact, and stared right into my face.

Jesus! She screamed so loud, jumped up so quickly, that I wouldn't be surprised if the guy's thing broke in two. Meanwhile, the John didn't know what the hell was going on. He thought she's playing, so he tackled her in the middle of the floor so she's now laying on her stomach and he aimed for a place nice guys shouldn't touch. She's yelled "He's under the sofa, he's under the sofa" so big boy spun around, looked under the sofa and thought he saw this broad's husband under there.

In two seconds he's out of the house, naked, and driving off in his car. The lady just laid there on the ground with her ass sticking up, yelling, "It was rape, it was rape."

I told her who I was, and I helped her put her clothes back on. Then we made a deal. The story would be that I saved her from a gang of kidnappers and I'd collect my full pay plus a bonus from a thankful woman. I'd keep my mouth shut about the romp on the rug and the lady promised to stick it out at home. I think she learned her lesson. We told the old man that the kidnappers would probably kill them both if they went to the police so they all lived happily ever after. The old guy got his wife back; she had a couple of weeks of rampant sex with some young stud; and I got paid for a change.

Now I had a chance for another missing person only I don't want the case. This babe is too nice to hire a bum like me. She really wants to find her brother and, for some unknown reason, I don't want her to know what I'm really like. After all, she thinks I'm some hotshot Society Hill detective. I could take her money, maybe or maybe not find her brother, and get away with it, but there's something special about this Miss Goldwyn.

"I would really like to help, Miss Goldwyn, but perhaps you should hire a detective that specializes in missing persons."

She made this sad face and her lips pouted in a way that made me melt all over. Looking like she was just left standing at the alter, all sad and depressed but trying to hide it, she said, "If you really don't want to help, I suppose I must find another detective."

I tried to explain. "It's not that I'm not concerned about you, personally, Miss Goldwyn. But I think you'd be better off with another firm. I specialize in major criminal and corporate investigations, not personal matters such as this. I'll recommend some firms that have excellent records in locating missing persons."

All of a sudden I'm turning down business and talking like a goddamn college professor, with this professional and detached expression on my face while my stomach feels like I'm ready to puke up a six-pack. Heather started to get up and turn around when she started crying; long deep sobs that shook her whole body. This I couldn't take.

"Miss Goldwyn, please."

"Forgive me, Mr. London, I usually don't fall apart like this." Each word came with another sob. "It's just that I had such high hopes that you could find my brother. Fred speaks so highly of you, I guess I never thought that you'd be too busy to help."

Fred? She's ready to put her hopes on someone recommended by our wino janitor, a guy that couldn't even stand straight half the time without sticking a broom stick down his pants? The same Fred who eats cat food because he thinks it will give him nine lives. Fred recommended me?

"Please understand. It's not that I'm too busy or don't care. I'm just thinking of what will be best for you."

At that she sat down on the sofa and started crying even louder, her face buried in her hands, her body heaving with each sob. So I sat down beside her, just to comfort her you see, and put one arm on her back and held her hand with the other.

"I'm so embarrassed," she kept on repeating, then she raised her head and looked straight at me, tears streaming down her face, those heavenly lips puckered into a pout. I was trying to be calm outside but some parts of my body had different ideas. She slid a little closer to me so my arm could wrap more around her shoulder. Now her face was about two inches away from mine and I was going nuts inside. Should I kiss her? Should I say something? Should I just sit there staring at her? What the hell did she want me to do?

I started to bend over real slowly to get a little closer to her lips. I was about a half inch away, so close I could smell her toothpaste, when she stood straight up and started to walk out.

"I understand Mr. London. I'd better be going now. Thank you anyway".

I'm a goddamn weakling.

"Heather, I mean Miss Goldwyn. On second thought, I feel I would like very much to take on your case."

Chapter 3

Call me a sucker for a pretty face. I'm stuck in the middle of the Trendle case and I'm taking on a missing John. I sat by myself for a long time after Heather left, trying to figure out what the hell's going on. Or to be exact, what the hell's going on with me.

Here I was, acting like a school kid promising to do some babe's homework for a kiss while I'm failing every subject myself. I suppose I was never the type to examine my own motives very well. Jobs came along and I did them. Maybe I just ran from job to job, not stopping to look closely at myself, because I was afraid what I'd see; like some ugly witch with no mirror in the house. Am I the real Reynold London? Is this what I'm like, as a detective, as a man? Was it work that really kept me alone and isolated, or was it something else?

Maybe all of these years I've been playing games with myself, letting something deep inside drag me down to its level. Like when was the last time I really stopped to think who I was? But who really did that these days, this self-examination shit?

I didn't try my best because I didn't get paid that well. I didn't get paid that well because I didn't try my best. I sort of learned to live with that over the years, saying that I could be a hotshot detective if only life were worth all that effort. So what kept me here, in this office, in Philadelphia, playing cop with everyone laughing?

I only tortured myself when I thought this way. Years ago I went through hell trying to be perfect. I studied, I practiced, I even worked part time for some big-time agencies to get as good as I could. But I could never get quite good enough to please myself. Sure the boss was happy but I'd just chalk it off to luck, not talent. "Oh, anyone could have done that." No matter how hard I tried, no matter how good I was, I could never make myself happy. So somewhere along the line I just stopped trying so hard. When I failed I just told myself, "It doesn't really matter, I didn't really try hard enough anyway." So I got used to failing.

But things kept nagging at the back of my mind, like some old fishwife screaming night and day in her old man's ear, "You're no good, you bum."

My life was like trying to walk down an up escalator. Whatever was making me this way just sort of won out, I got too tired fighting with my own mind and just gave up, letting the conveyor belt drag me wherever it went.

Escalators, conveyor belts. Enough of this introspection crap. I had some big businessman and his Karate Lady after me. I had Sim who'd just love to make a woman out of me with a 38. I had this killing headache. And all I can think about was Heather's lips when she talks. I'm a goddamn moron; a middle-age, overweight, incompetent, balding, weak-willed moron who'll probably be dead within a week and never get a chance to hold Heather in my arms and feel those lips on mine. Okay, just slightly overweight.

And I had two choices. One, try to stay alive and find the tapes that are missing. Two, risk my life by spending my time locating Heather's brother. But I'll think about that in the morning. I rolled up my jacket into a pillow and relaxed on the sofa. I was tired as hell.

In the morning, I took everything I had on the Trendles down to Bennite. He didn't ask me about last night but paged through my folders, reading.

"I'll say this for you, London, you keep good notes."

"With my memory", I said, "if I don't write it down right away it's gone forever."

Bennite continued. "For three days Trendle acts just like a card salesman. He goes from store to store, doing nothing special.

His company checks out, they're clean, and so does Trendle. No record, no known criminal contacts, just an average guy with two grand in his savings account and a paid up mortgage. Your typical John Doe."

"So why's this John Doe found with a fortune of cash and a knife in his gut? Why's his wife iced and his house torn apart, at least one room?"

"Got me, London," Bennite said. "But as of now it's none of your business. It's mine."

"Hey look. I'm mixed up in something and I'd like to know what."

Bennite looked hard at me, and then said, "London, you're mixed up in nothing. You were in the wrong place at the wrong time. Twice to be exact. But unless there's something more you haven't told me, you're out of this now. Leave it to the professionals."

He emphasized that last word a little too much and kind of sneered a little. Maybe he was warming up to me, so I just forgot to mention that as far as I was concerned I'm still in on this.

I got out with my license intact and a decision to make: life or Heather? What the hell? I went back to my building and up to Heather's apartment. She answered the door in this little short outfit. Oh Jesus, did she look good. The shorts ended just above her knees and a belt accented her small waist. On top she wore one of those thin soft blouses that looked like it was made in India. It was loose fitting but you could tell what she was carrying, and it was unbuttoned just enough to show some skin but no cleavage. She turned to lead me in and I saw that the shorts were just tight enough to frame a perfectly sized and rounded rear-end. Isn't God wonderful?

Okay, so I'm a pervert. Sue me. This is a person, a human being, and not some sex object. She is a troubled woman, a person in pain because her brother is missing. She is depending on me, leaning on me, as a professional who can ease her pain. So why can't I stop thinking about that rear, as it rocks back and forth as she walks. Of that little waist, of those shapely legs, of those lips, that tongue. Of how she smells and how soft her hand felt when I held it last night. Of her smile and bright eyes.

Oh, shit. I'm there to find out about her brother and my hormones are running wild, my body starting to do these embarrassing things that I remember from teenage days, things I thought were dead by now. I flopped down on a chair before she turned around, then I took out my notepad, real professional like, and started the interview, trying to keep my eyes down on the paper.

"Tell me about your brother," I started.

Heather explained that her brother, Robert, was a college student in Long Island, majoring in computer science. He came into Philadelphia to visit her and some friends at a local school. He met them at some sort of convention a few years ago and kept in contact. He was a very serious student, a real bright kid but not one of these eggheads who could only talk about computers. She explained how he was getting interested in the theater and its history, and how he enjoyed doing research and writing. For about a week he spent the days with his friends while she worked, but they would spend the evenings together. One morning, before breakfast, he ran down to the store for a paper but never came back. She called the one friend of his that she knew about but he hadn't seen him in a couple of days.

"So why didn't you go to the police?" I asked.

"Well, Robert's a pretty good kid and never got into any trouble, but you know how college kids are these days. I really didn't know his friends and thought that maybe he was just high or partying somewhere. I thought of going to the police. But what if he were up to something, you know, in some kind of trouble. I wouldn't want to get the police involved if it were something I could handle myself."

"Is that why you didn't use your real name when you called the police from my office?"

"I suppose so. I just thought it would be best if no-one asked why I was visiting a private detective."

She started talking about Robert again, about his childhood and whatever she knew about him since she left home. As she talked I looked around the apartment a bit. This lady had good taste in everything. The place was real neat but with little trinkets all over, like small statues, vases, fancy books; kind of Victorian but without the clutter. And everything was clean. The carpet looked vacuumed, the windows shined, the place smelled as good as she did. I saw a couple of diplomas on the wall but I couldn't read them from this distance. That's when I realized I didn't know what Heather did for a living.

I interrupted, "What kind of work do you do?"

"I'm a college professor. In biology, at Penn."

Okay, hormones, at ease. She's great looking, neat, and smart. This babe won't have anything to do with a slob like me once I find her brother. I mean talk about from two different worlds; I got as much chance with this broad as Fred the janitor.

I pointed at the wall. "Where are the diplomas from?"

"My doctorate is from Princeton, but I did my undergraduate work at NYU. I moved down here for the job at Penn about five years ago. But that has nothing to do with my brother, does it?"

A goddamn doctor, yet.

"Any personal background, even that of his family members, might be of help," I said in my best professional voice. "Can you give me the names and phone numbers of any of Robert's friends, both here and at home?"

"I only know of one here, and just a few at home. Robert

and I haven't been that close since I moved down here. I mean these past five years have been important ones in his development -- graduating high school and starting college. Sometimes he seemed like a stranger to me."

"How so?"

"Do you have any brothers or sisters, Mr. London?"

"No."

"You'd understand if you had. When we were growing up our lives centered on the family. We played and fought, and joined forces to manipulate our parents, even though I was much older than he was. But as I got older my attentions went elsewhere, to a social life, then college, and graduate school. I lived on campus when doing my doctorate work and only saw him a few times in two years.

"Yet this was an important time in his life as well," she continued. "You know, a young boy maturing and learning the social graces. I missed sharing all of that experience with him. After a while, we became like brother and sister by familial accident only. I really didn't know the man he had become, just as he didn't know me as a woman."

"Did he act strange when he was here?"

"No. Not really. Remember, I hardly saw Robert in the last eight years or so. I couldn't tell what would be strange behavior for him."

"I mean was he nervous or upset about anything? Did he complain about anything? Were his friends weird, drugged, drunk, gay?"

She looked a little annoyed and said "I never really met any of his friends here, just spoke with one on the phone. He sounded normal. But actually, Robert was quite excited most of the time."

"About what?"

"Oh, this research he was doing about the theater, the early days of burlesque."

"I thought he was a computer science major."

"He was. But as I said before, he developed this interest in theater. I guessed he got involved in an elective at school, or even fell for a theater major or something. I didn't ask him a lot of questions about his social life."

"Did you talk about your social life?" I asked her.

"What would that have to do with anything?"

"I mean did he meet your boyfriend or any of your friends? Could he have become involved with any of them?"

"Unfortunately, I haven't had much chance for a social life. Working on my doctorate, now writing and researching for tenure, doesn't give a girl much of a chance."

Thank you, Lord.

"Now if you don't mind, I better get to campus. I don't have any summer classes but I do have a few students to advise. One's coming in about 30 minutes, but I'll be happy to meet with you later if you need more information."

We parted ways for the day but I took her last comment as a social invitation, not a business one. She had given me a picture of Robert that was about ten years old. "When he still seemed like my brother," she said. She promised to call home and get a more recent picture as soon as she could.

I drove down to the campus to find the one friend Heather knew about. It was another hot day and the traffic was murder. Center City Philadelphia was laid out neatly in squares but with mostly one-way streets, so if you turned the wrong way you had to go around in a circle for blocks. I finally got past town and went straight out Market Street till I got to the campus and found this guy's apartment. It was one of those college type apartment buildings filled mostly with upper level students too independent to stay in dorms. I took the elevator to the seventh floor, walked down the corridor to his room and knocked.

A female voice yelled, "I'll be right there, Ken." Then the door opened and this half dressed teenage girl appeared wearing real short shorts, and I mean real short, and a top that looked like a bra.

"You're not Ken."

"And you're not dressed."

"Oh, I always wear this around here. It drives the guys crazy. Listen, if you're looking for Stan, he's down at the computer center. You can come in if you want, but he might be a while. I'll be leaving in a few but you can make yourself at home, I guess."

"You don't even know who I am."

"If you're a friend of Stan's, you're okay."

She led me into the apartment. You know how you feel when you're really down and out, but you meet someone worse off then you? Sort of makes your own troubles look small. Well, this place made my own apartment look as clean as a goddamn hospital. There was crap all over, on every chair and table, all over the floor so you couldn't even see the rug, if there was one. Empty cans and bottles of beer were all over, and half empty bags of chips and pretzels. Dirty clothes were hanging from the lamps and from pictures on the wall, books and papers were scattered around. There was a small fish tank filled with what looked like brown water and a few fish floating on top. I couldn't see anything swimming, or even alive, inside.

"Have a seat," she said.

Have a seat? There was no clean place to sit down.

"Do you know most of Stan's friends?" I asked.

"Oh sure. They're here all the time. The guys from the computer club, the ones he studies with. It's like one big party."

"Do you know someone named Robert Goldwyn?"

"Goldwyn? Let me think. I don't think so."

She rummaged around the clothes on the floor. "Where did I put that top? I need it for class."

"He's a friend from out of town. Came in about two weeks ago, from New York."

"Oh, here it is."

She pulled out this t-shirt from under a pile of rubble, and then took off this bra thing she was wearing so she's naked from the waist up. She was about to put on the t-shirt but she just stood there thinking, almost naked, right in front of a total stranger. Kids.

"You know, there was a new kid around last week. Bob, I think they called him. Had this accent. Was that him?"

She saw me staring at her chest so she put her hands under her breasts, cupping not covering them, and pushed them up.

"Nice, aren't they?" she said looking at them like she's admiring a pet cat or something. Then she let go of them and pulled on the t-shirt that was printed "Touch 'em and you're dead" with an arrow pointing to each side.

"That sounds like him," I told her. "Do you know where he is now?"

"Nope. He just hung around a couple of days. Went with Stan to the computer center a few times. Then I think they went to work or something. Nice kid but a little up-tight."

"Did he talk about anything special? Did..."

"Well I'd like to chat but I'm off to class. Hang around if you want. I'll be back in a couple of hours. God knows when Stan will get back. Oh, if Ken ever shows up will you give him that box over there." She pointed to a small box on top of the desk, and then just walked out the door, leaving me standing in the middle of the room.

Kids. How the hell did they live like this? If I were Stan's dad I'd put him over my knee and beat the crap out of him. And if I were that girl's dad, I'd lock her up with some psychologist or social worker for about two years.

Now that I was alone in the room, and not distracted, I could really look around. It was worse than I thought. Pieces of some unknown food were over the floor, growing this white and green fuzzy stuff. I opened the closet and a few drawers, but found just more dirty clothes and papers in no apparent order. The refrigerator was filled with beer and about three half-eaten pizzas still in their cardboard boxes, and the freezer was empty except for some strange round green thing.

The books lying around were mostly about computers, a subject I knew nothing about. There were a couple of other books sitting on top of a counter, but they were closed, looking almost brand new. I started looking through the papers, more computer stuff, when the front door opened and this kid came in.

"Where's Sue, dude?"

"She got dressed and went to class. You Ken?"

"Yeah. Who are you?"

"Just a friend of Stan's. Call me London."

"Hey, call me Paris. Did Sue leave a box of disks for me around here?"

"You mean that box over there? She told me to make sure you got it."

"Yeah that's it, dude. Who'd you say you were?" He walked over and took the box.

"London, a friend of a friend of Stan's. Bob, from New York. Remember him?"

Ken looked at me strangely for just about a second then said,

"Yeah, I remember Bob. Kid with an accent. Was here the other day."

"What day was that?"

"You'd better ask Stan, dude. I'll go get him." He backed out the door, not turning around and not taking his eyes off of me.

Weird kids. I started looking through the papers again. I didn't know what any of them meant but most of them didn't look like college papers to me, just business memos, computer reports, client lists, that sort of thing. Some of them smelled, others were all dirty and crumbled up, like someone just threw them away and they landed here. Most of them seemed to come from an insurance company, Philadelphia Mutual, so I folded one of the letterheads and put it in my pocket when the door opened again.

Ken came in with this other kid, a big ugly guy with wild hair and a torn shirt. His old lady must really be proud.

"Who the hell are you, dude?" the kid yelled.

"You Stan?" I asked.

"Yeah, I'm Stan and you're in my place. Now who the hell are you?"

"Sue told me to wait here until you got back. I'm a friend of Bob's sister. The name's London."

"Hey man, I don't know no Bob. Why don't you just back on out of here, dude."

"I see you're an English major."

"Get the..."

I interrupted him before he got to the best words. "Bob's sister is really worried about him, and Ken told me Bob was here just a few days ago."

At that Stan glared at Ken and called him something having

to do with his mother. Then Stan started yelling at me, "I told you, dude, I don't know no Bob. Now get out of here."

"Listen you weasel ass." I always start out nicely to make friends. "Ken already told me that Bob was here the other day. Sue told me the same thing. Just tell me where he went so I can make his sister happy and you won't get hurt."

"So I won't get hurt, dude. That's a good one."

He looked over at Ken, nodded his head in my direction then the two of them ran right toward me. Stan came barreling at me with both arms out straight like he's going for my throat. I just stepped to the side and tripped him so he plowed head first into the refrigerator. By that time Ken was on top of me and threw a punch I could hardly feel. Didn't they teach physical fitness at college any more? I felt sorry for the sap until he hit me a few more times, then I gave him a quick jab with my left and a mindbender with the right. He went down into a heap on the floor. I heard a yell and I turned around in enough time to see Stan charging, so I stepped aside again and he went right into the door with a bang.

I may be dense but something told me these two guys had something to hide, so I grabbed Stan with a headlock and dragged him into the bathroom. That was a real mistake. I thought the room was a mess until I saw and smelled that bathroom. I won't even describe it, okay. I grabbed Stan by the hair and stuck his head in the toilet.

"Tell me one more time that you don't know Bob." I pulled his head up and he's gurgling out water.

"I don't know Bob."

One more dunking, then with his head out of the water I put on the final treatment.

"I could drown you if I want, but that would be too quick."

I flushed the toilet.

"See that suction pulling out the water? If I flush it again real fast, I can get your head down so the pressure would just hold it in. You wouldn't drown cause the water will fill up above your head but you'd never be able to pull your head out with all that suction."

He really started struggling now.

"Instead, you'd be in that toilet with your mouth wide open with only a little air and lots of shit backing up through the pipes. You'll suffocate either way, lack of air or over-abundance of shit. It doesn't matter to me." I reached down and flushed the john one more time, then started to push his head down into the bowl.

"Okay, Okay, I know Bob," he yelled, actually believing that suction routine.

I held his head down just far enough so the spray from the toilet hit his face.

"What was he doing here and where is he now?"

"He's just a friend, dude, just a friend. We had a few beers, a few girls, a good time. Then he just left a couple of days ago."

I pushed his head a little further into the bowl and touched the handle like I was going to flush it again.

"I swear man, I don't know where he is."

Sometime in life I learned how to tell if a person was lying. No matter how scared Stan was of me and that toilet, something was scaring him even more. I could just feel he knew something he wasn't saying.

Me? I'm not really an animal, and I didn't know if I could get his fat head stuck in the john even if I wanted to. So I dragged him back into the room and just threw him on the floor.

"I don't really believe you, asshole, but I don't have time to play Mr. Plumber anymore. If you're lying to me you better clean that john real good. It'll be your home for a long time."

Ken had already run out, maybe for support, so I stuffed a few more of the loose papers in my pocket and left.

The first thing I did when I got out was find a washroom and scrub my hands real good. The next thing was wait outside to see where Stan went.

Ten minutes went by until toilet head came out, his shirt still soaken wet. He looked around a little, mounted a small cycle parked on the sidewalk, and then took off down the street.

I started to pull out but some damn Ford cut me off and stopped right in front of my car, then these two hulks got out and came straight at me. Now these guys looked tough and one had his hand inside his jacket like he's reaching for a gun. With my car blocked, there was no way I could drive out, so I crawled out of the passenger side door and dove around the corner, these two guys following me. I just had this bad feeling.

I was pretty tired after my little experience with Stan, and no matter how fast I moved these monsters were getting pretty close. On both sides of the street were just college office buildings, no large stores where I could duck in and get lost in the crowd. Meanwhile Kong and Son were getting closer, looking real angry that I didn't stop to be chewed up, so I finally swung into this door where I saw a group of kids standing, hoping there was an office or someplace I could hide inside.

Goddamn college. There was one long corridor with small classrooms on both sides. The walls were all glass so you could see what's inside as you walked through -- not the best place to hide. Kong and Company weren't in the building yet, if they did see me enter, so I rounded a corner and took the steps up to the next floor. More of the same.

It's time to take a stand, I figured. I turned the corner where I could hide behind a wall yet still see anyone who came up to that floor and entered the corridor. Standing real still, I tried to control my breathing, catch my breath so I didn't sound like a wind tunnel testing out some jet plane, and then waited. Only kids came up, no hulks. Five minutes went by, ten, then twenty. Good going London, you gave the goons the slip. Looks like the old instincts were starting to sharpen after all.

With a new sense of worth, I slowly turned the corner to make sure it was safe, then headed back down stairs and out of the building. Still no sign of the two guys. Great. Moe and Curly must have given up. Still moving cautiously, I headed down the street and back to my car. The Ford was no longer there and my Tercel was just where I left it, half parked and half in the street, so I jumped in the car and started the engine. That's when I felt this arm grab my head and a cold rod of metal stuck at the front of my throat.

"You must be Larry," I said.

"The boss wants to know if you found his property yet." I didn't recognize the voice. It wasn't Sim or the boss himself, and it certainly wasn't a lady, the hand was too hairy.

"Are you guys following me around all the time? Maybe we should car pool." I could see the guy in the rearview mirror; he wasn't one of the monsters from the Ford.

He pushed the gun a little tighter into my neck. "Did you find them yet?" he repeated. This guy had no sense of humor, I thought.

"Not yet, but I think I'm getting close. Just tell the boss to give me a little space, some time. I'm getting close." I figured I could stall them just until I found Bob and could really start looking for the tapes. Instead of saying anything this guy just sat there, like he didn't know what to do next. I looked down at the gun, just to make sure his finger wasn't twitching. This jerk's holding a Bauer 25 caliber automatic, a woman's gun, with the safety still on and his thumb near the bottom of the grip, too far away to push the safety off in a hurry. Bennite was right; these aren't professionals. First of all, no real strong-arm would be caught dead with a piece like that. Second, you can't get very far with the safety on, and a professional would have his thumb on the lever, ready to slid it down just before he pulled the trigger.

So they sent some clown, who's probably holding a gun for the first time, to shake me down. I said, "Tell the boss I need at least two weeks. I think the tapes are out of town and it'll take me a little longer to find them."

"But..."

"Just tell the boss what I said and get the hell out." I was starting to feel a little cocky knowing that I was dealing with amateurs. You see, this guy was sitting in my back seat, of a two-door car. He couldn't get out of my side unless I got out first. So he slid over to the other side and reached down for the lever to release the front seat so he could reach the door handle. Only he couldn't find the lever and started to panic, like he's trapped inside the car with a guy he just threatened with a gun.

I was in love. I started the car, fixed the mirror, and turned on the radio, all very slow and deliberate. Meanwhile, he was trying to squeeze his hand, the one still holding the automatic, to reach the lever on the side of the seat, but he still couldn't reach it.

Okay, no traffic, I just pulled out and started driving away.

"Hey, stop. Let me out," he started yelling with a stutter.

"What's a matter hot shot? Can't get out?"

"Oh, yeah." He tried to pull his hand back out, to threaten me with the gun, only his hand got caught between the seat and the door. If the gun's safety were off, he'd probably shoot off his fingers.

Now he was really in a panic, but I got this strange thought and didn't want to play anymore. I pulled over to the curb and reached over to release the seat. It went flying forward dragging the guy with it; screaming because his hand got pinched in the mechanism. Then he opened the door and just ran out.

Something bothered me. This guy was a real clown, strictly an amateur or a rank beginner, but the two monsters in the Ford looked pro. They couldn't be from the same place.

Chapter 4

Kong and friends made me lose sight of Stan so my plans for the day were shot. I went back to my place, showered and scrubbed my whole body. If you'd been in that bathroom you'd take a bath in bleach. Then I rested up a while, trying to sort a few things out.

First, there were two different groups after me: the pros from the Ford and the clown with the Bauer. If one of them were from the Boss, who sent the others?

Second, what were Stan and friends up to? What were all of those papers all over the floor?

Third, clown or no clown, I'd better start looking for the missing tapes. Maybe they weren't professional and maybe they didn't kill the Trendles; but someone did, and the tapes were the reason. Of course, I really had no leads; Warren and his wife were dead and I couldn't yet identify the Boss or Karate Lady.

I relaxed on the sofa and looked at the papers I scooped off of Stan's floor. One, on the letterhead of Philadelphia Mutual Insurance Company, was a note from some vice president to the company's agents, announcing a hike in rates for the next year. Most of the rest were computer printouts, on wide paper with holes along the side. They had three columns, a name on the left side, and two columns of numbers toward the right. There weren't any headings or anything else on the pages, just the three columns. One last paper was also on a computer sheet but marked CONFIDENTIAL in big letters. It had two columns; one was just 6-digit numbers, the other was combinations of six letters followed by four numbers.

None of the crap made much sense to me. It could have been from a part-time job or a class assignment of some sort. I figured if I ran out of leads I could look into Philadelphia Mutual. but for now, Karate Lady seemed the best place to start. A quick look at the phone book and I made a list of martial arts studios in the area. Maybe I could get a lead on her at one of these, if she still trained. There were quite a few, so I decided to start that night after I rested. Anyway, I wanted to avoid Heather since I really didn't have any good news for her. Sure, I could place her brother up to a few days ago, but knowing Stan was the last person to see him wouldn't be too reassuring.

After dinner, I started visiting martial arts schools. It was some experience. I always thought that all karate was the same, but there seemed to be as many different forms and styles of martial arts as there were languages on the planet, such as Kung Fu, Tae Kwon Do, Hap Ki Do, Shotokon, and a lot of other names I couldn't even pronounce.

At each school, I explained that I saw a demonstration of martial arts and wanted to learn the same style. I described Karate Lady, saying she was the one who gave the demonstration, and tried to explain the style she used. The instructors would ask me how she stood and held her hands; where were her feet, were her hands open or closed, what type of kicks did she use. It wasn't very easy to explain since I'm not very coordinated and I was more concerned with saving my ass than studying her style, although she did have a great form.

The first nine schools struck out, none of the instructors seemed to recognize the lady but just gave me the hard sell to sign up for lessons. The instructor at the tenth school didn't know her either, but said the form seemed like Hap Ki Do, a Korean style of karate. He took out the phone book and wrote down a list of schools in the area specializing in that style. So the next day, Saturday, I narrowed the rest of my visits to those on the list. The fifth one paid off.

"Yes, I know the woman of whom you speak, although I was not aware she presented demonstrations." Master Kim was a young man, about 35, thin and strong looking like Bruce Lee. He was a Tae Kwon Do and Hap Ki Do instructor at a school about 20 miles from center city.

"Well, it was more like a private demonstration, among friends." I explained.

"She is a very talented woman, although she still has much to learn. Black belt, third dan."

"Dan?"

"Dan is the black belt level. The woman has a third degree black belt in Hap Ki Do and a third dan in Tae Kwon Do." Master Kim explained that he had a sixth dan in Tae Kwon Do and a fifth in Hap Ki Do. He started studying martial arts in Korea when we was just a young boy, then moved to the United States a few years ago to teach at his uncle's school.

"You know," I said, "I never really got the lady's name at the demonstration. I was just so impressed that I forgot to ask. Does she train here?"

"At times. She is no longer taking formal lessons. Unfortunately, her energies are devoted elsewhere, but several times a month she joins a class."

"What's her name?"

"Perhaps you should start training, and ask the woman yourself."

Is this a face you can't trust? Master Kim seemed to think so. Maybe he was just protecting the privacy of an honored student. Maybe he thought I was some nut off the street. After a few more subtle tries, and failure, I figured the best way to meet the lady was on her own turf, here at the studio, so I signed up for an introductory course, received a karate outfit and a schedule of classes. Tomorrow, I'd take my first class.

The class that night was at 6:30 so I killed the rest of the day around campus trying to get another lead on Bob. I stopped by the computer science department, the computer center, and the student center. No one recognized my description of Bob. At about 3 p.m. I decided to look up the Biology Department where Heather worked. I didn't think she'd be there on a Saturday but I just wanted to see her office, feel that I was close to her a little. Pretty childish, I know.

By looking at one of the campus maps, I found that the Biology Department was at 38th and Hamilton Walk, a pedestrian walkway that dissected the campus, starting near Baltimore Avenue and running east to west. It was housed in an impressive old stone building marked Zoology but called the Leidy Labs. Heather's room, 203, was listed on the faculty directory hanging in the entranceway so I went up to the second floor, taking two steps at a time.

Heather was impressive enough, but this place really made me feel like a dummy. The second floor was mostly laboratories filled with complicated looking equipment and computer printers buzzing away. Even though it was Saturday, students were working in most of the labs, and I heard conversations in English that sounded like a foreign language to me. I didn't know what the hell they were talking about but I just knew that these kids were damn smart. I turned right and walked to another hallway, then took a look at the room numbers hanging on the wall. Heather's office was just to the right but I took my time, looking in the labs on both sides of the hallway.

In one lab, four students or teachers, I couldn't tell the difference these days, were sitting around a small table. The lab was filled with odd-shaped glass tubes and bottles, powerful-looking microscopes, and electronic devices with blinking lights and meters. I stood in the doorway listening until one of them turned around and gave me a "what the hell are you doing here, fatso?" look. I took the hint and moved on.

All of the labs and offices had a large window on the door but most professors had white paper taped over it for privacy. It didn't cover the whole window so I could still peek in even if the door was closed. Some labs and offices were neat, with plants hanging up and little personal touches like pictures; others were a mess, with papers and test equipment covering every surface. I tried to picture Heather's.

Her office door was closed but I could hear that she was there speaking to someone, so I sort of peeked into her window, almost entirely covered with a poster of some plant thing with names and little arrows pointing everywhere. Looking in one direction, I could see a computer on a table, a pile of books sitting next to it. Looking the other way I saw something I wish I hadn't; Heather sat talking to Stan and Ken.

Okay, so she was probably their biology instructor. Okay, she probably knew when they last saw Bob. So why the hell didn't she tell me?

I hung around outside the office for a while trying to look like I belonged there when a few people walked by. But the more I waited, the more this thing got under my skin. Something was really scaring these guys; so you'd think they'd avoid Heather, the sister of the guy that touched off our little romp down Urinary Lane.

No, Heather couldn't be involved in anything. She's too sweet and naive. Maybe she doesn't connect her student Stan with Bob's friend Stan. After all, it's possible she even doesn't know they are one in the same person. That's got to be it, I told myself over and over.

It still bothered me, though, and I changed my mind about seeing Heather just now. If there was something going on I didn't want her to connect me right now with her visit with Stan and Ken. I figured I'd see her later that night and maybe put it to her straight.

I was just walking out of the building, back to my car, when somebody grabbed my right arm, almost twisting it out of the socket and behind my back. Then I felt this other hand grab my left shoulder. Sure enough, the two heavies from the Ford.

"FBI, London. Please come with us, peacefully."

The goddamn feds! I ran away from the goddamn feds!

"Hey, why didn't you just ID yourselves the other day instead of scaring the crap out of me that way?"

"You didn't give us much a chance, London." As we talked they were gently pushing me toward their car, my arm still twisted behind my back.

"So what the hell's this all about? Elliot Ness after me for having a drink or something."

The two feds didn't say a word, they just led me over to the car, opened the door, and made me get in, pushing my head down so it wouldn't hit the roof.

"Hey, watch the hair fella, it's all I got left." Once we were inside the car, and the doors shut and locked, Moe let go of my arm and Curly started talking.

"We'd like to know why you were up in Kensington's room yesterday and what you were looking for?"

"Who the hell is Kensington?" I asked him.

"Stanley Kensington, computer science major, apartment 705, Oslen Hall. You entered the room at about 3:15 and were alone inside approximately 15 minutes."

"Stan? That living example of unclaimed freight?"

"Why were you there and what were you looking for?" Persistent devils, these feds.

"I was just visiting; looking for a friend of a friend. The brother of a pal of mine, just came in from Long Island."

"What's your pal's name?"

"Listen, why don't you tell me what this is about first. Did I break some law or something?"

"What's your pal's name?"

"Don't you guys have to read me my rights, let me call my lawyer, put me under a heat lamp and pull my fingernails out or something?"

"Don't bullshit us, London. Yesterday you show up in Kensington's room. Today, you're lurking in the hallway after him."

"I don't lurk. I resent that."

"You might resent 10 years in the federal pen even more, London."

"Ten years for what? Staring at some coed's chest?" At that these two guys looked at each other real fast and then back to me. It was an inside look that I don't think I was supposed to see, so I took a chance.

"You know, I thought that babe's breasts were too nice for just a coed. She's undercover. She's a fed like you, isn't she? Well, not quite like you", I said looking down.

"London, you're getting into some murky water here. So murky that you might not be able to get yourself out if you fall in all the way."

"Come on guys. Did you ever see that chest?"

"Stay away from Kensington. Stay away from his room and his friends. All of his friends. We'll let you know when you can look for your friend again. All you have to know is that this is federal territory."

"Nice nipples, big and..."

The larger of the two guys hit me hard in the stomach, cursed, and then said, "Lay off of it, London."

I started to talk but they opened the door and pushed me out. I landed on the sidewalk with a bang.

"You're being a little rough for public servants," I yelled.

Then son of Kong moved into the front seat and they drove away into the sunset. Isn't that romantic?

Holy shit. The FBI is involved in this. What the hell is Stan up to? And do Bob and Heather have anything to do with this? I mean Heather is some babe, and I'd do anything to impress her if I thought I'd have a chance, but where do I draw the line?

After all, I wasn't used to being in the hot seat. Divorce cases, repossessions, minor league stuff was my stock in trade. Nothing to do with the feds, and nothing where I could get hurt. Now all of sudden Reynold London seems mixed up in two hot projects.

That reminded me that I had a karate lesson soon, and perhaps a chance to meet Miss Karate. I jumped in the car and made it to the studio at about 6:15.

Kim's studio was in a strip of stores in a nice middle class neighborhood near the end of Philadelphia. You walked into a small waiting room, now filled with shoes and a few onlookers. His office was on the left. The entire back of the store was mostly one large room, plywood floors, plain walls, American and Korean flags hanging above a mirrored back wall. There was a doorway at the back, maybe leading to the outside or a changing room. Ten or twelve white uniformed students were inside, stretching and talking quietly.

"Welcome to your first class, Reynold." Master Kim had come out of office and was standing next to me. This morning he wore civilian clothes but he was now in a starched white uniform laced with black.

"Please go into the back room and change. Mark!" he yelled to a student in the class who snapped to attention and yelled "Sir."

"Please show our new student how to tie his belt and properly enter the dojang." Then turning to me, he said, "That is what we call the training room."

"Yes Sir", Mark yelled. He ran out of the training room, turned and bowed to the flags, then turned again to me. He explained that every student had to bow to the flags when entering or leaving the training room, the dojang.

"And always address Master Kim as Sir."

On the way to the back, to where the changing room was, I noticed that the oldest student must have been about 25. There were as many men as women, all thin and trim, stretching or doing splits on the floor.

In the back room, Mark demonstrated how the belt was tied, he reminded me to call Master Kim Sir, and to stand and bow when Kim entered the room. He then went back into the main room.

I didn't have any trouble with the pants; they just pulled up and tied with a cord. The jacket was another matter. It had two sets of ties, two ties on each side. I pulled the right side over and tied it to a strap on the left. Then I did the reverse with the left side. The white belt was about twice my waist size so I wrapped it around two times and tied it in a knot before walking back out into the training hall.

"You're supposed to take your shoes and socks off." It was Mark waiting for me. "Put them in the back, and then I'll show you how to properly tie the belt."

Mark took off my belt then lined up one end right in the center of my stomach. He wrapped the other end around me twice, and then twisted it so there were equal lengths remaining on both sides. Then he looped one side under and around, brought the other side around and down and pulled tight.

"Stretch a little until Master Kim enters. When he does, stand up and bow. Say 'Good Evening Sir' and wait till he tells us to line up. Then stand in the back of the room, behind the higher belts."

Kim didn't come in for about ten minutes so I had time to look around. The room was bare except for some padded things in one corner and a couple of punching bags hanging near another. Most of the other students were pretty young, I'd say teenagers. Mark was about the oldest, and one other kid probably near twenty. He was talking to a young girl about cars, obviously trying to impress her, but he wasn't too bright, a perfect example of when cousins marry. I mean he reminded me of that old joke "What has 300 legs and seven teeth? Your family."

This babe was stretching and bending like the goon didn't exist, and he's going on about wide tires and wire wheels, the size of his engine, and how fast he can go. Whoever the hell said our future lies with the young never saw this kid.

Just then Mark yelled something and everyone jumped up to attention, facing the front door. They bowed at Master Kim, who was standing in the doorway, then muttered something in Korean.

"Okay, line up," Kim said. He looked at me. "Mark, help our new student."

Mark snapped to attention, yelled "Yes Sir" then ran over to me. "Stand in the back and follow what I do," he said. "Don't worry if you can't do everything today. It takes a long time to get into shape."

I kind of resented that. The girl standing in the front row yelled something, everyone jumped to attention and bowed again. They saluted the flag then got down on their knees into some meditation pose. This is pretty easy so far, I was thinking.

Kim stood, the rest followed, and then we went through a series of stretching and bending exercises. I did everything I could to follow them. So maybe I couldn't exactly touch my toes or bend all the way over, but I was keeping up until the twenty jumping jacks. Then everyone jumped to attention yet another time, bowed, and Kim yelled, "Middle punch". In unison, except for me, they snapped into a straddle and punched out hard with their right hand, the left held in a fist at the waist. As they punched they let out this loud yell, just like in the kung fu movies.

"Low. Bend your knees and kiap," Mark told me.

Just then I heard someone take their place behind me in line, and as we punched out with the left hand I heard the same yell she gave when she came at me at the Trendle's.

Chapter 5

I couldn't see her in the mirror at the front of the room, too many bodies were in the way, but I knew it was her. Jesus, does she know that I'm standing in front of her?

We punched a few times, and then Kim yelled "Low Block Middle Punch." I was trying to watch Mark so I could follow him while keeping my face straight ahead. We're moving up as we're doing this thing, then after a few steps Kim yelled, "Turn around."

I was getting caught up in the karate stuff and forgot why the hell I was there, so I just spun around and saw Karate Lady staring right at me, smiling. She didn't say anything or do anything to me; she just turned around and followed the rest of the class.

I'm in goddamn trouble, I thought. I had Karate Lady in one direction and a room full of Bruce Lee junkies all around me. This time, I'm stuck between a rock and hard head, my own for getting started in this thing in the first place. Now I was thinking so much about saving my own ass that I didn't know what the hell was going on. The class was going back and forth, blocking and punching, and I was just flailing around like a flag blowing in the wind. They turned one way, I turned the other, but always a few seconds later. By the time I figured out what they were doing, they started doing something else. Meanwhile, Karate Lady didn't say a word to me, she just followed the class.

I was sweating all over and feeling like an uncoordinated hippo dancing Swan Lake. I was in the middle of doing something and gave this yell, when I realized everyone else was standing at attention again. As I screamed, everyone turned around and looked at me.

"Joanne, please help our new white belt," Kim said, and behind me I heard Karate Lady answer "Yes Sir."

"Please come to the back of the room with me," she said. While the class went on with their training, Karate Lady and I were standing by ourselves at one end of the room.

She said, "Stand like this" and she got into some karate stance. "Your front foot is facing straight ahead, your back foot pointing to the wall, in a back stance. Bend both knees and shift your weight to the back. Hold your hands like this."

As I tried to follow her, I noticed she had a bandage on her forehead; probably where I connected with my "scared shitless lamp attack" maneuver.

I was standing there feeling like a real idiot. Remember, I'm no lightweight kid like the rest of these students. I'm old enough to be their older brother, with less hair and more weight, and I'm taking instructions from a broad who tried to mash my brains not too long ago.

Karate Lady, Joanne, walked to my other side, so her back was facing the front of the room and the rest of the class.

"Hold that stance. What do you want?"

What do I want? I said, "Hey, I'm sorry about that lamp but..."

"What are you doing here? What do you want from me?"

"Lady, you're the one that tried to tear me apart. Maybe I'm here learning how to defend myself."

She put her hand on her forehead. "You seem to do that rather well, Mr. London, and by using techniques we do not learn in the dojang."

"Why the hell did you attack me?" Now keep in mind that during this whole conversation, I was in this crazy back stance with all of my 225 pounds being supported by two 48-year-old bent knees. My legs were shaking, my arms were getting tired, and I still didn't want to move.

She looked around the room to see if anyone was in earshot.

"I am very sorry about that Mr. London. I really did not want to hurt you. I just wanted to retrieve something very important to me."

"Well..."

Two other students walked by. "Now stand this way," she said. "Both feet facing directly forward, spread so the back leg is straight, the forward knee bent. Keep your back straight and your hands like this. This is a front stance."

"You could have just asked if I had it," I said as I tried to mimic her position. "I didn't know what the hell you were talking about."

"Hopefully, Mr. London, the matter is closed now."

I yelled "Closed?" and everyone looked toward us.

"Keep your right hand closed like this," she said, embarrassed that Kim's attention was drawn to us.

"Mr. London, please speak lowly."

"Closed?" I was now whispering. "Your goddamn boss is threatening to kill me, Sim or whatever his name is wants to shoot my balls off, and you say the matter is closed. That doesn't sound goddamn closed to me."

"Profanity, Mr. London, is for those who lack intelligence and imagination." She looked over at Kim then back to me. "Now do this, a low block. Cross your arms over your right shoulder, bring your left arm straight down parallel with your forward left leg, and your right fist to your side. A low block."

I followed her instructions.

"Something is terribly wrong, Mr. London. You're life should not be threatened."

"Tell your goddamn boss that."

"Mr. London, we must find a place to talk privately. Can we meet after class in the restaurant several stores down?"

"If I live that long."

"Oh, you will live that long Mr. London. I'll see to that. Now do this. Step forward with your right leg and execute a low block. This time cross your arms over your left shoulder, bring your right arm straight down parallel with your forward leg, and your left fist to your side."

For the rest of session, Karate Lady showed me how to do more blocks and some other stances. At 8 p.m. we were all called to attention and Mark led the class in some school oath. Then we saluted the flags and meditated again, bowed to Kim and were dismissed. I changed with the rest of the guys in the back room.

"How did you like your first lesson?" Mark asked.

"It was interesting, alright."

"You're lucky. Joanne is a great student. It was an honor that Kim had her help you."

"Do you know anything about her?" I asked.

"Not much. She's been studying since she was a little girl in Korea. She shows up about once a week and trains with us."

"What about her personal life? Does she work? Is she married?"

"Got the hots for her, hey." Everything laughed.

"Well, let's just say I'm interested in her form."

"I don't know too much. I know she works for some big company. I heard her talking to Master Kim about it. But I don't know anything else."

One of the other students joined in, "She must be pretty rich. I've seen her a couple times being dropped off here. Big Lincoln, chauffeur and all."

That must be Sim driving, I guessed. "What does the guy look like?"

The kid looked at me suspiciously. "The driver? Short, ugly, real squirrelly looking."

    Sim, all right. I figured I'd better not ask too many questions. I was the new guy around here. But if she got dropped off before class, she was probably picked up afterward. That meant that we wouldn't be alone after class, and she didn't mention anyone else to me. I thought that this could be a trap, but it was the only lead I had, so I thanked Kim for the class, telling him I'll be back, and peeked out the front window. No Lincoln, and no sign of Karate Lady inside the school. Maybe I was just being too careful.

    The restaurant was small but nice looking, with plain wood tables and chairs, and a long counter at the back where you ordered food. Just a neighborhood pizza shop. Karate Lady was sitting at a table furthest from the window and as I sat down across from her I couldn't help but notice what a knockout she was.

    There was always something about Oriental women that drove me crazy. Maybe it was the long straight black hair, maybe the dark complexion, or maybe the stories about Geisha girls that I used to hear about as a kid. Sitting across from me, though, was now the perfect example of that fantasy woman from the Orient; dangerous and sensual, mysterious. She was dressed very casually in one of those wide-necked sweatshirts that hung over revealing one shoulder. Did this lady have skin! She had a perfect shoulder and neck, a flawless face with clear sharp eyes. She didn't look capable of harming anything, just causing immense exotic pleasure. In fact, she seemed almost shy and embarrassed as I sat down.

    "I hope you enjoyed your first class, Mr. London."

    "Call me Reynold."

    "Studying the martial arts can be quite rewarding."

    "Yeah, I felt how rewarding it could be," I said, feeling sorry the second I finished. From her tone, I could tell that she really believed in martial arts training beyond just the physical; from her face now it was obvious she was sorry what had happened at the Trendle's.

"Mr. London, Reynold, I am terribly sorry that occurred. If I could make up for the event..."

"Why don't you just tell me what this is all about?"

"That, I am afraid, I cannot do. I can just apologize for what occurred and promise that no further harm will come to you."

I stated raising my voice. "No harm will come to me? Your boss has already threatened me, even sent some weasel after me with an automatic."

"That cannot be, Mr. London." She really believed that. She really thought that sort of violence was out of the question. "We are a business, it is beyond us to threaten or cause harm to anyone."

I saw her discomfort and lowered my voice. "You better have a long conversation with your Boss and Sim."

"Sim?"

"That's the name he called the shithead who was with you that day. Sorry, for the language."

"That is not his name. John was my driver. He's been transferred to another office."

"Let me guess. Your new driver is a short ugly scumbag with real hairy hands, stutters when he's nervous."

"How do you know that?"

"He's the one that came after me with an automatic."

"No, it can't be. But I'll find out. Bruce will be picking me up shortly."

"Bruce?"

"My new driver."

"Tell you what. Bruce will lie his little stuttering head off if you just walk up and politely ask him. Let me ask him. When's he going to pick you up?"

"Any moment now."

"And if I can prove that I'm telling you the truth, that my life has really been threatened over this, will you let me know everything?"

"I'll tell you as much as I know. Even I do not know everything."

"Deal."

We got a couple cups of coffee and just sat drinking, talking about karate. The lady really loved the sport, for the physical benefits as well as the psychological ones. I learned that martial arts was a lot more than Bruce Lee beating the crap out of the bad guys in those awful dubbed movies. It developed self-confidence and self-control, concentration and a respect for human life, not violence.

"It is only the truly ignorant, or those that train for just a short time, that give martial arts its bad reputation," she explained.

When we heard a horn, she looked out the window and saw her car waiting. I gave her some quick instructions then ducked below the window where I could watch the car without being seen. Bruce got bored in a few minutes and started reading the paper. I waited until he was engrossed, probably in the comics, and then I slipped out of the restaurant and quickly into the back seat of the limo.

Bruce thought Joanne had entered. He said "Okay, Miss, where to now?" then turned around.

Just as he saw me, I put one hand over his mouth and the other at the back of his head, and twisted.

"Bruce, if I twist with all my might your neck will snap right at the spinal cord. You won't die but your body will turn into a paperweight."

He tried to speak but my hand was too tight over his mouth.

"You know, even if you cooperate I still might be tempted to snap your neck. Then you'll have to drag yourself around with your tongue."

I could tell he was getting ready to cooperate at this point; he was mumbling now, slobbering all over my hand, and shaking his head violently.

"Now Bruce, I'll let you go but you have to promise me a few things. Okay?"

He started shaking his head Yes.

"First, keep your mouth shut and speak only when asked a question. Okay?"

Yes.

"Second, don't even think of pulling a gun or trying anything stupid."

Yes.

"Third, don't even think of lying. One lie and I'll shove my 38 up your ass and give you a lead enema."

Yes.

I let go of my hands slowly, and then wiped the slobber off on his shirt.

"Now listen real closely. I want you to close your eyes and put your head down as far as it will go." He started to speak. "You won't get hurt as long as you cooperate and tell the truth."

"Okay, just don't..."

"Do as I said. Now!"

When his head was down, I motioned for Joanne to join us.

She slipped into the back seat next to me, not saying a word, so Bruce would think one of my own pals had joined us.

"Now Bruce. Who told you to come after me the other day with the automatic?"

"Mr. Green."

I looked over to Joanne. Her eyes opened wide and she looked like she couldn't believe what she had heard. I continued questioning Bruce. "Who's Mr. Green?"

"My boss at the company."

"What company?"

"Philly Mutual."

Jesus. "What company?"

"Philadelphia Mutual. The insurance company."

What the hell's going on?

"Why did Mr. Green send you?"

"He wanted me to scare you, that's all. He gave me the gun and told me what to say. He promised I couldn't get hurt. He said you were a fat ass who would scare real easy."

Joanne started to speak but I cut her off.

"Why did he want you to scare me?"

"I don't know."

I grabbed the back of his neck and started to squeeze. "One more lie and you're human kitty liter."

"I don't know. I'm telling the truth. He just gave me the gun and told me to scare you."

"Okay, you did real good Bruce. Now keep you're head down for five minutes, then drive away."

"What happened to Miss Paek?"

"I saw her get a ride home. I guess you were late and she

thought you had forgotten her."

"But, I was..."

"Don't worry Brucey. You won't be fired. Now keep your head down for five minutes. We'll be able to see you. Lift your head up before that and you'll have only one moving part."

"Okay, okay."

Joanne and I slid out of the car and back into the restaurant. I told her to stay away from the window until Bruce drove away. This asshole must have really been scared, he kept his head down for fifteen minutes before he looked up and tore off as fast as the limo could go.

"I didn't want your boss, Mr. Green, to know you were talking to me. There's no sense putting you in danger."

"You don't really think that..."

"I think your Mr. Green might do anything at this point. He already got you involved in a killing."

"We had nothing..."

"You were at the scene of a murder, you assaulted me, then you left the scene before the police arrived. You're very involved."

She closed her eyes and kept very still for a minute, without saying a word. During that time, her expression turned from one of worry and fear, to peace-like. Whatever she as doing was making her calm, relaxing both her body and mind.

"Joanne?"

"I'm fine." She opened her eyes, looking so much at ease you'd think this past week never took place.

"Do they teach you meditation along with breaking bones?"

"Martial arts training is really about control, not force," she said. "That's what separates those who really believe sincerely in the form from the kids who learn it to impress people."

"What were you just doing?"

"I was controlling my breathing, clearing my mind; trying to regain control of my emotions. It's impossible to act wisely, to take the correct steps, when your mind is overrun with conflicting thoughts." Then she added, "I'm just sorry I didn't take the time to think when we last met."

This was some special lady. Lean and powerful like a jungle cat, with sharp instincts for her own protection. Yet, like the same jungle cat, beautiful in form and graceful in movement, even when the moves are against you.

"Listen, Joanne. There's a lot happening here, people have been killed, other's threatened. Now you know that your boss is mixed up in this. What's this about?"

She closed her eyes and concentrated again. But when she opened them her face was one of resolve, like she just thought of a course of action.

"I'll tell you everything I know. But first let me make a phone call. It will clear up a lot."

I nodded okay and she slid out of the booth and walked to the back of the restaurant where I assumed the phone was. She really did move like a cat, sure-footed and controlled. Her shorts revealed lean shapely legs, the same perfect skin as on her shoulder. For all of the strength in them, they weren't overly muscular, like a weight lifter's, but still sexy and enticing.

Sitting still now, and alone, I had time to feel my own muscles after the exercise. Everything hurt. I could feel the pain emanating downward from the thighs into the calves, wondering why people go through that torture voluntarily, but then I pictured Joanne sitting in front of me and knew the answer.

I wondered whom she was calling but it didn't bother me. Being a good judge of character was my strongest point. No matter what happened at the Trendle house, I knew I could trust Joanne now; she was on my side, not fighting against me anymore. If she said she'd tell me everything, she would.

Yep, the way I could size up people was my greatest asset.

In ten minutes, when she didn't return, I walked to the back of the restaurant to find her. There was no phone, just the back door. Bitch.

Chapter 6

Sunday morning, I was stiff as hell when I got up, stiff and mad. I got suckered again, taken in by a babe with smooth skin and a story to match. Meditation, shit. All the time she was probably planning on walking out, laughing inside at the sucker sitting across from her.

"Oh, honorable detective. I will shaft you right up the rear."

And me, like a royal ass, nodding my head and sucking up that crap like a vacuum in a portable toilet. Now where the hell was I?

Some insurance company bigwig was after my scalp, looking for his tapes. Tapes that got Warren and his old lady put away. Tapes from a company that's plastered all over Stanley's dump. At the same time I'm trying to find Heather's brother, getting hounded by the feds while she's playing something with Stan and not telling me.

So what do I do? I sat down and made a list of assets and liabilities. Not money, but facts. The assets were things I knew for sure about these cases; the liabilities were questions that I still had. If I believed what Joanne told me last night, my assets were a little longer:

Mr. Green was the bigwig and Philadelphia Mutual was the company.

Joanne and Sim had nothing to do with the murders but just stumbled into things as I had done.

Joanne really didn't know what Green was capable of doing.

Now for the other case:

Stan, who was knee deep in some federal stuff, had seen Robert a few days ago. The feds warned me off, but unofficially as far as I could tell. If it was official they'd have called me into the office and been a little more professional about it.

Heather may be playing me for a sucker.

Sue, with the nice chest, may be a fed working undercover.

Stan's place was covered with papers from Philadelphia Mutual.

Okay, I thought, what do these two cases have in common? I got to Stan through one channel, Joanne through another. Except for the Philly Mutual papers, there was no connection. But then I thought about Heather, a thought that I didn't like very much. When did I meet Heather? Right after Green and Sim played cricket with my head.

I figured it's time I try to get something out of her, confront Heather about her connection with Stan, a link with her missing brother that she somehow forgot to mention. Only I really didn't want to find out if Heather was jerking me around. There was something real special about her, something that went beyond that face and body. It was that look on her face when I first woke up after Sim creamed me, with Bennite standing over my head screaming my name. She really looked concerned for me, like she really cared if I ever woke up.

It had been a long time since anyone really cared about me, about ten years since Nancy left me to marry that scuba diving instructor from Camden. A goddamn scuba diving instructor, not a brain surgeon, or some rich lawyer, but a rejected frogman with the brains of a toad and a personality to match. I mean, I'd understand if she left me at the altar for some good-looking playboy, or even an old millionaire about to croak. Croak, frogman - now that's funny. But she left me for Norman the frogman, Norman who never made more than twenty grand a year escorting middle class thrill-seekers into the dangerous depths of the YMCA pool. What the hell did she see in him?

We were going to be married and I promised to give up

detective work for a real job. We talked about moving out to the suburbs, having a family, all that normal shit. Then one day I come home and found her letter, smelling of chlorine.

Dear Reynold:

I just couldn't tell you this in person so I'm writing this letter. Norman needs me and I think I need him. He's mature and sensible but very vulnerable now.
We're moving to California where Norman can find more work, maybe a career. I hope you don't hurt too much, or for too long.

Love,

Nancy

My first reaction was to call every Y in California looking for the scum. I was really hurt, but the more I thought about it, the happier I became. Did I really want to give up detective work, the business I was working so hard to build? Was I really the suburban type, mowing the grass, walking the dog, reading bedtime stories to some turd kids who would grow up and put me in a home?

Nancy and Norman deserved each other. In a year, I bet, he'd be out of his wet suit selling shoes or insurance, trying to pay the mortgage on their little picket fence. Nancy would be fat and ugly. The suburban dream.

These past ten years made me forget the pain I felt, but not the loneliness. Drinking buddies just aren't the same; you can't open up with your true fears, or feel like there's one person who really shares your life. Nancy was the closest I came to being married, the closest I got to feeling love. Maybe until now.

Heather. I decided to start the morning with her, to find out exactly where she stood in all of this. She opened the door in a halter top and short shorts, and my heart dropped right down to my big toe, giving my chest this hollow feeling and making my head spin. Her eyes shone and she gave this broad, wide-awake smile that melted the enamel right off of my teeth.

"Reynold, I'm glad you came this morning. Come in. Can I get you some coffee?" Bright and cheery, she was attentive and alert. Her attitude was different too, like she sensed my feelings for her and wanted to return them. She called me Reynold, not Mr. London, and treated this like a social visit, not business.

"Not yet. We have to discuss something very serious," I said trying to be professional and cool, yet feeling like someone set my shorts on fire.

"Oh, can we have some coffee first?"

"Goddamn it Heather, we have to talk." My conflicting feelings were playing havoc with my temper. I wanted to grab her, hold her tight, and kiss her more passionately than any woman thought possible, but at the same time I wanted to shake her yelling, "What do you really know about Stan!"

"Reynold, bad language does not become you." She gave this fake pout, like a mother scalding her child, but her puckered lips just made my body tingle.

"I'm sorry." Now I'm standing in front of her with my head down, like a guilty child cowering in front of an angry father.

"Sit down and let me give you some breakfast. You didn't eat yet, did you?"

"No, I just got up a few minutes ago and..."

"Good. Sit down and relax. I'll be right in." She was good at giving orders; it must be the teacher in her; so I sat down, dutifully, and waited with my hands clasped listening to her work in the kitchen.

"I've got a lot to tell you," she yelled from the other room. "I finally met Stan, Robert's friend, yesterday. He's such a nice kid. I'm glad Robert has friends like him."

She came in carrying a tray with coffee, plates of eggs, and toast. Sitting the tray down at a table, she waved me over. "We'll eat over here while we talk."

"How did you meet Stan?"

"He came to my office on campus, with another friend. He told me he heard that Robert was missing and wanted to help. I had to go in yesterday, to finish some paperwork, and he just showed up at the door."

"I'll bet." She looked at me and frowned with a "please behave" look. "What else did he say?"

"Robert came to see him a few days before I last saw him. They just talked about school, about friends. Robert seemed in a good mood, not depressed or worried about anything. Stan said he'd ask some questions around campus, call a few other friends they had in common. Wasn't that nice?"

"Did Stan tell you that we met?"

"You met Stan? No, he didn't mention that. Did you tell him I hired you?"

"Yes. But he was a little flushed after our conversation."

"Oh." Her face showed wonder, not an inkling of the real encounter.

"Did he say anything else?" I asked.

"No. Just that he really liked Robert and was worried as much as I was. What did he say to you?"

"About the same. Real nice kid."

The eggs were delicious, so were the coffee and toast. Sitting there, eating with her across from me, I felt right at home, like Mr. and Mrs. Joe Average having breakfast together before going off to work in the morning. I began to relax and grow more at ease, comfortable, enjoying the conversation and watching her lips as she ate and talked. She told me a little more about herself, her struggles against the male academic establishment, her efforts to get tenure at the University. She talked a lot about her younger days, about her very strict parents who didn't want her to date, how she developed an intense interest in biology, a love for scholarship. At one time, she explained, she wanted to be a medical doctor, but that evolved into an interest in pure science, research into biological functions that she could pursue in the academic world.

I started comparing her life, these noble and intelligent pursuits, with my own career.

"You look sad," she said. "Did I say anything wrong?" She had that same expression of concern that I first saw after waking up in my office.

"No, it's not that. I just really admire what you've done in life. I feel kind of inadequate."

"Inadequate? Why?"

"Well, first of all, you're goddamn smart. Sorry." She didn't like bad language. "Second, you're trying to make a name for yourself, with your research, helping humanity. Pretty far from my life."

"But you help people every day. You solve their problems, you give them the answers that they need. And you're as smart as any of the eggheads at the University any day."

"I wish it were like that," I told her.

"Fred told me a lot about you."

"To be honest, Fred's no rocket scientist; nothing against

janitors."

"No." she laughed. "But he's an honest man with a heart of gold. Fred told me how you've helped people, people that couldn't afford to pay your fees, people that couldn't find help anywhere else. How you helped him when his son was in trouble with that gang."

"Fred just exaggerates. It's the wine running through his veins."

"Why can't you just admit it?" She was looking at me, seriously and concerned. "Why can't you be honest with yourself?"

"I'm sorry."

"And stop saying you're sorry. Were you sorry when you saved Fred's son from that gang? Were you sorry when you got that old lady's money back for her?"

"Fred has a big mouth."

"No, Fred just loves you, for what you did for him and his son. And for others."

"Listen, Heather. I'm just a detective trying to make ends meet, that's all. It's not a noble profession. I'm not trying to save the world, just my own a...," I caught myself, "my own career."

She reached across the table and took my hand in hers, stroking it slowly and looking into my eyes.

"I think that some people know you a lot better than you know yourself."

We just looked at each other for a minute, her with that caring expression, me with that dumb blank "I'm in love" look. Then she let go of my hand and started clearing the table.

"What's your next move?"

"To find Robert? I called the numbers you gave me of his friends from home, and struck out. I do have a few leads that I can follow up on today. I don't want to say any more until I'm sure of some things yet."

She finished clearing the table and stood beside me. "Is there anything I can do?"

"Not really. Well maybe later." We just looked at each other for a couple of seconds. "Listen, Heather. Don't try to make more of me than I really am. Fred will get carried away for anyone who slips him a gallon of Thunderbird for Christmas."

"I think Fred is a lot more than that, and you know it. As for you..."

This thing was starting to get scary. An hour earlier I wasn't sure I even trusted this babe, now I'm wearing my guts on the outside for her. "Let's just say I'm trying the best I can to find your brother. Then maybe we can talk about other things."

I walked over to the door. She followed and took my hand before I left. "If you need anything, please call. Can we meet tonight, uh, to talk about your progress?"

"Sure, I'll give you a call when I get back."

She leaned over and kissed me on the cheek; a sweet sisterly like kiss, but more than that, like the kiss of a young girl with her first boyfriend. She quickly looked down and closed the door, leaving me standing in the hallway, alone, with my hand touching the spot where her lips touched.

Something happened to me right there, but I'm not sure exactly what it was. It could have been love. Or maybe resolve. Maybe it was all my feelings of inadequacy erupting, filling me with guilt that Heather trusted me to find her brother. I was confused as hell. Encouraged by Heather's attitude this morning, I was worried, in my own neurotic way, that it was just hope on her part for her brother. I was afraid I'd read the signals the wrong way, made too much out of her familiarity.

And Fred. I'll kill him. That wino of a janitor giving out my

No Waiting To Die

life story, broadcasting the few lucky things I was able to do in my life, like I'm some saint. Just a quart this Christmas for sure.

Chapter 7

I still wasn't sure of any connection between Stan and Robert, and the Trendle case, but if I were one of those television detectives this was the time to visit the friendly police captain. What the heck. I called the station looking for Bennite, sure that he'd be off duty on a Sunday, freeing me from an unpleasant chore on a day that started so nicely. Unfortunately he was there and I arranged to see him in an hour. Then I went back to my place, shaved, and put on a pressed shirt and jacket.

Bennite was sitting at his desk when his sergeant showed me in with about as much respect as a hooker gets at the Lady's Auxiliary.

"What can I do for you, London?" It was obvious he considered this a nuisance visit.

"I'm fine, thank you. And you?"

He looked down at his desk and started shifting some papers around. "If you came to waste my time, get out. It's Sunday. I want to do my reports and go home."

"Do you have anything more on the Trendles? That's all I want to know."

He looked up. "You're off of that case. Far off."

"Nothing official. Just curious."

"Just curious, uh?" He didn't believe me, but his eyebrows started to lower, showing he was giving in a little. "We did come across something that you might be interested in."

"What?"

"A body. Female, oriental, 35 years old. Name of Joanne Paek."

My God! I tried to hide my emotions, pretend the name didn't mean a thing to me. "What about her? Why would that interest me?"

"Well, she seems to match the description of your alleged attacker the other day, and she was killed by a karate blow to the neck. One chop, no waiting, to die. We picked her up late last night. Someone dumped her body in the middle of Chinatown. Looks like robbery."

"You know anything about her?" I tried to ask casually.

"Not yet. So far she's just another body. Lansing has the case. It's not mine, and it's not yours. Go back to divorce cases and the scum work you do so well."

"Any clues. About the Paek woman?"

"Listen London..."

"It could be important to me. Please."

He put down his papers, stood up, and walked over to me. "London, you are officially and permanently off this case. As far as you're concerned there is no case. You have no client, you're cleared of any charges with the Trendles, just consider yourself lucky, and stay out of it."

"Just anything you have, something little."

He struggled with himself for a minute, making faces at me, and groaning. I just sat there, smiling as nicely as I could, behaving myself.

Finally, he said, "Okay, but you didn't get any of this from me." He sat down again and watched the door as he spoke. "Joanne Paek was the wife of In Ho Paek, the guy that started some big insurance company in town. He was much older than her, and he died about five years ago, leaving her with a kid, a daughter, and controlling interest in the company. Only when he died, the directors of this company tried to squeeze her out. Proxy fights and all that. From what I gather, she's been holding on these past years, but just barely, thanks to a few company execs that are still loyal to her and her husband's memory.

"She had a lot of money, but also a lot of enemies." He looked over to me and continued. "Not the type that would kill her, if that's what you're thinking. Mostly company execs and board members who wanted control to go to some guy name Peterson."

"Where was Peterson last night?"

"We thought of that angle. He has an alibi. But why would they do it now, after almost five years of infighting? Anyway, all of her stock now passes to her daughter, who will get control when she reaches 21."

"Who controls it now?"

"Her strongest supporter on the board, Paul Green. He's stuck with the Paeks all the way from when they first came over from Korea. He's the girl's guardian until she comes of age."

"Does it seem strange to you that a robber killed her with a karate chop?" I asked Bennite. "Wouldn't your average hood use a knife or bat?"

"Who says it was the average hood? You know these people, with all their Kung Fu and all. You think only the good guys learn that?"

"She wouldn't have been taken too easily." I was sorry I said that.

"How do you know? So help me if you're hiding something..."

"I only mean that she looked pretty good when she attacked me at the Trendles', if it was the same lady. Can I see the body? Then I'll be out of it for good."

He thought for a minute. "Sure, why not. It's your lunch."

Bennite arranged it with the Coroner and I drove out to 38th street where all of the stiffs are cooled. It was the first time I was ever in this building, the medical examiner's office. Along the outside were loading doors, not for furniture but for the bodies being brought in by police or rescue trucks. They loaded them on carts and wheeled them down to a cold room where the bodies were stored until the examiner could get a knife in. Anyone who dies outside of a doctor's care has to take this detour to heaven, or to hell, so the place is open seven days a week, twenty-four hours a day.

I've seen them do it in the movies a hundred times. Some weird, ferret-faced looking guy in a white coat pulls out the slab, like he's opening a filing cabinet. D for dead. The sheet comes off and you see the relative nod their head in pain and revulsion. That's really how it is.

She was laying there, Joanne, on the slab. He lifted the sheet up just enough so I could see her face, that beautiful controlled and peaceful face. There was a large mark on the side of her neck where I suppose the blow had connected.

"One chop, that's all it took. Snapped the neck in one chop," ferret-face said, almost in awe. "Don't get to see that too often."

"You're lucky day, I suppose."

"Don't mean anything by it mister. Sorry if she was a friend or something. It just must have been a really talented guy to do that. That's all I meant."

Talent is a wonderful word, something to admire. Even if it is a talent for killing, it seems.

I turned away from the body. "Couldn't any karate expert do this?"

"Maybe, maybe not," he said putting back the sheet. "This was no housewife. You could tell from her muscles, her feet and her hands, that she was pretty good at the stuff herself. And the blow was placed perfect, right where the least amount of force would do the most amount of damage."

"Can you tell anything else?"

He looked around, and then said, "Well, it looks like she

went down fighting."

"How can you tell?"

"She had other bruises, places where you'd get hurt in a good fight, made about the same time, and she had blood on her own hands, like she drew it in the fight." While he probably just read this stuff in the report, he spoke with so much pride you'd think he did the autopsy.

"Any clues?"

"I'm not supposed to give them to anyone. The boss would have my head, there are rules you know."

"And you know that Detective Bennite himself called about me. We're working on this together."

"Well, it'll come out soon. Just don't say anything."

"Okay, sure."

"No rape, and it doesn't look like robbery."

So Bennite lied. "Why not?"

"She had over a thousand bucks in her bag, and this large diamond ring."

"On her finger?"

"No, in her bag. You'd think she'd be wearing a rock that size. You know, show it off. And she didn't die where they found her. Looks like she was killed someplace else, driven over in a car, and just dumped."

"How do you know that?"

"We found small particles of automobile carpet stuck to the blood on her hand. It must have been some drive, not real local, because the blood had time to coagulate, trapping the threads, and there was no sign of a struggle where they found the body."

He was being pretty cooperative, so I figured I'd go the whole route. "Can I see your report?" I stressed "your" to make him feel important.

"Why not, I've already told you everything."

He rolled back the slab and it slid effortless into the wall, almost with obscene ease, like what it carried had no value, no importance. But he didn't do it without feeling, as a bored secretary would close a file with a flick of her hip while chatting about her boyfriend. He did it slowly and carefully, with respect.

The report had Joanne's address, which was what I really wanted. I couldn't believe that she was dead, even if she did run out on me. It had to do with the Trendles, and maybe it was my fault because I told her the truth about Green, but why did someone kill her?

Joanne lived in a condo in Society Hill, not far from my own office. It was one of those exclusive places, with a real doorman and real security, paid for by the upper crust that could afford it. From the outside it looked like a concrete and glass prison, keeping out the low life that didn't belong there, definitely a place that wouldn't let me just waltz in and up to her place on the 16th floor.

But I came prepared. Years ago I did a favor for a friend, a guy who made extra money doing small time forgeries. Nothing major, things like diplomas and transcripts for instant college graduation, state cosmetology licenses, stuff like that. He paid me in ID's; a collection of over 100, making me everything from a city building inspector to Her Majesty's Lord Lieutenant from Scotland. Each included a photo ID card, ten business cards, a badge where appropriate, and fifty sets of stationary. I kept the kit in the trunk of my car so it was handy whenever I needed it.

For this job I was L. Reynolds, city elevator inspector, on a surprise round at all the high-rises in Society Hill. I flashed the ID at the doorman, who didn't even check with security, and I told him I'd be inspecting the elevators and their operation as tenants rode up and down.

"And don't tell anyone in Engineering I'm here or I'll have

your job." A closing threat works wonders.

As I learned years ago, I got off two floors below the one I wanted and walked up to the 16th. This way, anyone who might be watching the floor indicators would be looking for me in the wrong place. For a high class security building this place was a joke: no cameras in the hallways or stairs, and doors that a ten-year-old could break into. I suppose rich people can be taken as easily as poor ones.

Nobody answered when I knocked on Joanne's door so I let myself in with a pick kit I got mail order about 15 years ago. It was an old skill but an important one. Like Joanne, the place had class; that sparse clean look that was homey but with nothing out of place. I didn't know what I was looking for so I just walked around a bit, getting a feel for the place, hoping something would grab my unconscious.

Something grabbed me alright. All of sudden I felt a shock to my back and a punch to my kidneys that rolled me to the ground, breaking about a thousand bucks worth of porcelain statues as I went. Then a hand grabbed and pulled up my hair while a foot pushed down on my back.

"Not the hair. Please not the hair." So I'm still a little vain.

"One move and I'll kill you. Who are you?"

Jesus, it's a ghost, I thought. The voice was Joanne's, in control but with a touch of fear. Like Joanne's but not exactly.

"Who are you?" the ghost repeated.

"London. The name's Reynold London. I won't hurt you." That must of been the dumbest thing I ever said. I'm laying on the ground, pinned between my hair and my back, and I'm promising not to hurt anyone. The hand and foot relaxed, then were removed.

"Oh, Mr. London. Please forgive me."

I turned and saw Joanne's daughter; it just had to be. The

face was almost a copy of Joanne's, the body the same just scaled down to fit a 16-year-old or so. She was dressed in white shorts and a black sweatshirt, looking just like Joanne must have looked when she was girl; fresh and beautiful, with that dangerous innocence of youth and the knowledge that it will last forever.

She peeled me off the floor. "Please forgive me. I didn't realize that it was you, Mr. London."

"How do you know me?"

"My mother talked about you all last night. She said you could be trusted, that you were an honest and good man."

"Your mother?"

"Yes, I am Lydia Paek, daughter of Joanne and In Ho Paek. Fifteen years old and second degree black belt." She said that with pride, almost boasting.

"Where'd you learn all that?"

She helped me off the ground and onto the sofa. "I started when I was six years old, in Korea. It was something I shared with my mother."

"Do you know about your mother?" It was hard to believe that she could be so open and brave when her mother was just killed.

"Yes, I do, Mr. London. The police told me about it earlier."

"You don't seem..."

"Upset or sad, Mr. London? Inside, my heart is torn into pieces, but I do not have time for childish tears. I must discover who killed my mother and see that justice is done."

While just a child, she carried herself like a woman, straight and mature, with the confidence of a tigress protecting her young. The resemblance to her mother was amazing, from the straight dark hair to the lean muscular legs, the sound of the voice and way she moved her head.

"Why don't you leave that to the police?" I told her. She just looked at me. "Tell me what happened last night. When did you talk to your mother last?"

Lydia stood up and paced around the room. "Mother came home late last night. I was already asleep but she came into my room and woke me up. That was the first time she ever did that, but she said she had something important to tell me. We sat right here, she was on the sofa, me on this chair facing her. She told me not to be worried and just to listen, without interrupting, even if I really didn't understand what she was saying."

She stopped and looked down at her hands so I couldn't tell if she was about to cry or just regaining composure. A child with remarkable strength, but too afraid to let her grief show, to act like the young girl she really was.

"Can you go on? It's very important if you can."

"Yes." She looked back up. "Mother told me that something terrible was happening at the company, that violence was taking over. She said that she wasn't really sure who was to blame, but that she had to do something about it, to maintain my father's good name.

"I remember the exact words. 'Your father is dead but his spirit will never rest until peace is brought to the company he founded.' She was very sad as she talked, but resolved that nothing would stop her." Lydia pointed to the kitchen. "Excuse me, I must get a drink of water. Can I get you anything?"

I shook my head, then with a feeling of deja vu I watched her walk out to what I assumed was the kitchen. It was almost the exact scene from the restaurant when Joanne excused herself to make the phone call, except her mother never came back. I heard a cabinet open and close, the refrigerator door open, and ice cubes clink into a glass. The water ran, and then Lydia walked back into the room.

"Mother said that she had an errand to run that would clear

everything up. Then she told me about you."

She looked at me like we were old friends, as if I would know what Joanne said about me. I said "Go on. What exactly did she say?"

"Oh. She said that you were a detective, someone who could be trusted, and that if anything happened I should find you and listen to what you said. She said that I could trust no one in this country except you. If I could not find you, I was to go back to my family in Korea and let the pack fight it out here. Those were her words, 'Let the pack fight it out here.' What should I do, Mr. London?"

"Well, who's going to take care of you? Do you have anyone to stay with?"

Lydia shook her head. "I have no family in this country now... but I can take care of myself, right here, at home. Perhaps my aunt or uncle will come over from Korea. Maybe someday I'll move back." She looked at me, saw my concern, and smiled. "Don't worry about me Mr. Reynolds, I'll be all right. I can take care of myself." She paused. "But what can I do to help you?"

I looked at this beautiful, brave, young girl, who deserved all that life had to offer, and wondered why God, if there is one, decided on this course.

"To begin with, Lydia, forgive me for not trusting your mother. I wasn't sure where she stood in this matter. In fact, when she left me last night I believed she had something to do with the violence that was taking place."

She looked up fast, as if I splashed cold water on her face. "Mother could never..."

"I understand that, Lydia. I really do now. The most important thing you can do now is to remain safe," I said. "Give up all thoughts of revenge for now. Maybe go back to Korea and stay with your family for awhile."

Lydia shot up. "I cannot do that. It is my duty now to take over for my mother."

"Take over?"

"Yes. In the company. And in putting my father's spirit to rest."

"But you're just a young..."

"A young girl, Mr. London? I am the last of my family; now the oldest Paek in America. I have responsibilities, duties, that I cannot ignore, to my mother now as well as to my father."

"Sit down, please. Let me see to your father's spirit, and to find justice for your mother's death." She didn't look convinced. "What would happen to your father's spirit if you were killed, if no Paek was alive to put it to rest?"

"Okay, I will listen to you for now; because my mother said you could be trusted. But I want justice done." She looked down at her hands, and then asked me how her mother had died. "The police just told me she was dead," she explained.

"Lydia, it's not very pretty."

"Mother said I could trust you. Will you trust me? Will you tell me everything? Don't let my age make up your mind."

I could see that her courage, her love for her mother and her father's spirit, would keep her strong, at least for now. She was only a kid, and I knew that someday the emotion and the pain would prove too much, but I thought she deserved to hear the truth and I told her everything I learned at the coroner's.

"What can I do to help?" she asked when I had finished.

She brought me all of her mother's papers, her briefcase from work, personal notes, financial records, and for a few hours I read as many as I could. The family had plenty of money; Lydia wouldn't have to worry about that. The other papers traced years of bitter struggle between rival factions in the company, starting almost the day In Ho Paek, Joanne's much older husband, died.

From what I could tell, Green was her major ally in the company and on the Board. The letters between them were friendly and sincere, showing support yet independence on a few minor items where they disagreed.

Nothing in the papers hinted of violence or fear, from within their own camp or from outside. Even mentions of Peterson, the rival, were respectful. It seemed that Peterson owned a large block of stock and had made an inside run to get control of the company. A few Paek loyalists, lead by Green, were able to fight off his advances, but one or two board members could swing in either direction. Most of the correspondence dealt with the maneuvering of these members into the various camps. It seemed like the only thing keeping them loyal to this point was the excellent financial shape of the company and how it was run, even after Paek's death. Green stressed to the Board that this was due to Joanne's personal involvement in the company and the fierce loyalty of rank and file employees; loyalty, he claimed, that would be lost if Joanne was replaced.

Like Bennite said, it didn't look like anything that would cause murder, but you never know when this kind of money and power was at stake.

I took a look at Joanne's will. Green was appointed executor of the estate and Lydia's legal guardian until she was of age. But oddly, Lydia had complete say over the Paek personal fortune even though she was a minor. Joanne must have really trusted her daughter.

Lydia promised me that she'd stay at home. I gave her my office number, and Heather's in case she couldn't reach me any place else. I also gave her Bennite's name and number for an emergency.

It was time I met Mr. Green. I had his address from the papers and decided to make a little unannounced visit to my old friend. I stopped off at my place first to wash up and change my shirt; it got pretty messed up when I redecorated Joanne's apartment thanks to a well placed kick and punch from Lydia. I was driving down Walnut Street when I noticed a blue Chevy following me; there was hardly any traffic this Sunday night so it stood out in my rear-view mirror. I turned down 10th and cut up Locust; the Chevy was still there. So I turned into 9th, going the wrong way down a one-way street, my final test to see if I was being tailed. Sure enough, the Chevy turned along with me. I couldn't see the face of the person in the car, it was just one person, male from what I could tell, wearing dark clothes and a hat. Whoever it was certainly didn't care if I knew I was being tailed, unless he was a rank amateur. He kept his distance but mimicked every change in my speed, every turn of the wheel.

Playing tricks, I made four or five more turns just to aggravate the guy, starting to be pretty confident that it must be some other clown from the insurance company. I was at the intersection of 8th and Pine when I noticed a red Plymouth two blocks down, running parallel to me, just offset by two blocks. It didn't worry me until I saw the same car at the next intersection, then the next. I was being teamed; one car right behind me, another running parallel, probably to pick me up if the Chevy got lost. Maybe this wasn't an amateur operation, after all.

But why make it so obvious? If they wanted to scare me, to let me know I was being followed, why run a team when one car would do the trick? I was thinking about this when I noticed where I was headed, down toward Front Street where I'd get squeezed in between both cars at a maze of dead ends butting Delaware Avenue. Then it hit me that I wasn't being tailed but lead; rather pushed like a rat being chased into a box with a broom. That's why they made the tails so obvious; so I'd concentrate so much on the car behind me that I wouldn't really think about where I was headed.

Their plans were to box me in, corner me at some dead end

with the Chevy in back and the Plymouth in front. One of me and two of them.

Idiot! Goddamn idiot! Getting soft in the head because of a couple of good-looking babes. The only way to get out of this mess was to find some alley or small street that I could quickly duck into, race down, and hope to get behind the Plymouth before they realized what was going down. Once behind the Plymouth, I could cut out in the other direction. The Plymouth would have to circle back to pick up the trail; meanwhile I could lose the Chevy. But I had to do it quick, before I got to First Street and hit the blockade made by I-95.

Then I had a great idea. If I could shake the Plymouth, maybe I could lead the Chevy into my own trap, get a hold of the driver and squeeze some information from him. It would be just one against one, odds that seemed a lot better than I would face if I fell into their trap.

There were no alleys in sight, and no small streets that I could think of. I made a few turns, ending up going north on 3rd Street, past Pine, Delancy, then Spruce. Then I remembered this little courtyard coming up, surrounded by million-dollar designer townhouses and accessed by a walkway wide enough to drive through except for a metal pipe temporarily stuck right in the center, locked into place so it can be removed to allow delivery trucks and the like into the courtyard. We were out of sight of the Plymouth so I gunned the car to throw his timing off. In sight of the walkway, a few feet from Willings Way, I made some quick observations, hit the brakes real hard and yanked the wheel left as hard and fast as I could. The car spun just right so it was straight across the street in the path of the coming Chevy. I saw panic on the driver's face as he braked real hard, sliding into some trash cans lining the sidewalk. When his head was down, I gunned the car again, barely squeezing the little Toyota between the wall and the metal stand, scraping both sides of my car.

I slowed down in case some residents were in the courtyard,

and I heard this crash behind me. The Chevy tried the same maneuver but was a little too wide; it was jammed stuck between the wall and the metal stand so both its doors were blocked. The driver was in a panic; he couldn't open either door and the wall blocked his window. He started to slide over to the passenger's window when I knew what to do. It had to be done fast, before the Plymouth got worried and circled back to find us. With my 38 out, the first time in a lot of years, I ran back to the Chevy and met the driver, a kid about 20, face-to-face as he was crawling out of the window. Now half-in and half-out, he found my 38 up his nose.

"Who sent you?" I held his shoulder with one hand, the 38 with the other, so he dangled out of the window. He just looked at the 38 in fear that I was going to shoot him. I took advantage of that. "Tell me who sent you, quick or you'll have three nostrils."

He started yelling, "Don't kill me! Don't kill me!"

"Tell me who sent you or you won't live to see puberty."

"Okay. Stan. It was Stan."

"Why?" The kid was still staring at the gun.

"To rough you up a little, that's all. Because of what you did to him."

"What's this all about? What's that little turd up to?"

Just then the Plymouth tore down the street and screeched to a stop just outside the courtyard. The driver yelled "Oh shit" and started running over with a little 22 in his hand.

I pushed the kid back into the Chevy and told him to stay down or he'd be dead meat. Then I moved to the front of the car, knelt down so the Plymouth's driver couldn't see me, and waited. When he reached the car and bent over to look in, I jumped up and pushed him head first into the window so the two guys bumped heads. I grabbed his 22.

"Listen you little asswipes, stay away from a man's game until you grow up. Roll up the window as tight as you can." The Chevy driver, who probably thought I'd still kill him, rolled up the window so his pal was hanging like a seesaw pivoting on his stomach. Without knowing why, I pulled his shoes off and tossed them into the courtyard, and then I drove out the opposite side of the courtyard.

Fed or no Feds, I couldn't have Stan and his band of pimple-faced hoodlums chasing me all over town. He'd be the next order of business.

Chapter 8

I was too tired to do anything that night. After all, I'm no kid anymore. Anyway, I wanted some time to think things out a little; it's only in the movies and cheap detective novels that everything happens at once.

Heather seemed upset that we couldn't meet that night. Her voice sounded sad on the phone but she said she understood.

Laying in bed, thinking alternately of Heather, Joanne, and Stan, I started wondering what these damn kids were up to. And I started thinking of my father.

My father was a perfectionist, just the opposite of me. He did everything perfectly, through a combination of terribly hard work and persistence. The old man never gave up. I remember him telling me a story about when he was a salesman and he was trying to get in with this big company. He couldn't get an appointment to see the chief buyer, so every day he showed up at the office, told the secretary he'd like to see the buyer, then sat down and waited.

For two weeks, the buyer never had time, but my dad would sit there, all day, talking with the secretary, making friends with the people in the office. The buyer would see other people without appointments but not my dad. At night he'd explain that there was tough competition in his area, and that some other firm was in real tight. Well, in the third week the buyer started to feel a little sorry for my old man. I really think the secretary put in a good word for him. So he called my dad into the office, heard his pitch, and gave him this small job to do, like a stick you'd throw to a dog to get him out of the yard so you could close the gate.

Well, that was all my dad needed. From that little job, he took over the entire account, and within a year he signed an exclusive contract with the company, worth over two million, and his commission set him up pretty good.

That was my old man. He stuck with something till he did it perfectly. He'd never settle for second best, never give up, and never be satisfied unless he was happy with what he did. I never really told my dad how much I loved him all those years. I felt second place to him. It just wasn't in me to work that hard, to want something that bad, but I really loved the old man.

About two years after he won that contract, when his dreams of financial success came true, when this self-educated man made it to the top and everyone could see, he died a terrible death that reduced him to a shell, laying in bed, being taken care of, wasting away. I couldn't face him much those days. I know it probably hurt him that I wasn't around much and it hurt me too. But I couldn't face the fact that it was my old man lying there. My old man was that super salesman that could do magic, and as he lay there, no more the king of the mountain, he reminded me too much of myself.

I never really told him how much I loved him.

The phone woke me up.

"Mr. London?" It was Joanne's voice. Lydia. "I found something you might be interested in. About tapes."

"Okay. Stay where you are. I won't be able to get there until later, but put whatever you have in a safe place, and stay home. Don't let anyone in."

"Did you speak with Mr. Green?" she asked.

"No, I had some car troubles last night."

" Mr. Green called this morning."

"What did he want? Did you tell him what you found?"

"He wanted to know how I was. And no, I didn't tell him anything. Remember, mother said to trust only you."

"That's good. Listen, Green was your mother's friend. Your

mother made him your legal guardian so she must have trusted him, but right now I can't be sure if he can be trusted. You did the right thing."

"Mr. London?" Her voice was hesitant, as if she was about to ask a question she really didn't want answered. "Do you think Mr. Green killed my mother?"

"Why do you say that?"

"I don't know. Last night I read over all of those memos and letters again. Mr. Green seemed to be losing patience with my mother, even though his words were words of support."

"Listen Lydia, let's not jump to an conclusions, but as long as we don't know who killed your mother we have to suspect everyone; Green, Peterson, or any drugged out karate-head on the street."

"It wasn't anyone on drugs, Mr. London. And if it was Green or Peterson, they only gave the orders. It was a professional." She sounded quite sure.

"Oh?"

"I thought about what you told me, how mother was killed. She could not be taken easily. You see, martial arts was more than exercise to mother."

I wasn't sure what she was leading to. "What do you mean?"

"Of course mother believed in the defensive aspects of the sport, and in the psychological advantages. But she was an experienced full-contact fighter."

"What's full contact?" I asked.

"Normally when you train, you pull your kicks and punches, not really making contact so your partner doesn't get hurt. In full-contact fighting you use all of your force, like in boxing. In Korea, mother was once the women's national champion. She could beat most of the men, too. She knew how to fight, Mr.

London, not just exhibit her skills or defend herself. The person who killed her was not drunk or on drugs. It was not a lucky punch. The person who killed her was an experienced fighter, a trained killer."

"Do you know anyone like that? From your own training?"

"Go to the dojang where you met mother. But Mr. London." She paused. "Be very careful."

To be honest, the conversation scared the shit out of me. I had my 38, and I knew how to use it, but the mystique surrounding Joanne's death, the vision of black hooded ninjas stalking me, gave me goose bumps.

Fear aside, I had a few reasons to take care of Stan first. Not only did I want to find Robert, but also I couldn't afford to be ducking the Bowery Boys any more, and I didn't want the Feds to think I was still mixed up in their case. Right or wrong, I still worked on the assumption that Stan and the Trendle case were not connected, that the insurance papers were just a coincidence. So if I could find Robert, I could then devote my full energies to getting those tapes and finding out who killed Joanne, for myself and for Lydia.

I ran over to the campus again and checked the apartment for any signs of watching Feds. The place looked clear so I went up to Stan's again. Sue answered, wearing less than before; just a pair of skimpy panties and one of those low cut bras that ended just above the nipples. That's all.

"Stan in?" I asked, staring at her chest.

"No, just me, big boy. Come on in." She turned around and sat on the couch with her legs spread apart, letting me stand in the doorway.

"Where do you keep your badge? Or shouldn't I ask."

"Come on in and sit down next to Suzy." She patted the

sofa so hard her breasts bobbed up and down like buoys floating on waves. "What badge?"

She was a Fed, or worse, just a kid, but I walked in and sat down anyway. "Wouldn't your two partners be a little upset if they knew you were talking to me?"

A puzzled look came over her. "Partners? Oh, you mean Stan and Ken?" She started running her tongue over her lips, moistening them in nice slow circles.

I tried to find some place to look, away from her lips, away from her breasts and legs. "Look. I don't want to play games and I don't want to get involved in anything...serious," I said.

She slid over real close to me and swung her legs so they were over mine, then put both arms around my neck and pulled real tight so her breasts were touching me. It was getting difficult to talk.

She purred, "I don't want anything serious either. Just a little fun."

I didn't know exactly how to act at this point. I had my arms stuck out to the sides, afraid that if I moved them I'd touch some part of her. She was rubbing her legs up and down on mine, creasing my pants, and pushing her chest into me. All the while she's doing that thing with her tongue.

"Don't you want to have fun, too?" she teased.

All I could do was count down from ten. I figured if it helped forget anger it might help here.

"Ten, nine, eight, seven...."

"Oh, seven ways to do it. How nice."

"Six, five, four..."

Her lips were now sucking my neck like a tick in heat. "Four people? That's sinful."

"Three, two, one."

"Blast off," she yelled, and then jumped right on top of me.

"London, you're an ass."

I heard that voice before; it was the Fed from the Ford. Sue jumped off of me as the two feds walked out of the bathroom.

"Powdering your noses?" I asked politely. The bigger one held up a camera while Sue rushed over to a cabinet and pulled on a top.

"You take nice pictures, London."

"So what?" I stood up, but real slowly.

"You got two choices big boy," he said. "If Suzy here is just a kid, you'll spend a few years away on molesting a minor."

"I think you've mixed up the molester and the molestee," I said. The scam was getting pretty clear.

The smaller one continued the sermon. "But if Suzy's a fed, we got some rather obscure but potent laws that were created to protect defenseless federal agents."

"Defenseless? With the 38s she's packing?"

By this time the two guys were on top of me. They shoved me down on the sofa while Suzy, now dressed in panties and a short top, started to run out of the room. She hesitated a minute, looking at the two guys standing over me. I thought she was going to say something but she just turned around and left.

"What'll it be, London?"

"Okay. Okay. Just tell me what you want?" I was starting to get just a little annoyed at seeing my tax dollars at work here.

"We told you what we wanted last time. You stay out of the case, away from Stan and his friends. It seems you decided not to make us happy, and we don't like to be sad." He snapped a few more pictures of me. "Smile real pretty."

I started to get up again but they pushed me down. "London, you're a real loser. Just can't keep it in your pants for the little girls, can you."

"Listen, I'm not getting involved in your case, Okay." I tried to explain I wasn't interested in Stan, just in finding Robert. "I don't give a shit about Stan or your case. I'm trying to find my girl's brother, Robert Goldwyn."

The two feds looked at each other, and then the big guy walked over and slapped me across the face.

"Let's cut this crap and get it over with," he said. "We've wasted enough time with this..."

The other one interrupted. "Let me handle it. Don't make us tell you one more time, London. Stay away from Stan and his friends. Leave town, go to Mars, jump in the Delaware. Do anything you want, but stay away from this."

Then Kong hit me one more time and the two walked out, slamming the door behind them.

I've never been known as a genius. I mean I just barely made it through high school and college, but I'm smart enough to figure out that something was strange about these two Feds. FBI agents aren't supposed to work like this; I've seen the TV shows. After all, maybe these two guys have a little ID kit of their own, complete with fake FBI badges. That would explain a lot.

I looked around the apartment again, but all of the papers had been cleaned up or thrown away. There was just boxes of disks, those computer things, around. Each box had a number on it and, inside, each disk was numbered. Some of the disks also had the word "Backup" written on the label. I figured these were duplicate copies of some others so I shoved one of the boxes under my jacket and left.

Just as the elevator came, I heard a noise down the hall and turned to see Sue reenter Stan's place. I now had a decision to make. If these two guys were feds, even lousy ones, I should stay away from this case and find another route to locating Robert. But if they were just goons pretending to be FBI agents, that was different. I decided to take a gamble.

Down in my car I reached into my ID kit and made myself a federal drug enforcement agent. Then I scooted back up to the apartment and walked right in without knocking. Sue was there looking through the boxes of disks like she was searching for something. She turned around when she heard the door close after me. "What are you doing here again? I thought..."

Real official like I pulled out my new ID and badge. "Before you say anything else Miss, let me formally introduce myself. R. L. Rinaldi, Drug Enforcement."

She looked like I was nuts but took a good look at the ID. Before she got too close I went on with the official routine. "I have to inform you that you are entitled to an attorney, that anything you say..."

Her eyes got real wide, almost covering her whole face, and then she fell down on the sofa crying. "Jesus. I didn't do anything. I didn't know you were a cop."

"...can be held against you. If you can't..."

"I needed the money. They said it was just a joke, no-one would get hurt."

"...afford an attorney, the court will appoint one for you."

She started yelling. "But I didn't do anything wrong. Really."

"Okay Miss." I sat down beside her and gave her the best fatherly look I could muster. "Why don't you tell me all about it. Things will go a lot easier for you if you cooperate."

Sue looked up at me, wiping the tears from her face. "Cooperate?"

"Yes, tell me all about the two men illegally masquerading as Federal agents. You know, that's a very serious crime and I am afraid you've been an accessory."

She started crying again.

"You've violated section 34B dot 456 of the Federal Penal Code 976 dash 01. It states that any one, even a minor, acting as an accessory to the illegal representation of being a federal agent can receive up to 20 years in a federal penal institution."

Now she started to get hysterical.

"With no chance of parole. Have you ever been inside a federal penitentiary, Miss?"

"I've never done anything wrong before!" I could hardly hear her over the crying.

"It's not a very pretty place, Miss. A young girl like you will be...I'd rather not say." I suppose I went a little too far; she started rocking back and force, screaming and crying at the same time. I thought she was going to have a heart attack so I pulled her head down onto my shoulder and tried to calm her down. "Now, now, Miss. If this is your first offense, and you cooperate, the judge may go easy on you. I'll put in a good word."

"Oh, thank you, thank you." She started to wipe her tears, and then asked if she could go into the bathroom to wipe her face.

"Okay Miss. But remember, I'll be right out here. I have to call Washington for permission to make a deal."

London, you're doing pretty good, I thought. Sue's so scared out of her mind she'll tell you everything. So she's not a fed, and neither are the two bozos from the Ford; just two goons trying to jerk me around, to scare me off for some reason.

Sue came out of the bathroom, all composed, and sat down on a chair facing the sofa.

"Feel better now?" I asked.

She nodded. "Much better. Thank you."

I took out my notepad and a pen. "Okay, now tell me everything you know."

She looked up. "I really can't tell you much." I didn't like the beginning. "The two of them hired me to make friends with Stan so I could get in his place whenever I had to."

My stomach started to turn. "What for?"

She started crying again. "I don't know. I swear. They told me to get in real good so I'd be able to let them in here whenever they wanted. To tell them if anything strange went on."

"And did it?"

"Nothing really. Maybe a little drugs, nothing heavy. Stan's just a nice dumb kid, with nice friends. I mean, I was getting paid to party."

"Miss, if you're not telling me everything..."

She stood up and started crying. "I swear, that's everything."

"What's your full name and address?"

"Suzy Williams. I...live here."

"What do you mean you live here? You have an apartment here? Are you going to college?"

"No. I mean, I live with the guys here, crash where I want to. I...ran away from home last year."

"What's your real address? I want to get in touch with your parents, to let them know you're okay."

She ran over, sat down beside me, and threw her arms around my neck. "Oh, please Mr. Rinaldi. Don't tell my parents." She started to push her breast on me again. "Please don't tell them where I am. They beat me."

"Okay, Okay. For now. Listen, I want you to keep on doing what you've been doing, for the two goons, I mean. But don't tell them about our conversation. I'll stop by again in a day or so and we'll talk." I stood up and walked to the door.

"I won't go to prison, will I?" She was looking up at me

with real sad eyes and a puppy dog "take me home" look.

"As long as you're telling the truth, no."

"Oh, I am, I am."

Stan must be in something pretty deep to have those two goons after him, and Sue was a setup. But now I didn't know what the hell to do. I mean so far I didn't seem to be getting anywhere, and it looked like I was getting in deeper and deeper. Typical of my progress, I thought. It reminded me of that robbery case I had about 6 years back.

An elderly couple came to see me about money and things being missing from their house. They explained that they didn't go to the cops because they thought their son and his friends were stealing from them. They wanted it stopped but they didn't want to see their son go to jail.

"Have you tried talking to him?" I asked.

"Well, we did. But we're afraid of him."

"You're afraid of your own son? Just throw the little shit out."

"Oh, Mr. London. We wish we could."

I was thinking that these two had to get their act together. After all, they're the parents, and it's their house. If that was my kid I throw him the hell out, after making his ass shine like a red light. But they looked so pitiful sitting there that I told them I'd take the case.

"Tell you what," I said. "I'll talk with your son. I'll tell him that you know he's stealing, and that he better stop it or I'll take him to the police."

They looked at me, worried for their son I thought. "Perhaps he should leave the house, for awhile."

I reassured them. "Don't worry. The kid only needs a little

scare. I won't do anything to hurt him. Tell you what. Is he home now?"

"Yes. Steve is home with a few friends."

"Okay, stay away for the rest of the day. I'll take care of everything. I'll tell him to take a hike and not to come back until he can show you some respect."

Easy money. I like cases like that. I figured I'd roll over to their place, scare the hell out of the little thief, and mail in my bill in the morning.

They lived in Kensington, a working class neighborhood that could be real tough if you let it. It took about 30 minutes for me to find the house; a nicely kept row house near the end of the block.

There was noise coming from inside so I knocked on the door real loud. The sound continued but no one bothered to come to the door. Maybe they couldn't hear over the noise, so I banged harder and yelled again.

"What the hell do you want?"

The door opened and one of the biggest guys I ever saw in my life was standing there. He must have been six five, over 250 pounds, wearing biker boots and a leather jacket with chains across his chest. A knife was stuck in his belt, and his arms were covered with tattoos.

"What the hell do you want?" He was not the friendliest kid on the block.

"Steve?"

He took a gulp of beer, spilling most of it down his chin onto his boots. "Who you looking for?"

"Steve. The boy who lives here."

He let out this roaring laugh, turned around and yelled "Some ass is here asking for Steve. 'The boy that lives here'."

Then he looked at me, his eyes piercing right into mine and growled like an animal. "There ain't no BOYS living here."

All of sudden, behind him, five more guys appeared; all big and mean, bikers like the guy that answered the door. "Why don't you invite your friend in?" one of the others said, and a big hairy hand grabbed my shoulder and pulled me in, almost lifting me off the ground.

I was surrounded by six of the meanest, ugliest, wildest looking bikers that ever spread their legs over a Harley. I felt like a weed in the middle of the Redwood Forest. They just looked at me, making faces and strange little noises with their mouths.

No time to retreat now. "Which one of you is Steve?"

"Steve's upstairs mister. You want us to get him?"

I smiled real politely. "If you wouldn't mind sonny." The rest of them laughed.

"Steve!" two of them yelled. Something crashed on the floor above makings the lamps shake.

"I think he heard you," I said, and then I heard footsteps on the stairs. Not really footsteps, like the sound of a fully loaded steamroller coming down the steps one at a time. The six bikers spread out so they were all behind me and reverently faced the stairs. One step, boom! Another step, boom! Now I could see a pair of boots appear on a top step. Another step, boom! The legs looked like tree trunks. Another step, boom! I was expecting to see branches shooting off at the sides.

With each step, Steve came more into view like the giant climbing down Jack's beanstalk. Yeah, that's what it was like; the old Abbott and Costello movie, Jack and the Beanstalk. I'm fat little Lou Costello waiting down on the ground and the Giant is climbing down after me to get the goose that lays golden eggs. Only, whose gonna be the goose here; I got six other giants watching me so I can't take an ax to the vine.

Step, boom! Step, boom! Steve's a goddamn bull elephant in leather, with enough chains around him to dock the Queen Elizabeth in a hurricane. Step, boom!

He reached the bottom, looked around, and then walked so he's standing right in front of me. First he scanned the six guys behind me, and then he looked way down at the top of my head.

"Can I help you?" he asked.

Now I wasn't too sure of myself at this point. "You Steve?"

"Yeah."

"Can we talk somewhere in private?"

Steve let out a roaring laugh that almost knocked me down. The six-man chorus started laughing. "Private? Why do you want to talk in private?"

"Your folks asked me to talk to you."

Silence. First Steve stopped laughing, then the guys behind me. He looked at me, grabbed my lapels then lifted me off the ground. "My mom and dad are dead. You're gonna be shit man."

I started screaming. "Your folks, the people that live here with you." Crash, he dropped me and started laughing again.

"My parents. They told him they were my parents." Chorus laughs.

I told you about my good sense of judgment, my instincts. Somehow I got the bad feeling that the lovely old couple left out a few details about sonny boy here. Like who he really was. Steve grabbed me again and lifted me up.

Chorus silent.

"And what are you supposed to tell me?" the giant asked.

I was now hanging by my lapels about a foot off the ground. I figured what the hell. "They want you and your friends to get out."

Chorus laughs.

"And what if we don't?"

"I'll make you."

Chorus silent.

Steve lifted me up about another foot. "And how you gonna do that?"

I was up so high that my shorts were cutting into my crotch and my shirt into my neck. I tried to talk but all I could do was gurgle a little with the saliva in my mouth.

Steve looked up at my face. "I asked you a question. How you gonna do that?"

"Let...me...down...I...can't...talk...this...way."

Chorus laughs.

"I...can't...breathe...let...me...down."

Crash. Steve let go all at once and I came straight down on his feet. He screamed with pain and tried to pick a foot up but fell straight back onto a console television, breaking its legs so it collapsed under him. The chorus panicked for a second, letting me get to the side and pull my 38. Four of the guys were trying to pick up Steve, who's cursing and screaming, and the other two turned toward me. I shot into the ceiling to get their attention. The blast was so loud in the small house that the four bikers lifting up Steve jerked around, letting him crash back down on the floor.

"The six of you, get out," I yelled, waiving my gun at them, hoping that they couldn't count -- "Duh, let's see; he's got six bullets, he shot one, that leaves five. But there's seven of us."

They looked at each other, then at Steve, who was rolling on the remains of the television trying to get up, but they ran out when I stepped forward and cocked the gun.

With the door closed it was just Steve and I. I sat on a chair and watched him struggle for a minute trying to get up.

"Just lay there, Steve, or I'll let the air out of you." I kept the gun pointed at him and one eye on the door; I'm not that stupid.

He was rolling around like a beached whale looking for a mate. "I'll get even with you," he mumbled.

"If I let you out of here alive." I waved the gun back and forth. "You know, you and the six pack tried to kill me. It'll be self-defense.   One look at your pals and the judge will give me an award. The keys to the city, maybe."

"You wouldn't do that."

I stood up and walked over to him, but far enough away for safety since wounded animals are pretty dangerous. "What makes you so sure?"

"My folks would be mad as hell," he said, rolling around trying to get up. "They told you to get me out, not kill me."

"Your folks? I thought they were dead?"

"I just tell the gang that. I don't want them to know I still live at home. They think my dad was a big biker."

I pictured that frail scared old man sitting in my office that morning, terrified of his son.

"So, they are your mom and dad?"

"Yeah. I didn't mean any harm. But the gang..."

"The gang thinks your hotter shit than you are."

He looked up at me. "Can you get me up? This hurts, man."

"How about a deal?"

He wasn't happy. "Okay. What is it?"

"I won't let the gang know your secret and you'll get out of here and leave your folks alone."

"But the gang..."

"Look, let's make this easy. You stroll out of here and brag how you took care of me. Then talk the gang into moving on, like

Alaska or something. I won't clear out till you're gone."

"And if I don't? We could come right back in here and kill you." Pretty cocky for a couple hundred pounds of blubber rolling around.

"How will the boys in the band feel if they knew you were lying to them, that mommy and daddy still took care of little Stevie, that you're just a little shit afraid to tell them the truth?"

"Okay, Okay. You got a deal. Now get me up."

That was the hardest part, getting Steve on his two feet again. I rolled him over onto his side then pried him up with a piece of the broken television console. When he was just about on his feet I backed off and pointed the 38 at him.

"Remember, momma's boy, we got a deal."

I hid out of the way when he walked out the door. For a dumb kid Steve did pretty well. I heard him describe my torture in exquisite detail; how he tricked me to help him up, how he broke my fingers and my toes, how he shoved my gun into my anatomy so I'd never sit again. The chorus laughed, although they were a little mad that Steve wouldn't let them come back in to see me. But he convinced them that this place was "just too hot now" and they disappeared. I never did see or hear their bikes.

Chapter 9

Now, just like then, I got the feeling that I've walked a little too far into the woods for my own good, without a compass and no moss on the trees. There was so much running through my mind that I decided to run over to Joanne's, Lydia's, grab the papers she found then spend the rest of the day at my office; I did have other cases, paying ones, beside these two. The doorman wondered why I was making another elevator check but he let me walk in like I lived in the place.

Lydia didn't answer the door. I rang the bell and knocked a couple of times, but no response from inside. I finally let myself in by picking the lock again, found the place empty, and left. Kids.

The rest of the afternoon at my office turned out to be good for me, it cleared my head a little and let me bill some clients for much needed cash, not that I was guaranteed they'd pay. By getting my mind off of my personal problems, I hoped I could come back to them refreshed, with some new ideas and leads.

I worked in the office most of the next day, with only a visit from Fred. About once a week he'd come up just to talk; about his family, other tenants, the Phillies, anything that went through his mind. A few times he'd be so stewed on wine I had to pour coffee down his throat and walk him around the room before he was coherent. Fred was a good man, even if he talked too much, but family troubles from the past got him on the sauce. While his life was smooth now he just couldn't break the habit, and he got tired of my lectures.

By 6 p.m. I had finished almost all of my paperwork, made my notes for the day, and was feeling pretty hungry. I called Heather and we arranged for a late dinner. I loved hearing her voice on the phone. There was just enough time for a shower and shave, change into casual clothes, and then I went to her place.

When she opened the door I could have fainted from her beauty. Her hair had a slight wave that I didn't notice before, the curls floating gently down around her ears. She was wearing a red and black dress, tight around her small waist and ample chest. Around her neck was a single strand of pearls that caught the light and drew attention to her smooth perfect neck. And her eyes shone.

She let me in. "I'm glad you called," she said.

I felt myself staring at her and became self-conscience. "Me too. Where would you like to go?"

She pointed to her table set immaculately for two. "Can we just stay here? I picked up some steaks on the way home. I think I'm really too tired to go out tonight."

"Fine with me. Can I help you get it ready?"

"No, just have a seat and let me get you something to drink."

"Just water thanks." I didn't want my head clouded by anything but Heather tonight.

She went to the kitchen to do something with dinner and returned in a few minutes with two classes, both ice water. She sat next to me on the sofa. "Reynold, I want to thank you for trying to find Robert."

"Not trying to find," I said. "I will find him. I'm just getting sidetracked with another case right now."

She took a sip of water, her lips caressing the glass. "I know you must be busy."

"Believe me, Heather. If this other case weren't so important I'd ignore it, but lives hang in the balance."

Her face showed concern, worry. "Are you in any danger? Could you get hurt?"

"Me? No" I tried to reassure her. "It's just getting involved, taking more time than I thought."

"Tell me about it," she said but not as a question or command.

"I'd like to, really, but it's really complicated and I'd rather not get you involved." She looked a little disappointed. "It's safer if you know nothing about it."

We chatted about our backgrounds. I told her some stories about past cases; she told me about her high school days but nothing about her work. I wondered if she skipped that subject because I made an ass of myself last time with my "you're smarter than me" paranoia. Talking to her was like sitting down with an old friend, easy and comfortable, without a hint of competitiveness or the need to mask feelings and thoughts. We talked about things I never mentioned to anyone, about my feelings for my parents, my days in the Corps, the early days of my business. You know, she never looked bored, never tried to change the subject.

At one point we were laughing about some story and my hand accidentally came down on her knee. I felt her muscles tighten and looked at her face for signs of disgust or fear. Instead, she smiled and moved closer to me, looked deep into my eyes, and kissed me on the lips, a sweet innocent kiss like the other day. Then she pulled away and looked down.

She said, "Reynold, I'm sorry."

"I'm not." I gave her a small tentative kiss then waited a second for a response, a word to stop or an indication to continue.

"Kiss me again," she said, closing her eyes and leaning over so her lips almost touched mine.

I kissed her once again then wrapped my arms around her and held her, her head on my shoulder. What a feeling, having Heather that close, smelling her hair, sensing her body in my arms. That warmth, the security I felt with her in my arms, was like nothing I had felt before, better than the few full-fledged sexual encounters I've had in the past. We sat there together for quite a while. I stroked her hair, kissing the top of her head, until she gently pulled away and put her arms around me. She held me tightly but uncertainly, as if it were a new experience, then let go and kissed me again; only this time it was a full and robust kiss, her mouth turning on mine to heighten the sensation, the physical contact.

"Oh, Reynold," she whispered as she looked up at me. We looked in each other's eyes, holding hands, until we stood up and I led her toward the bedroom.

You'd think I'd be crawling out of skin by now, another triumph, but it was just the opposite. I wanted to please her so much, to give her the kind of pleasure that went beyond the act of sex itself. I wanted to satisfy her emotionally, psychologically, as much as physically. And I was scared as hell I'd fail.

We went into her bedroom, sat down on her bed, and held each other as we had done before. I was afraid to kiss her, afraid to begin the rite that might end in disappointment for her. Would she scream when she saw my middle-aged spread? Would she find me oafish? Did I wash well enough?

For some time we just sat there, holding and gently kissing. I loved the feel of her neck, her face, her hair, on my lips. I loved the pleasure that shot through my body when I'd tighten my arms around her. Then we gently slid down on the bed so we were on our sides, still holding on to each other and kissing. Time just stopped in her arms, I had no idea how long we just held each other like that on the bed. But my arm, the one under me, started to fall asleep, to tingle and ache. So I shifted around so she was more on her back and I was facing down at her.

"Heather, I want this to be right" I said, still really unsure of her feelings.

"It is," she answered.

I sat up, pulling her with me, then reached around to undo the buttons on the back of her dress. They must have killed her laying on them like that. I could feel her body tense just slightly but her eyes were filled with pleasure, desire for me to continue. As I slipped the top of her dress down she tightened her arms around me; and when I unhooked her bra she pulled so tight it almost hurt.

"Heather, are you sure?"

"I've never been so sure in my life."

I stood up, bringing her with me, and she stepped out of the dress. She was magnificent, not just in the physical sense, although that certainly was the case. She looked away shyly as I took off my shirt and then slipped out of my pants. We sat down, and then laid on the bed again, just holding each other.

Her hands starting stroking my back and her kisses became longer, more forceful as I slid my hand down her back and inside the lace of her panties onto her buttocks. With the other hand I pulled her tight so I could feel her erect nipples on my skin and nuzzle my nose on her neck so I could smell her hair.

When my fingers reached the soft wet ringlets between her thighs she shuddered and pulled me tighter and our kissing became more intense.

I moved my hand up her back again and pushed slightly away. "Heather, I want you to know that you can trust me. I...I don't have anything."

She looked at me and laughed. "I'm sorry for laughing. What do you mean?"

"I'm clean. No diseases, nothing like that."

She said "Oh, Reynold" and pulled me to her, kissing me strongly. But then she stopped and pushed away. "Reynold, what about..." She couldn't finish her sentence.

"What about what", I asked.

"You know. Birth control." She was embarrassed, even though we were lying in bed, almost totally naked.

I looked at her. "I kind of thought you might be...taking something, pills, you know."

She turned around so her back faced me and said "Oh, Reynold!"

Did I hurt her? "I'm sorry, did I say anything wrong?"

She turned back around, her hands touching my face. "Oh no, you're perfect. It's just that...just that...I've".

"You've what?" I said.

Her eyes started to close. "I've...I've never".

I tried to complete her sentence, thinking that I could help her get over the awkwardness. "You've never used birth control pills."

She smiled. "Well, yes. But..."

"Heather, you can tell me everything. I mean it. Don't be embarrassed." After all, I thought, you're lying in bed with me, with my hands all over you. What could be more embarrassing than that?

"It's just that I've never...this is my..." She couldn't get it out. But it finally hit me.

"You've never made love before? This is your first time?"

She grabbed her face with her hands and started crying. "Oh Reynold. Yes, I'm sorry. My parents were very strict, and I've been so occupied with work and research. It just never happened. I never felt this way before, I even was starting to think that I was...that something was wrong with me."

"Heather, stop crying. What have you got to be sorry about? I'm the one who should be sorry for rushing you."

Through her hands and tears I could hear her say "But I wanted this to be perfect for you."

I gently pried her hands apart and kissed her forehead. "Listen to me. Holding you is perfect. Talking to you is perfect. Having you near me is perfect. Do you think I have to have sex to make it any more perfect?"

She started to talk. "But...".

I put my finger across her lips. "But nothing. No matter how you feel, or felt a few minutes ago, you just might not be ready." I remembered the wetness on my fingers. "And I don't have any...any birth control with me. I'm not that type of man."

She laughed. "I know."

"After all," I said, "I'm not that easy you know," affecting a high-pitched voice with a twist of my head.

I wiped the tears from her eyes and held her again, kissing her face, stroking her neck. She purred with pleasure and kissed me in return. We fell asleep in each other's arms.

Chapter 10

I woke up before Heather, my right arm stiff and tingly from holding her all night, a sure sign of age. She looked like an angel laying in bed; her knees bent slightly, face half hidden in the pillow with her soft hair around her eyes. I didn't want to wake her but I was hungry as hell since we seemed to have forgotten all about those steaks last night, so I slipped on my pants and tiptoed out of the bedroom.

In the kitchen, I found two baked potatoes sitting cold in the microwave; two rib steaks, now ruined, I suppose, out on the counter waiting to be broiled; and two ears of corn in a dish of water next to the microwave. It would have been a good dinner.

For 35 years I've taken care of myself, made my own meals, so it was my turn to take care of some one else. Figuring Heather would be as hungry as I was when she awoke, I decided to make her an All-American breakfast of eggs, bacon, toast, and coffee.

First I put up a pot of coffee. She had a bag of some special flavored blend in the refrigerator, the type you buy at the gourmet shops in the mall. It smelled a little like almonds.

Then I started defrosting the bacon in the microwave before melting butter in her electric frying pan. It was the first time I ever used a microwave but there were some instructions printed on a panel behind the door. I set the timer for one minute and put in the bacon still wrapped in aluminum foil from the freezer. I was just getting the butter from the fridge when I heard this zapping, sparking, noise from the microwave. Pop, zap, zip. I didn't know what the hell was going on so I just opened the door to turn it off. I got the butter started in the pan then looked around for some instruction book on the microwave itself.

She had a collection of books in a cabinet and one of them was the manual that must have come with the microwave. It was a pretty simple thing to use, after all. The book said not to use metal in the oven, like the aluminum foil surrounding the bacon. That's the problem. I unwrapped the bacon, laid the frozen lump on a plate covered with a paper towel and put it back in the microwave after resetting the timer for a minute.

Then I heard something else popping and I looked up to see smoke coming from the butter, now burning in the pan. I had forgotten all about it! I couldn't fry eggs in that so I unplugged the pan, dumped it into the sink and turned on the cold water to wash it out. Only as the water hit the pan, hot butter and smoke started spitting out, all over the cabinets and counter top.

Then I did the wrong thing. To stop the popping I whipped the pan out of the sink spilling the greasy water all over the floor. When I was just about done cleaning the floor I heard the microwave buzz, letting me know the one minute time was done for the bacon. It seemed an awful long minute, though. I just let the bacon sit there and finished the floor. Before cleaning out the pan and starting the butter over I looked in the microwave. The bacon was burnt to a crisp; I must have set the timer for 10 minutes, not one. It was the last package of bacon Heather had, and I couldn't find any sausage. Oh, what the hell, too much cholesterol anyway.

So more butter into the pan. I watched it carefully as I went to the fridge for the eggs. No eggs! What kind of kitchen has no eggs in it?

Well at least we could have toast and coffee. I found the bread in the freezer and put a couple of slices in a toaster-oven combination on the counter.

The coffee was starting to smell real good. I took some cups and plates into the other room, cleared the unused dinner dishes, set the table again and lit two candles she had on the table from last night. Okay, everything was ready.

I slipped into the bedroom, sat down beside her, and kissed her gently on the forehead.

"Wake up," I said.

She stirred a little, rolled over on her back and opened her eyes, slow and sleepy like.

"Good morning, Heather" I whispered. She smiled.

"I've got a little breakfast ready for us. I have to go soon. Why don't you get up and join me?"

She sat up and put her arms around me, kissing me on the cheek. "I'll be right in," she said.

As I started to walk out I heard this alarm sounding.

"The fire alarm!" she yelled. She jumped out of bed, remembered that all she was wearing was her panties, and then grabbed my shirt that hung over a chair. "That's the smoke detector. Reynold, there must be a fire."

She started gathering up some items around the room while I ran out of the bedroom. The apartment was so filled with smoke I could hardly see. I put my hand over my mouth to help me breathe and then opened the apartment door, but there was no smoke in the hallway. Heather ran out of the bedroom yelling, "Reynold, where are you? Are you okay?"

"I'm here. Go into the hallway," I screamed. "I'll take care of this. Do you have a fire extinguisher?"

"In the kitchen. But don't..."

I left her standing out in the hallway, her arms wrapped around a few belongings she had gathered. Neighbors were now coming out of their apartments, shouting questions. I ran into the kitchen to get the extinguisher and saw the two pieces of toast smoking madly in the toaster oven. Oh shit! There's no fire, just breakfast. Waving the smoke away, I unplugged the toaster, then went back into the other room and opened the windows.

Meanwhile Heather was outside yelling "Reynold, Reynold, oh please be careful" and the neighbors were screaming.

There she was, classy Dr. Heather Goldwyn, the proper Long Island lady and college professor, standing in the hallway wearing only panties and a man's shirt, unbuttoned but held closed by her arms full of clothing. Half of the neighbors were standing behind her, getting a great view of those long legs, while some half-dressed man was running around her apartment. And not just any half-dressed man; the underemployed slightly overweight detective from downstairs that most of them snub their remodeled noses at.

I walked out of the apartment. Heather yelled "Oh Reynold" and she dropped the clothing to wrap her hands around me. As she did, the shirt opened wide and I could feel her breasts against my chest.

"It was the toast," I whispered.

She looked at me. "What?"

I repeated, "It was the toast. I burnt the toast."

"The toast. Just burning toast?"

I closed my eyes waiting for her to hit me or something but instead she just grabbed me tighter and kissed me. "I was so worried about you," she cried.

Then we heard the neighbors screaming, "What was it?", "Where's the fire?", "Is everything okay?", "Nice legs." Pervert. I couldn't help myself; I started laughing. Heather looked at me then started laughing too. She turned around to explain the situation to the neighbors, saw the look of shock on some faces, and realized she was standing there in nothing but panties and an wide open shirt. Some old man yelled "Well, hello doctor!" before his wife hit him on the head. She pulled the shirt closed and tried to explain.

"Everything is okay," she said. "Just a small kitchen accident. You can go back home."

Most of the audience walked back into their apartments,

except for a few men that had to be dragged away by their wives. Then she turned, grabbed and kissed me hard.

It took about 30 minutes to clean up the disaster, have a cup of coffee, and kiss goodbye. I had work to do and Heather was already late for some appointment. We didn't say a word about last night, about what did and didn't happen. What good would it do, within an hour the whole building would be full of a hundred different stories.

As I changed into a clean shirt in my office, which I always kept there for emergencies, and I took a good look at myself in the mirror. What in the world did she see in me?

I got a few odd looks as I rode down the elevator and out the front door. Fred slapped me on the back and winked "Have a good night?" I growled at him and headed to my car only to find two uniformed cops waiting for me. "Can you come with us, Mr. London?"

"Planning a shopping trip?" I said.

"Detective Bennite would like to talk to you. Now."

No one has a sense of humor anymore, I thought, as I went into the squad car. The trip was short but all I could think about was Heather. Not Bennite, not why he wanted to see me. Not the Trendles or Stan and the fake feds. Just Heather.

Bennite was obviously waiting for me in his office, wearing the official scowl and chatting uncomfortably with two well-dressed men I didn't recognize. One of the uniforms opened the door for me.

Bennite looked up, frowned. "Sit down London. And this is no time to be a wise-ass."

I smiled. "Good morning to you detective. Nice to meet you gentlemen."

The two guys just nodded.

Bennite pushed a buzzer on his desk. "London, I want you to

meet somebody."

The door opened and a uniformed policewomen walked in. She looked a little familiar but I couldn't place her. "You two have already met," Bennite said.

I looked at her face. "I don't think so. I can't remember."

She looked at me, started to cry and said "Oh, thank you, thank you. I didn't do anything wrong."

I knew the voice! It was Sue. Suzy wasn't a fed or a nympho, but a cop. A city cop.

"Jesus. I didn't recognize you with clothes on." That's all I could say. "You look so...normal."

Bennite waved her away. "Thanks officer. You can go now."

Turning to Bennite, I said, "That's some cop you got there. Bennite. Did you ever see her...?"

"Shut up London. Just shut up and listen." He was obviously disgusted with something, but I wasn't sure it was me. "These two gentlemen are from the FBI, the real FBI." They nodded. "We've been working with them for six months now on a very important case. The officer you just met has been working with them as well."

I put on my best pervert voice, "I'll bet."

"London, shut up and just listen." It was one of the feds, the real feds.

Bennite continued, looking straight at me. "You stuck your fat ass in the middle of something that even I don't know all about." He looked at the feds. "And that doesn't make me happy." Then back to me. "These gentlemen have asked me, told me, to speak to you. To give you a little message for them." They smiled.

I looked at them. "Cat got your tongue," I said.

Bennite started to stand up. "London, for Christ's sake..."

"That's okay detective." The fed could speak. "I'll explain this to Mr. London."

He stood up, paced around a second, and then faced me. "London, you've interfered with a federal investigation. Right now, you could get six months, easily. Keep it up and it'll be years."

I was listening to this but thinking that the two jokers from the Ford made better feds than these guys. "Six months for what?" I said. "No FBI agent, no real one, ever identified himself to me, or ever officially notified me to keep my nose out. You know, clown..."

Bennite reached the end of his rope. "Shut up, London. For God's sake shut up." He put his head down in his hands.

I continued, "Now look what you've done to the poor detective here."

"London, I don't need your help."

The other fed spoke, not very politely. "Maybe you do Bennite. You're the local around here, it's your jurisdiction. Can't you keep this jerk in line?"

"Who you calling a jerk?"

"London, please."

Both feds looked at each other, and waved to Bennite to calm down.

"Mr. London," one fed said. "We are formally notifying you that your actions relating to Stanley Kensington are interfering with an on-going federal investigation. We are relying on your civic pride, your willingness to cooperate with the law enforcement agencies of the United States, to have no further contact with Mr. Kensington or his associates."

I nodded with approval. "Very polite."

The fed continued. "However, if you continue to interfere with this investigation, we will obtain an injunction to halt your activities and we will file a criminal action in the Federal Court for violation of Federal regulations. If you want we can cite the specific code numbers. Well, Mr. London?"

"Nice speech, boys. I'd be happy to cooperate in any way I can. Just one question."

"What is it London?"

"What the hell is going on? Does Robert Goldwyn have anything to do with it? What's the story with Sue? Did you ever see her...?"

"London, not again." It was Bennite this time. "Can't you for once keep your mouth shut and your mind open?"

The feds looked at me. "Detective Bennite was correct when he said that even he didn't know what this was about. No one at this jurisdiction does. As far as you are concerned, Mr. London," with the emphasis on mister, "this is a highly classified matter. Just do your duty and stay out of his."

"How about if you do your duty, dog duty, right on your own shoes." I thought that was a good one.

"That's it," Bennite yelled. He turned to the feds. "Gentlemen, you are right about one thing, this is my jurisdiction. We're cooperating to the fullest; and I will make sure Mr. London does so as well. Now, do you have anything else you'd like to discuss with Mr. London or myself?"

"No," the fed said. "Just make sure, Bennite, that London stays clear. Your badge is on the line."

"I know my job. You worry about your own. You can see yourselves out, can't you?"

The two feds left the room as Bennite sat down. He really took a stand and got those two jerks out of there, and off my back.

"Thanks, Bennite," I said. "Those two guys..." I stopped when I looked at his face. He was looking at me, or rather right through me like he was staring at someone sitting directly behind me, except we were the only two people in the room.

"London, don't thank me."

"It's just that..."

"London, it may turn out that I'll be the last person on this earth who you want to thank, because if I find out that you're in this again, that you even go near Kensington or his apartment, or any of his friends, I'll stick your ass so far down in this jail that your hemorrhoids will hurt every time a subway goes by. If you so much as mention this case to me, or anyone else. If you investigate this case in any way. If you...Oh just get out."

I started to move.

"London?"

"Yes, Detective?"

"Do you understand what I'm saying?"

I nodded and snapped to attention. "Yes Sir, Detective Bennite."

"I mean, do you really understand?"

"Yes Sir, I do."

Then he just sat down, silently, and starred.

On the way out I passed Sue, or whatever her name is.

"Hello Police Officer Sue," I said.

She looked at me and chuckled. "What was that London; section 34B dot 456 of the Federal Penal Code?"

"Dash something or other," I added.

Dressed in her blue uniform, her hair done in a more mature style, she looked a lot older than I remembered her from the apartment.

"Did you make all that up just then?" she asked, laughing.

"Oh, finally a police officer with a sense of humor. And a lot more than that," I added.

"We do what we have to do. Did they read you the riot act in there?"

"Yeah. Stay away, far, far away."

"I'd take that advice if I were you." She had a kind face.

"What about you?" I asked. "Aren't you going back?"

"No, the feds are afraid you've compromised my cover. They're worried that...the two guys you met might not want to keep me around too much longer."

I nodded my head, like I understood what was going on even though this garbage smelled to high heaven. "So, how come you're talking to me now. Aren't you afraid the feds will get mad."

She looked around the room, and then turned to me. "They're not here. You know, they gave me hell for telling you as much as I did." Then as an afterthought, she added, "I met a lot of scum in that apartment, some of the kids, but a lot of outsiders. It took an awful lot for me to do what the feds wanted. I'm really not like that, you know. But you kept your hands to yourself, really seemed to care...even when you started that penal code stuff. I feel bad about what went down with you. I kind of want to make it up."

"That's okay Officer Sue. You gave me some nice moments there yourself."

She blushed and looked down as I winked and left the building. There are some good people around, I thought.

The cops had driven me down but not back. I hailed a cab back to my office and had her drop me off down the street from my car. From about a half block away I saw the two feds, the fake feds, standing across the street from where my car was parked. For some reason these guys are coming after me now, not waiting till I tripped into their territory. I was in no mode for charades; the visit downtown, except for my talk with Sue, gave me a headache, and I just wanted to get on with finding those stupid tapes and Robert. Somehow, finding Robert meant even more to me now. I did promise Bennite I'd stay away from his case, but this was different, the case wasn't staying away from me.

I went into the building and found Fred. He's helped me with some minor things a few times, and I've slipped him a few extra bucks. Luckily he was relatively sober. We mapped out a few plans, and then I gave him the keys to my car.

Fred walked down the street to my car, opened the trunk, and moved his hands around like he was looking for something. Then he stared right at the fake feds, slammed the trunk down and ran as fast as he could into the parking level of the building. The goons took the bait and came running after him. One thing Fred could do was run, sober or drunk. He ducked into the building, waited to make sure they saw where he was headed, then turned down a long hallway out of sight. As he passed me and went into the storage room, I waited till I heard their footsteps, and then I pulled open the door to the boiler room.

When they made the turn it looked like someone just went in there in a hurry and couldn't get the door closed in time. I ducked in the storage room joining Fred. The two thugs stopped when they turned into the hallway. They must have seen the boiler room door swinging because I heard them whisper something to each other, enter the boiler room and shut the door. They probably didn't notice that the door had a padlock on the outside.

Gotcha! I crept out and put the padlock on the boiler room door. They must have heard me because someone from inside violently turned the handle and tried to push the door open. They started cursing.

"Cover your ears, Fred," I said, although Fred was still hiding in the storage room. "Now listen you two jerks." I had to yell so they could hear me through the door and over the noises from inside. "I know you're not the FBI. I knew all along. I also know that it's hot in there, and it'll get even hotter as the day goes on."

They just kept cursing and threatening me.

"Now be polite boys. I could leave you there a couple of days, but you'd probably die from the heat. Or I could let you out. It's up to you."

More cursing.

"Okay, I'll be back next week. Have a nice day."

"London! What do you want?"

"Now that's more like it. Who sent you?" Silence. "Okay boys you had your chance. See you later."

"Wait!" They paused for a moment, probably discussing what and how much they should tell me. "We work for...Nassau Mutual."

Another insurance company. This was getting strange.

"What do you want from Stan?" I yelled.

There was another pause then bang! The two guys started slamming their bodies against the door trying to break out, and the doorframe started to separate from the wall.

"Don't even try it jerks," I screamed. "This is a security door." They kept on banging, now with a nice even pace, a rhythm like scullers rowing along the Delaware. Of course, I had no idea if the door could withstand the pressure so I just kept yelling at them to stop wasting their time, with all my weight pushing against their force.

"Fred! Fred! Get your ass out here and help."

Maybe the two of us could hold the door in long enough to

discourage these two, but Fred wouldn't come out. I kept on yelling for Fred even as the frame came further away from the wall, far enough for one of the goons to squeeze his arm through the opening trying to grab for me.

"Fred! I need you. Get your wino ass out here!"

I kept moving my head to avoid being grabbed while trying to keep the pressure against the door. Meanwhile, they were still pushing so the doorframe was coming further and further away from the wall without the lock opening or breaking. When this guy's whole arm was out of the door, and some of his shoulder, I figured it was time to split. They'd probably hear if I ducked back into the storage room next door and I didn't have time to get all the way down the hallway and into the parking area; so I scanned the hallway for some other place to hide.

There were just three other doors in the hallway. One went into a small utility room where Fred kept the supplies he used most often: brooms, mops, and the like. The second was to a small, narrow, closet that housed the main telephone box. The third door, the farthest away, had a high voltage warning sign on it and held all sorts of transformers and electrical devices. I knew that all three doors were supposed to be locked but I also knew Fred. He had enough trouble finding his feet let alone keys, so he usually opened all the doors in the morning, locking them when he went off duty at night.

The trick was to get into one of the rooms without the goons seeing or hearing me as they came crashing into the hallway. Once there, I either had to lock the door from the inside or hide well enough not to be found. The telephone closet was out; it was too narrow so at least two inches of my gut would stick out of the door. So was the supply cabinet unless I wanted a few brooms up my...well, you know.

To give me some time, I managed to get my 38 out and smashed it full force on the hand groping for my neck. The guy screamed with pain and the pressure let from the door, my cue to dash down the hall and into the electrical room.

The room was dark, I could barely see, and I was scared out of my mind of being electrocuted. Remember, the sign said something about 50,000 volts and Fred once told me a story of this cat he once found in there, or rather the remains of the cat. I worked myself to the back of the room, stepping over this small railing that surrounded a large device with wires running into it and warning signs posted on all sides. Being real careful, and I mean real careful, I squeezed between the device and the wall, and crouched down so I'd be out of sight to anyone looking casually from the other side of the room.

For a while I didn't hear a thing except yelling. The two guys must be screaming at each other. Then ram, ram, ram, bang. The boiler room door must have given way and the two guys probably careened into the wall opposite.

More screaming, and I heard a door open and close. They must have checked one of the other rooms. Then a second door that sounded a little further away, probably the storage room. I didn't hear Fred yelling so he must have ducked out of there sometime during all of this. Then a door sounding a little closer, the utility room, then the closest door where the phones were stored. Then silence.

It seemed like hours, but seconds later I heard the door to the electric room open slowly. I balanced the 38 in my hand in case I needed it, and shifted my weight a little to the right when my foot hit something on the ground. It was too dark to see what it was so I reached over with my left hand and felt around on the ground a little. It was a dead rat, stiff as a board.

Meanwhile the slice of light from the door was getting wider and I could hear the two goons walking into the room. One of them must have bumped against something because I heard this bang and a curse.

I didn't exactly want a shootout. Trapped next to the wall, surrounded by high voltage fryers, I wasn't in the best position in the world, and there were two against one. I thought about it for a minute and figured I could probably get off two shots, maybe hitting both of them before they knew I was there, but I wanted a little better odds than that.

The rat. I picked the rat up by its tail, holding my breath because it stunk to high heaven, and put it on the ground to my left. Then I slid it as hard as I could to the other side of the room.

Boom!

One the guys must have seen it moving and took a wild shot at it; the bullet hitting the ground just in front of where the rat was laying, the impact pushing the rat back onto some transformer or something. I heard one them say "Jesus. Just a rat" when I smelled singed hair and smoke, and then with a wuff the goddamn rat burst into flames.

"Let's get out of here," one of them yelled and the two slammed the door closed and ran down into the parking lot.

"Jesus, London, that was close" a voice said out of the darkness, making me jump a foot off the ground. I turned and saw Fred stand up from his own hiding spot about two feet from the burning rodent. "A few more feet and I'd be roast beef," he said.

"What the hell are you doing here? Why didn't you help me out there?"

"I may be nothing but a wino, but I'm no dummy." He grabbed a broom that was standing in the corner and, using the handle, slid the rat away. Stomping on the burning creature he said "I knew that piss-ass door wouldn't hold those guys in that room. Shit, this rat could knock it down with his nose."

"Why the hell didn't you tell me?"

"You're the smart one around here. And if I were you I'd

climb out of that spot real careful like. There's fifty thousand volts running around your head. Jesus, I can't figure how you got in there without burning in the first place."

Chapter 11

It was time to regroup. I went to my apartment, showered and changed. The office was my most comfortable surroundings, except for the stiff neck and back I'd get when sleeping on the sofa. The apartment was different. I spent little time there, outside of sleeping and a few meals. It was almost foreign to me, less of a home than the office was, but a place where I could get away from everything.

Although I lived there for ten years, I didn't know many of the neighbors, and because I used my business address for everything official I hardly received any mail here, just those things marked 'occupant'. In fact, very few people even knew I had the place, I suppose, thinking that I actually lived in the two-room office in Society Hill.

All of my money went into the office and business, so the apartment was furnished in early thrift shop; reconditioned everything that I picked up at second hand shops and flea markets. It wasn't dirty or messy, or anything like that, just pretty impersonal and plain.

The building was a five-story townhouse near South Philadelphia, not too far from the Italian Market where street vendors hawked everything from live chickens to fake designer jeans. Filled with a variety of ethnic smells and languages, and little kids running up and down the stairs, it could have been right out of some novel about immigrant America, a melting pot in the heart of the city, a mixing ground for the spice that seasons our country.

I rested on the bed and gave Lydia a call, but the damn kid still didn't answer so I couldn't get those papers she had found. I did, however, know a few more facts from all that went down that day. The feds, the real ones, were after Stan, along with two other goons from Nassau Mutual, if you could believe them. It had to be pretty important to stick a policewoman in there under those conditions and to push the feds into threatening an outstanding citizen like Reynold London. I also realized that things deep inside of me had been reawakened; that emotions long suppressed could be aroused, that instincts really never died, they just became dormant from misuse or repression.

But that's about all I had, not a significant addition to my store of knowledge regarding these two cases, and no closer to finding Robert or the missing tapes than I had been days ago.

Except now I realized another emotion had surfaced: fear. Not for myself, but for people I started to care about; like Heather, her brother who I've never seen and probably should dislike, and for Lydia, the girl-woman who can't follow orders. All of a sudden Reynold London had something to care about beside himself, and that frightened me. Frightened me not only because it was a new experience, but also because it complicated matters, disturbed the neat compartments of my mind where rationales and excuses had provided sanctuary for my failings. Sure, I could convince myself but not the others; the others whose safety was now important to me, and who I wanted to think more of me than I thought of myself.

So even though my heart was filled with Heather, my mind was still playing tricks, pitting one force against another to control the path to my sanity. I didn't like the feeling, I certainly didn't need the aggravation, but I realized it was now a part of me, a part I couldn't have cut out, drown in booze, or throw away.

I guess I was more tired than I thought, because the next thing I knew, it was nine in the morning and I was in bed with my clothes on. I called Heather; she was at her office and we talked for a while on the phone. She sounded like a little girl over the wires, a little girl with a wide smile and wide-open heart.

That night, the dojang was more crowded than last time, but now mostly with little kids from 8 to 12 years old. I stood out because of my size, and because I never washed the uniform since my last lesson, I just rolled it up in a ball in the trunk. Master Kim welcomed me to class, smiling, either unaware of Joanne's death or uncaring. I was sitting on the floor trying to spread my legs and bend over my fat middle when Lydia walked in, uniformed, from the changing rooms.

"What the hell are you doing here?" I couldn't believe she came there.

She sat down beside me and started stretching. "I just couldn't sit at home and wait, Mr. London."

"What do you think you're doing? What do you hope to accomplish?"

She looked around the room to make sure no one was listening. "Maybe I just came here to train. It's been some time."

"Listen, Lydia, don't give me that. You already warned me that it could be dangerous. You told me you'd leave it to me for a while."

Master Kim walked by and smiled at us. Lydia smiled back but her faced changed when he walked away, then she faced me again. "Trust no one, Mr. London." She just got up, walked to the front of the room, faced the mirrors, and started kicking the air.

The lesson went just like the last. After the ritual bowing and meditation came warm-up exercises then several series of blocking, punching, and kicking routines. It was tiring, but the workout must have triggered someone inside, endorphins or hormones, because I felt invigorated and alert, enjoying myself even through the sweat and pain. This time I didn't get any personal assistance but sat for a while and watched the higher belts perform more complex moves, high jumping kicks, and forms. A form is a series of choreographed moves that simulates a combat situation. I couldn't imagine how these little kids remembered all of the steps.

Lydia stood at the front of the room, near Master Kim, the place of honor earned by her high degree. Today she was the oldest student in the class, next to me that is, and the best; her kicks had power and height, her body flying high in the air with control and grace. What amazed me was her face at the moment of impact, when her leg was extended full in the kick and she kiapped, giving that yell martial artists do to scare the enemy. At that moment, her pretty little girl face turned savage, full of hate and fury toward the imagined enemy.

Master Kim watched her closely and barked comments as she performed. "More power," he'd yell, or "Keep leg straight", even though she looked perfect to me. Several times he stopped class, demonstrating a kick or move for the students to see. He'd do it once slow, and then several times at full speed showing power and speed that I thought was faked in the kung fu movies. His arms and legs would whip through the air making woosh and snap noises, yet he never sweated or seemed to tire.

When the lesson was over, I cornered Lydia before she went back to change. "I want you to get out of here. Get back to your place and wait till I call."

She pouted. "Mr. London, I am not a little girl."

"You are to me. Go home. I'll call when I'm done. I still have to get those papers you talked about, the ones that mentioned the tapes."

"I have them here."

I couldn't believe it. "You brought them with you? Didn't you think that was dangerous? Your mother was killed over those tapes."

"Is everything okay?" It was Master Kim.

"Yes, Master Kim. Lydia and I were just talking about training."

Kim nodded, then walked away.

"Where are they?" I asked.

She pointed toward the changing rooms. "I have them in my bag, back there."

"Okay. Listen. Go change and bring your bag out here, but keep the papers inside so no one can see them. Wait till I get out then just leave your bag next to where I'm standing. I'll do the rest."

She looked puzzled. "Won't anyone notice that you're walking out with a bag you didn't come with?" she asked.

"I don't think so. Anyway, I'm hanging around late to talk to Kim. Everyone else should have left by then. Now get going."

She didn't look satisfied but she went back to the women's changing room anyway. I changed in the men's locker, rolling my uniform up in a smelly ball tied with my white belt, just as it was when I came in.

The waiting room was filled with kids drinking water or waiting for their parents to pick them up. Most had already changed into their street clothes; a few were still in uniform. The lights in the training hall had been turned off. I stood near the doorway to the hall, half in and half out of the darkness so when Lydia came out she put down her bag and went to the cooler for a drink. It looked very natural with all of the noise and movement of the kids. She talked casually to a few of the students then went out laughing with a group of four or five of them. No one said anything about her bag.

I kicked it out of the way, on the side of the sofa, and then knocked on Kim's door.

"Yes," he said.

I opened the door. "Excuse me, Master Kim. Can we talk a minute?"

He stood up from his desk where it looked like he was

recording the roll for the last class. I could see a book open with a list of names down the side and dates along the top. "Come in and sit down Reynold," he said, and then he sat down and closed the book. "What would you like to talk about?"

"Joanne. Joanne Paek."

He looked down at the desk then mumbled "Oh yes. Joanne. What a sad thing."

"Do you know what happened to her, Master Kim?"

"I heard she was killed." He looked up. "Killed by some thief in the street. A sad thing. Especially for little Lydia."

"Do you think it was just a thief who killed her?"

"Why do you ask? That's what the police said, is it not?"

"Well, Lydia doesn't seem to think so."

He seemed surprised. "Oh?"

"She says her mother was too...talented to be killed by just some thief in the street."

"She did, eh?" He stood up and came to the front of the desk, then sat down facing me, very close. "Sometimes, Reynold, children see too much in their parents; things that aren't really there but that they wish to see anyway. Yes, Joanne was very talented, but she was not invincible."

"Master Kim, I have to tell you the truth. I didn't come here just to learn a martial art. I'm a detective trying to find out who killed Joanne."

He smiled. "I thought so, Reynold," he said.

"The police told me that the blow was a very good one, right where it would do most damage. Could a lucky person do that?"

He stood up, walked back to the other side of desk. "Reynold, I have been teaching many years, in Korea and now here, in the United States. Luckily, we have not had many accidents over the years, but I have seen students, even high belts, hurt by aggressive beginners, just by accident."

I wasn't sure how far to push the issue. Although he was calm and friendly, I didn't know him well enough to judge at this point, but I needed something to get started. "Master Kim, can we assume for a minute that it was not luck but talent, that the person who killed her, the thief, knew exactly where he was hitting."

"He or she, Reynold. It could have been a woman."

"Yes, I'm sorry. But if it was not by accident, what type of training would be required?"

His face was deadpan, no expression. "Tell me everything the police told you about the blow."

I explained what the medical examiner's office had told me and what little else I put together. He sat there and listened in silence, then sat for a minute after I finished before speaking. "If we assume, Reynold, that the person did not hit her by accident, then we have to assume the person who killed her was very advanced in training. Joanne was indeed good. But if you insist on eliminating luck from the matter, her killer was extremely talented and knowledgeable. The blow that you described," be continued, "hit a very sensitive nerve point that is buried deep under the flesh and difficult to reach. The strike would have to exact and forceful. Like this."

He came around the desk, and before I could move or even flinch, he struck out with a knife hand chop toward my neck. The strike had speed and power, his arm one blur in the air, yet it braked just before the moment of impact so all I felt was a rush of air.

"That blow, Reynold, would have killed you instantly. That is how Joanne was killed." He looked at me. "But don't be worried Reynold. I wouldn't have hurt you. Just a demonstration of what could happen."

"Do you know of any people with that type of training?"

"Do you mean those who could have killed Joanne with that blow?"

"Yes."

"Reynold, there are many in this city who could deliver a blow like that, but perhaps only a few who could have done so in combat with Joanne. Striking an untrained person, as I could have done to you just now, is one thing. But striking a trained fighter like Joanne is another."

"Can you tell me who they are?"

"That's hard to do, I may not be aware of them all. But let me consider the question and we'll talk again after your next lesson."

I thanked Kim for his time and bowed before leaving the room, then I grabbed Lydia's bag from behind the sofa and walked to the car. I couldn't tell for sure, but it seemed Kim was watching me through the window of his office.

Chapter 12

I was sitting in my living room, reading the paper with a beer in my hand, when the doorbell rang.

"Who is it?"

"Lee Marvin. I'm an insurance agent."

Damn salesmen. "Go away. I gave at the office."

The doorbell rang again.

"I said go away."

"Charles Bronson, insurance agent."

"Go away!"

Ring, ring.

"Will you get lost!"

"John Wayne, insurance agent."

"Hold on, I'll be right there." I didn't need any insurance, and insurance salesmen to me are just above salamanders in the evolutionary scale, but I'd do anything to meet John Wayne. So I ran into my bedroom and put on a cowboy outfit that my parents bought me. It had a brown cowboy hat, dark brown shirt, light brown pants with fringed chaps, and brown boots engraved with pictures of cows. I tilted the hat just right then opened the door.

John Wayne was standing there, in a three-piece suit with a holster and six-shooter around his waist, a large briefcase in his hand.

"Well, hello partner. Can I come in and show you some universal life?" It was the Duke all right.

"Sure Mr. Wayne. Please come in and sit down."

"Now, son," he said, "have you ever thought what would happen to Heather if you died? Would she be financially secured?"

"She has a good job," I answered.

"A job just isn't enough these days, son."

"But Mr. Wayne, I really don't need any insurance."

"I'm not selling insurance, son." He looked at me real sincerely. "I'm selling security. Universal life isn't just insurance. It's protection for you and Heather, an investment that you can always count on."

"I suppose you're right, Mr. Wayne. I'll take a million dollars of universal life."

He opened his briefcase and took out about a thousand sheets of paper. "Here's the policy, son. Just sign here and all your troubles will be over."

I made a big X on the dotted line.

"That's all we need. Come in boys," he yelled.

The door blasted open and in rushed Stan waving a plunger above his head, behind him was Sim carrying a giant nutcracker. The two fake feds where behind him, carrying coils of wire with electric sparks shooting out in all directions. They all stopped and made a pathway on both sides of the door, came to attention, and then bowed.

Lydia walked in holding a basket, like a flower girl at a wedding except she was throwing little white pills around the room.

Puffs of smoke appeared, and then flames shot through the doorway, thunder shaking the room, lighting bursting through the roof. John Wayne gasped, got down on his knees and bowed his head. "She's here son. She's here," he screamed.

In the smoke I saw a woman's figure but I couldn't make out the face. She walked slowly, majestically, through the smoke, as if she were floating an inch above the ground. The four men standing by the door turned to face me and mumbled something in a foreign language while waving their arms up and down in karate movements. The waving started to clear the air so the woman became visible from the floor up. First I saw her white nurses shoes, then a white lab coat. There was a large chastity belt tied around her waist and between her legs. She was holding some old books in one hand and rolled-up diploma in the other. It was Heather.

The alarm rang in my ear, warning me it was 7 a.m. I turned over and thought about staying in bed the whole day, but it was a day long overdue, a day that I promised myself would show some progress. After I got washed and dressed, I ate a small breakfast then called Lydia, waking her, letting her know that I had the papers, and that she should stay around her place as much as possible.

I had read the papers last night before going to bed. They were a series of memos from Sam Stein, a disaster planner at Philly Mutual, detailing backup procedures in case of a major fire or other problem destroyed the firm's computer center. From what I could gather, a New York company had been contracted to make tape copies of critical data every night, and then store the tapes in some secret location.

Each memo emphasized that the company was bonded and highly reliable. "Our records will be safe" was repeated in each correspondence. I had no idea if these were the tapes I was looking for, but it was a lead, another direction to go on.

Heather must have already left for school, there was no answer at her place, so I called the college.

"I was worried when you didn't call last night," she said.

"I'm sorry."

She lowered her voice. "It's just that I was expecting you to call."

"I'm sorry..."

"Stop saying that, Reynold."

"I got back late and didn't want to disturb you. Are you okay?"

"I've never felt better. How are you?"

We sounded like a couple of distant friends, not lovers.

"Never better myself. Listen, Heather, about the other night."

"Yes." She sounded worried.

"Well, I...I mean..." I was having trouble getting the words out, trying to apologize if I pushed her into something too soon.

"Are you sorry about it?" she asked, her voice low and hesitant

"No, nothing like that. It was...very special for me. I only hope..."

"That I don't take it seriously?"

"Of course not. Listen Heather, I took it very seriously. I mean take it seriously. You're very special to me."

"Oh, Reynold."

"What's the matter? Do you have regrets? I mean I'm not the best catch in the world..."

"Please stop, Reynold. You don't understand. Oh, this is embarrassing. I just don't know...I don't know how to act. This is stupid." She regained some control, now sounding like the college professor. "I feel like a schoolgirl with her first crush."

"I'm glad it's for me," I told her.

"I'm afraid I'll do something wrong, say something stupid, to scare you away. I don't want to be possessive."

"There's nothing you could do to scare me away. Just relax, let nature take its course. Possess me."

"Then what did you want to say about the other night?"

"I hope that I didn't rush you. Maybe I should have taken it slower."

"Reynold, you were perfect, so understanding and warm. I loved...sleeping with you." She paused for a second. "I only hope I didn't disappoint you. You know..."

Here were two rather mature adults, who should be enjoying the fruits of the sexual revolution, but sounding like two kids playing spin-the-bottle for the first time. She's worried I'm disappointed, while I'm worried I tried to rush her.

"Heather, nothing about that night disappointed me. It was...the most wonderful night in my life. Just being with you, holding you, was wonderful."

"I feel the same. It's just that you're...so experienced and I wanted to make you happy."

"Happy is just being with you. I don't have to...you know...to be happy with you."

"Oh, I hate to do this, but I have students knocking on the door. We'll talk later?"

"Sure will." I made some quick calculations in my head. "I'll be working on a case most of the afternoon. How about dinner? Say early, about five."

"I'd love it. See you then. Bye, Reynold." She hung up the phone but I kept mine to my ear for a minute longer, thinking about her, her voice lingering in my head. She was a real contradiction, if that's the right word for it. Smart, mature, great looking. A doctorate in biology, but still a little girl in some ways, shy and inexperienced, unsure of herself. The inconsistency, though, made me love her more, wanting to lean on the strong part of her while protecting the other.

Philadelphia Mutual Insurance Company held the top three floors of one of the city's newest high-rises, with two special elevators going non-stop past the lower 25 levels. I gave my card to the receptionist and asked to see Mr. Green.

She rang his office. "Mr. Green, there's a mister L. R. Linden to see you, from the Securities and Exchange Commission." I whispered something to her and she added, "He says it's very important and highly confidential."

She hung up the phone. "Mr. Green is very busy today but he'll be able to see you. Please have a seat, someone will be down in a moment."

It was one of those very efficient offices with the receptionist acting like a traffic cop, directing the flow of people from their lobby on the 26th floor to the other offices and floors of the firm. A few other people were waiting in the lobby; they looked like salespeople, going through papers preparing last minute for their presentations. One guy had his briefcase open on his lap so you couldn't see inside; another was thumbing through a thick binder full of papers. If I were a salesperson I'd sit there with my hands folded, or maybe casually reading a magazine like I didn't have a care in the world. I wouldn't want someone to think I wasn't prepared, or see me awkwardly close my briefcase when summoned into the bowels of the firm.

On the opposite side from me was a sharply dressed lady in a suit, one of the tailored jobs. She had her legs crossed so her skirt rode up well above her knees, revealing nice thighs in dark stockings or pantyhose. From time to time I noticed the other guys sneak furtive looks at her legs; quick stares then back to their papers. I wondered how short her skirt was when she stood up. Now I'm all for women's rights. Equal pay for equal work, no sexual harassment and all that. A woman is just another person, deserving the same respect as a man, but human nature is human nature. How would I feel if she were in front of a conference room giving some presentation or sales pitch? I'd be looking at her legs, feeling guilty as hell for it, probably not hearing a word she said. Just couldn't take her seriously.

"Mr. Linden."

"Mr. Linden."

I realized they were calling me.

"Yes?"

"Mr. Linden, I'm Miss Santini, Mr. Green's executive assistant." She was a youngish woman, most likely in her early twenties, dressed conservatively in a black skirt, white blouse, and man-tailored jacket; not the most flattering outfit but probably just right for a place like this. "Please follow me. I'll take you to Mr. Green."

She turned sharply, almost militarily, and walked through the lobby to a doorway. I followed her in the door to a small private elevator down the hall. She pressed the button for floor 3, which I assume was actually the 28th floor in the building, and stood at attention as the doors closed and the elevator lifted.

"Mr. Green is quite busy today," she said offhandedly, staring directly ahead of her at the elevator door. I just nodded.

When the elevator stopped, the doors opened, revealing a plush smaller lobby with dark thick paneling on the walls, real art on the walls, and one large desk with a stern older woman behind.

"Mr. Linden for Mr. Green," my guide said.

The older woman rose from her desk. "Please follow me, Mr. Linden." Like the changing of the guard, the younger woman went back into the elevator and my new guide waved me into a doorway on the right. "Mr. Green is quite busy today, he only has a few minutes. If you'd like, I can schedule a follow-up appointment when you are done." She talked, her back toward me, as she led me down a small hallway framed with paintings of older men in dark gray business suits. She waved her hand toward the wall. "These are the former directors of the company."

"All dead?" I asked. She didn't answer. She stopped, knocked politely but firmly on a door then opened it, letting me pass. Following me in she said "Mr. Green, Mr. Linden. Can I get you anything?"

"No thank you, Mrs. Rocco. That will be all."

I recognized the voice immediately; it was the man who came into my office with Sim that day, staying out of sight behind my back. He rose from his desk. "Mr. Linden...from the SEC, isn't it?"

Green looked at me strangely, like you do at a person you think you met before but just can't place. I remembered that my back was to him when we met in my office. "Haven't we met before?" he asked.

"Yeah, maybe this will help." I turned around and bent over so my ass stuck up in the air. "Sim's footprint finally disappeared," I said.

"London. You. What are you doing here?" I turned around as he was pressing the intercom on his desk. "Get out."

"Not so fast, Green." I drew my 38, walked close and then pressed the barrel to his forehead.

"Yes, Mr. Green?" the intercom buzzed.

I whispered, "Tell her that you don't to be disturbed." He obeyed.

Green was a medium sized guy, a clone of all those hanging in the hallway outside, with a dark gray suit, graying hair at the temples, an executive look. About 50 years old, he had a golf course tan with cold eyes and a steady face, calm and in control even looking into the 38.

"What do you want, London?"

I pointed to a chair on my side of the desk. "Sit down,

Green. Not behind the desk, around here." I changed places with him, sitting in his chair as he sat down in the one intended for me.

"I always wanted to see what it felt like, sitting behind a desk like this."

"Is that why you're here, London? To see how my chair feels?" He was cool.

I put the gun on the desk and started looking through the papers on his desk. "I'm here to return your social calls; Sim and the other clown you sent with your little automatic. Just being polite, that's all." The papers were boring business stuff.

"If you don't mind, London, can we get on with whatever you came here for? I'm a busy man. If you're here to kill me, get it over with. Otherwise say your piece and get out."

I admired how cool Green was. He sat on the chair, looking relaxed, but I could tell he was coiled like a snake, ready to strike. It seemed out of place for a business executive. "It's about the tapes."

He looked up. "Did you find them?"

"Let's say that I'm getting close. But before we talk about them, let's talk about Joanne."

"What do you know about her?" he asked.

"I know she's dead. Why don't you tell me more?"

"Listen London, get to the point."

The little worm was really asking for it. With the 38 in my hand, I walked around to his side of the desk and aimed the gun at his kneecap.

"Did you ever see a man's kneecap shot off, Green?"

"You wouldn't dare?"

"Think I couldn't get away with it, don't you? Shooting you in self defense after you've already sent two hoods with guns after me?"

"You don't have the guts."

I noticed that he really didn't look worried, but was very much in control of his emotions.

"It's not like a bone that can be set, the knee. They can't stick a piece of plastic bone in there."

"You're bluffing, London."

"They just stuff the muscle back in, close it up, and give you a cane. Like having a pole up your pants."

"You don't scare me."

I brought the butt of the gun down near his knee.

"London, stop playing games and get on with it. What do you want?"

"That's good. Very cooperative Mr. Green. First, what do you know about Joanne's death?"

"Tragic. Just what the police told me, what I've read in the paper."

I started toward his knee again.

"Listen, I was her ally, her only one still on the board. I can prove that. Without me she'd have been out a long time ago."

"Why did you help her? What did you get out of it?"

"We go back a long way. Before the company. Even before she was married."

"Tell me about it."

He straightened up a little, keeping both hands on his knees. "I was stationed in Korea, in the army. I needed some extra money so I did some part time work for a small electronics firm in Seoul. Joanne's father owned it. The old man was good to me, kept the deal private."

"Go on."

"Joanne was just a kid back then, spending all her time

learning karate, playing with her girlfriends. She was a beautiful child."

"A beautiful woman, too," I added.

"Anyway, when I got back to the States, I kept on writing to her father. We made a deal and I represented his company here, and I made a nice little living out of it. Then Joanne married Paek, moved here and they eventually started the insurance company. They brought me on board. I was like an uncle to her."

His eyes watered and he put his head down in his hands. "I loved the girl. She was like a daughter to me."

"About the company. You two agreed on everything?"

He looked up. "No. Not on everything. Oh, in front of the board I'd side with her on everything. But we often disagreed, had our private fights on smaller issues, where I thought she was wrong, from her inexperience. But we put up a united front to outsiders."

"Did you see her the night she was killed?"

"No. I spoke with her, on the phone. She found out that we were putting pressure on you, scaring you, that's all. We would never have hurt you. She was furious at me. She yelled at me, claimed I was shaming her husband's memory, dishonoring my friendship with her father. I tried to explain to her but she hung up. The next thing I heard, she was killed by some thief in Chinatown."

"I don't think it was a thief, Green. I think she was killed deliberately, stalked and killed by an expert, an assassin."

"Who would...?"

"Listen, you told me yourself how much money is involved in this. You even sent people after me with guns..."

"Just to scare you so you'd look for the tapes," he said softly, resigned.

"Do you really think that others won't kill for that much; that businessmen will just fight in the boardroom? I've seen people killed for loose change in their pocket. You're talking about millions here." Green started to speak, to deny that big business could lead to violence. I wouldn't let him. "You sit in your paneled office, protected by secretaries and the organization, like the dictator of some mosquito-ridden country. But you're facing a revolution like it's a gentlemen's disagreement. Don't be so naive. This is a real revolution. People are getting killed, like Joanne, the Trendles. And more people will die until you face up to the truth."

"Which is?"

"That someone out there is playing this for real. They're using bullets and fists, not memos. It's no game to these people and they'll do anything to win. What's your position here anyway?"

Without looking up, he explained that there were two executive vice presidents who really ran the company, him and Peterson. Paek, Joanne's husband, was president until he died about five years ago, then the infighting began. Joanne was put in as president but just as a figurehead only. A rather unique situation, Green said, because of the intense loyalty to the Paek family, but the two vice presidents really took care of the firm. One of them, Green or Peterson, would end up as president once the board stopped arguing among themselves. According to Green, the company was doing fine this way and a few key members of the board wanted it to stay that way until one of the vice presidents proved especially worthy of the promotion.

"Now tell me about the tapes," I said.

Green stood up and paced slowly around the room. He stopped in front of the window and stared. "The tapes contain our backup system, a complete record of our business, clients, tables, figures...everything." He waved his hand like everything included the entire world. "They were supposed to go to a security location in New York, in the event of a computer disaster here. That way we'd be back in business in a matter of minutes."

"Why are they worth so much?"

He looked at me. "For a lot of reasons. First, if we lost our computer system, with no backup we'd lose millions a day. Lost income, lost clients, interest penalties. In one week we'd lose so much we might never come out of it.

"Second, the competition might have them. They'd know everything about us, they'd be able to undercut us with our own customers, slice just a little off, ruin us."

I felt there was still more. "And third, Green?"

"And third, if the board knew about the tapes, we'd be done. Joanne, the Paeks, and me. Peterson would use this to prove our incompetence, get us thrown off of the board, get complete control. Data processing is one of my departments, and Peterson would use this incident against me if he ever found out that the tapes were missing."

"You'd lose your fat paycheck," I sneered.

He hesitated. "Yes. But more than that. Joanne's family would lose face, plus the legacy that should be theirs, that should be Lydia's."

"Okay. Now tell me about the tapes." I was getting impatient.

Green looked in control as he explained what had happened. It seemed that somehow a set of backup tapes waiting to be picked up by the security firm just disappeared. One minute they were on a secretary's desk, the next they were gone.

"Then we got the call," he explained. "They wanted a quarter of a million to return the tapes. If we didn't pay, they'd auction the tapes off to the highest bidder among our competition or in the other camp here. It had to be someone knowledgeable about our internal problems and about the value of those tapes to us if they got into the wrong hands.

"We agreed to pay. It was set up that someone would take the money to the Bourse building. At a certain time, our representative was to leave the money in an elevator on the east side of the building, then walk to the west side elevator where the tapes would be waiting. It was the day the Trendles were killed. But the Trendles blew that."

"Explain."

"That's the funny, I mean odd, part. I don't really know what happened. At about 2 p.m. we got a call from the thieves. They were furious. They claimed we paid Trendle to steal the money back from them. They threatened to bomb our building, to steal another set of tapes, to destroy us. Of course, we had no idea what was going on, what this guy Trendle had to do with it. They told me that they'd taken care of Trendle, that was their words, but they weren't done with us.

"Well, we traced Trendle through the police report." He noticed my expression. "Oh, you'd be surprised at the contacts we have with the police, Mr. London. Joanne volunteered to visit Mrs. Trendle to see if she could shed some light on the subject. She had just gotten to the Trendle house when you interrupted."

I looked at him like he was crazy. "Do you really expect me to believe that's all you know?"

"It's the truth. We have no idea how Trendle got the tapes, if he did in fact ever have them at all, or how he got our money. I can only assume that he was somehow involved, but was killed by the thieves in the bargain."

"So why didn't they take the cash?"

"Good question. Perhaps they were too interested in locating the tapes themselves. Or maybe they thought the money was marked someway. I wish I knew."

"Why didn't you tell all this to the police?"

"The police? We didn't want the board to know about the tapes. I mean if Trendle was mixed up in this he probably deserved what he got. We just didn't see the...profit in letting this get public yet."

The conversation reminded me that a quarter of a million bucks of the company's money was sitting in the police station.

"What about the cash, the money that Trendle had on him? Are you getting it back?"

He shook his head.

"Right now that would be a real problem. The police don't know this story, remember. If we make any claim against it then the whole story will come out. We'd be ruined. I suppose until the case is solved, the money is some type of evidence. Maybe it'll go to the Trendle estate."

"How the hell did you come up with that much money anyway, without Peterson finding out?"

"Oh, don't ask," he moaned. "Some of it is my personal money, some we siphoned off from various discretionary accounts under our control. It's just a mess. A real mess."

Green filled me in on Peterson, the rival, and then I left him alone in his office. Mrs. Rocco, the secretary, didn't want me to get on the elevator without being escorted out, but when I told her she'd better check on her boss she quickly ran down the hall leaving me alone in the outer office.

I used the time to copy some names, numbers, and addresses from her card file and check Green's appointment book that was on her desk. His calendar was clear for the day Trendle was killed. I also took a look at some papers she had laying around and was going through her filing cabinet when she returned.

"Can I ask you what you're doing?" She had one of those annoying voices that felt like someone was filing your brain with sandpaper.

"SEC business," I said. Then I just walked over to elevator, waited till it arrived and got in, all the while Mrs. Rocco was leering at me, madly checking her papers to make sure I didn't steal anything.

Well, that certainly wasn't productive, aside from a little revenge on Green. I still didn't know what Trendle really had to do with this, and no idea where the tapes were. Green's coolness, how he carried himself, even when threatened with a gun, perplexed me. I wouldn't think some insurance executive had that much control.

At this point, though, I couldn't give a damn about the Green and the tapes, but I did care about Lydia and making sure she got what she deserved, finding her mother's killer and getting her share of the company. So I figured the tapes were still my business. Anyway, the reward offer probably still stood.

Chapter 13

Peterson, the arch rival, seemed the next logical step but I wanted to see him at his home unsupported by company staff and security. It was still early enough so I buzzed over to the campus hoping to get some other lead on Robert. Heather had given me a more recent photo of him that she got from her parents, and I started showing it around wherever I thought he might have been.

After lunch, my dumb luck paid off. As I was driving down Spruce I passed Stan going by on his scooter. I made a u-turn, nearly crashing into a pizza truck, and started following him, several cars behind. The kid was nuts, he was cutting in and out of traffic, going up on the sidewalk, making him damn hard to tail. Luckily his bike was one of the small imported jobs that didn't go very fast, so I could catch up on the straight ways. I didn't know why I was following him at all. I'd already been warned off by the FBI, and begged by Bennite, but I hadn't exactly been Sherlock Holmes in getting a lead on Robert. Except for a few minor possibilities, I wasn't getting anywhere in either case so I figured what the hell, I might as well tag along with Stanley for a little while; it's no crime driving down Spruce Street in Philadelphia, yet.

Stan drove out Spruce, turned left on 38th, then right on Baltimore. He went left onto Woodland, then followed it straight out to 51st Street, deep into West Philly past the pharmacy college. He turned right onto 51st then pulled his bike onto the curb, about halfway down the block, between Woodland and Greenway.

Maybe he was just visiting friends or doing research, but the way he looked around before going up to the door made me think something else was on his mind. It was a typical West Philly row house, with no lawn and a facade that had seen better days. Stan knocked on the door, paused, and then knocked again. Someone I couldn't see opened the door and let him in.

I had pulled over to the curb near the end of the block, between a faded green Chevy, about early 80's, and an '85 Mustang in orange primer. My Tercel looked pretty good in that company. While I watched the door where Stan disappeared I tried again to sort things out.

My life had certainly changed in these past weeks, going from a two-bit unknown detective working crap jobs to a two-bit madly-in-love detective, with the police, FBI, and college hoodlums up my ass, getting nowhere on what may be the two most important cases I'd ever handled. Talk about complications. And what was I going to do about Heather? Could I ever really expect she'd feel the same way about me, once she got over this naive infatuation. Maybe she was clinging to me out of fear for her brother, or maybe I provided her with some temporary escape, but could a classy broad like that ever really fall for me? And did she deserve getting stuck with me even if she did?

I was half unconscious in thought when I saw movement from the doorway. Stan came out, screamed something at the doorway, then hopped on his bike and took off. I wondered about the house now more than Stan, so I waited till he was clear then strolled back and forth past the place a few times trying to get a peek in the door or windows but every shade in the place was down, the door was closed tight.

It was one of those blocks with a narrow alley running up the back of the houses, shared by those on this street and the next over. I counted the houses then walked up the alley using the count to locate the back of the same house. There were some metal trashcans tucked under what seemed like the kitchen window with the shade only half drawn. As quietly as possible, I climbed onto the strongest looking can and stood on my toes, grasping the windowsill so I could just get a glimpse inside the place. Like Stan's place the kitchen was mess; cans and bottles, empty pizza boxes and take-out bags were all over the place. The refrigerator was open and some guy's ass was hanging out like he was looking for something. I ducked down as far as I could so I could move out of sight as soon as he stood up, but he pulled back and turned the other way, facing the sink, with a box of fried chicken in his hands, a leg sticking out of his mouth.

"Last chicken. If you want it get in here," he yelled.

Then a voice yelled something from inside the house, the guy cursed a few times, stuffed another piece of chicken in his mouth then turned. I ducked under the window but the shift made me slip and lose balance. Trying to stay up, I sort of tiptoed over the trash can lid for a moment, but the can won, and I went crashing down onto the lid then sliding down feet first into the garage door. Sounded like a goddamn truck plowing into the house. I was laying there, with my back bent between the garage door and a pile of cans, staring straight up expecting the kitchen window or downstairs door to open up. But nothing happened.

Christ, they had to hear that racket, even if chicken-man didn't see my face before I collapsed. But no one yelled or came out. It was hard to get up but I managed to get onto my knees, then my feet, and walked around to the front of the block. As I turned the corner I saw five guys run out of the house and into a car. My eyes were still a little blurry from the fall but I knew what I saw: one of them was Robert, Heather's brother.

As they sped past me in their car I tried to flag them down, get them to stop, but they just zoomed by.

That little jerk ought to be tanned, I thought. Making Heather worry so much about him, all the while running around with Stan and his friends. What the hell were they up to?

I went to the house and, finding the door wide open, invited myself in. The living room was bare except for four tables set up with computers, each one with a phone wire running over to a box near the wall outlet. There were papers all over the place but they were filled with nothing but numbers. Except for the food in the kitchen, the rest of the downstairs was bare, not a stick of furniture in the place.

Then it hit me that these guys were more afraid of me, or at least of someone, than I was of being caught by them. At the first sign of an outsider they left this expensive computer stuff and ran out as fast as they could.

I don't know anything about computers but I knew that this stuff must be able to tell me something about Stan and his friends, but I couldn't figure this hardware out. The only person I knew smart enough was Heather. She was at her office and agreed to drive over here. I didn't tell her anything about her brother yet, just that I needed some help on a case. She was pleased to help and made it in about 30 minutes.

"You see those wires going to the phone box," she said. "They're attached to modems inside the computers. The modems are used to let these computers communicate with other computers at the other end of a phone connection. It looks like they have T1 lines."

"What would they be doing here?"

"Well, from the looks of things I'd guess some illegal activity. Maybe a computerized numbers operation, electronic theft, something like that."

"Could it be just a group of kids playing around?"

"You mean hackers? I don't think so. Look at the equipment here, and the rest of the house. This isn't just some home. I mean no one really lives here; this place is just set up for this phone operation. And the hardware is pretty expensive. Here, let me show you."

She sat down and turned on one of the computers, then started hitting keys. "You see, these machines are using synchronous communications cards used to talk with mainframes." I must have had this dumb look on my face. "Large computer systems," she added, "the type businesses would use. Not home computers. I'm sure you've already planned to contact the phone company for a lead."

"Of course," I lied.

"Whoever owns this stuff just ran out when they heard you?"

"Yeah. Within a few minutes after...after I made myself known to them; they were out the door. Left it wide open."

She scooped up some pages that were lying on a table then quickly scanned two sheets. "I'd guess it wasn't numbers. These don't look like betting slips, the numbers are wrong for that."

I acted surprised. "And how does a nice girl like you know so much about numbers?"

"I've been around in my own way. From the looks of these papers it seems that they're professional hackers, not kids out for a lark, but a well organized and financed team out for big money. Take a look at these." She held up a pack of papers that were lying on the floor. "These look like password sequences and access codes; the numbers needed to gain entry into sophisticated computer systems."

"Hey, I knew that."

"Four separate lines mean they were working to break into more than one system at a time, or using a multiple approach."

"Can you find out anything by looking at what's in the machine?"

"What's in the machine? You mean what's stored on the disks. Give me some time." She turned on all the computers, moving back and forth between them, hitting keys. As she worked, I took a look around the second floor. No furniture, like downstairs, just some dirty clothes, a couple of blankets, a book of poetry with no name inside, and a pair of sneakers with holes in the soles. I carried the stuff downstairs and laid it on the floor near the door when Heather called me over.

"Just found a couple of programs and some data so far," she said. "These guys were too smart to leave too much else on here. The programs are code breakers. I can't tell for sure without seeing the code, but they look like AI programs designed to gain access into systems."

I felt like a moron but I asked anyway. "What's AI?"

Without even looking up she said, "Artificial intelligence, a program that sort of learns by itself, by its mistakes. Two of the computers use synchronous communications boards, the other two asynchronous. They could be used for some less expensive systems. From what I could gather, all of the results were printed on that printer over there, the four computers share it through that box on top. There's nothing else on the disks except a few small data files that I can't make anything out of yet."

"Okay. Is there anyway to take those files with us?"

"Sure. I'll take some of the disks they have around, and there's a box of CDRs over there, recordable CDs. I'll copy all of the files that can fit. Just take a few minutes, depending on the speed of the drives."

It took her about 30 minutes to make the copies and turn all of the computers off. "Just in case they come back, I erased their programs," she said. "We can take all of the CDs with us so it might put them out of business for a while. Not too long I'm afraid."

She gathered up her things while I scooped up the clothes and book I came across, hoping I might learn something from them later. But all of a sudden Heather stopped dead and slapped me hard across the face.

"How could you? How could you know and not tell me?"

"Heather, what are you talking about?"

"You found Robert! You found him and you got my help in linking him with something illegal, without telling me."

She went to slap me again but I caught her hand. "What are you talking about?" I asked.

"That book. The one you're holding. It's Robert's."

"What?"

"I gave that book to Robert years ago. I can tell by the mark on the spine, a little code we used to have between us when we were young. How could you?"

"Listen, Heather. The truth. I knew Robert was here. He was one of the guys that ran out of here. I tried to stop him but couldn't. I wanted to tell you but I didn't want you to know if he was involved in something wrong, not yet at least. I didn't know what was going on in here until you told me just now."

"I'm sorry, Reynold." She put her arms around me and cried. I was holding her, kissing the top of her head when I heard a car pull up outside and voices getting closer.

"They've come back," I said. I looked around then started up the steps, pulling Heather by the arm.

She protested, resisting my pull. "It may be Robert. Where are you going?"

I continued to pull, this time hard enough to move her. "And it also might be some hood who financed this operation."

She started talking louder as I dragged her onto the steps. "No one would hurt us, especially if Robert's involved. He wouldn't get involved in any violence. Can we at least wait and see?"

I had her almost at the top of the stairs when I heard the voices getting closer outside. Luckily I had shut the door when we came in. "I don't know who's out there, or what they are capable of doing. But you're here and I can't take any chances. Just be quiet, very quiet, and stick with me awhile."

We ducked into one of the rooms then into a closet. I put my hand on her mouth indicating that she should be very quiet, then I closed the door almost the whole way and we knelt down in the darkness. The voices were muffled but I was able to make out most of what they said. I heard two voices, one yelling much louder than the other.

"I can't believe you just left this stuff here cause you heard a noise," he yelled.

"Hey, it was our ass on the line, not yours. Where the hell would you be if it were the cops?"

"I'd be getting you out of jail, you moron. But it wasn't the cops, maybe just a rat or some kids playing."

"Someone was looking in the window, in the kitchen. I'm sure of it. Then I heard at least five of them banging on the garage door downstairs."

The loud one called the other some unkind names. "Then where the hell are they? We drove around this block ten times. No cops, no broken doors. Just all this crap sitting here with the door unlocked. Take a look around."

"For what?"

"Maybe someone was here when you were gone. Maybe the cops are hiding in a closet to scare you. Just look around. Start upstairs."

I heard footsteps on the stairs, then in the hallway outside our room, but no sounds of doors being opened, of a search taking place. I figured this guy was too scared to really search.

"Find anything?" the loud one yelled from downstairs.

"Nothing up here. I'm coming down."

For a long while I heard them talking, trying to figure out what to do. They were screaming at each other, the cursing getting worse and worse, and then it got quiet. In the darkness of the closet, however, I just held onto Heather, stroking her hair trying to comfort her. "Does either one of them sound like your brother?" I whispered. She shook her head.

There wasn't much room in there. Our legs were touching and we held each other tightly to balance each other from falling. I was worried about her safety, but equally anxious to see who was downstairs, maybe hold them for the cops. When I started to whisper to her, she turned her face toward me so her lips where just a breath apart from mine. I didn't want to kiss her. Well, I did but I didn't want to forget why we were hiding in the closet. But she smelled so good, her body felt so warm next to mine, that my own desires took control. I pulled her face toward me and kissed her, a long, hard kiss with my tongue stroking the inside of her lips, her teeth, then finding her tongue. Her hand came down my side and onto my thigh, squeezing it, moving up, then squeezing it again, until her fingertips were almost between my legs. I moved my own hand down her slender neck, caressing as I went into the top of her blouse. Then we both fell over sideways, rolling out of the closet and crashing onto the floor of the room. As we fell, my hand got caught in her blouse and the front ripped straight down, scattering the buttons out into the room.

Chapter 14

I put my hand over her mouth and held her so she couldn't move. One of her hands was still between my legs, the other around my back. Her blouse was wide open and I could see a delicate lace bra, a pale yellow that looked sensual against her tan skin, low cut, showing some cleavage and the smooth round tops of her breasts. The lace was half way down, far enough so I could see the outline of her nipples, pink and erect.

If anyone were still in the house, they'd be running up the steps soon. I listened, preparing myself to roll off of Heather, grab my 38 and get a clear aim at the top of the steps, but I didn't hear a sound except a muffled giggle, a laugh that Heather was stifling under my hand.

"What's so funny?" I whispered, removing my hand.

"How we just rolled out of the closet. Now I know what a bowling ball feels like." She started to laugh but covered her mouth with her hand.

"Very funny. Listen, they must have gone out. I'm going to take a look."

"Don't..."

"I'll be careful. I want you to go back in the closet and wait there till I come back. Don't make a sound." I kissed her on the lips then bent down to kiss the silky skin of her chest.

I started slowly out the door on my knees, with the 38 in hand, while Heather crawled back into the closet. I tried to be as quiet as possible but I put my knee down on one of her buttons and gasped. No response from downstairs. I was just about at the top of the steps when I heard the door open. They had returned.

"Get that computer over there. I'll look around for the disks," one of them said. They must be packing up the hardware. I crawled to the top of the steps and, flat on my stomach, craned my head down the top step so I could see under the railing.

There were two of them. One was unplugging cables from a computer, throwing them into a bag. The other guy was looking everywhere.

"Where'd you put the disks?"

"Over there," the other said, pointing to a table.

"Well, they're not here. Where the hell did you put them?"

"They got to be around. I'll take this one out." He picked up a computer and walked out the door while the other kid walked into the kitchen.

With only one of them in the house now I figured I had a chance to get the drop on them. I crawled down the steps on my stomach, a technique I learned in the Marines, only with barbed wire and bullets flying over my head, and then got to my feet when I reached the bottom. It sounded like he was panicking looking for the disks that Heather had in her handbag upstairs. He was slamming drawers and cabinet doors, cursing. With all the noise I was able to walk into the kitchen and grab him around the neck before he knew I was there.

"Shut up and listen," I said. I put the 38 to the side of his face. "Don't make a sound, just nod your head if you understand."

He nodded.

"Is your friend coming back?"

He nodded.

"Okay, we're going to turn around real slow so you're facing the door. When he comes in, call him into the kitchen. Understand?"

He nodded.

The turkey was a strongly built kid about 21, with long sandy-colored hair, dirty and unkempt. He didn't say anything but I could tell he was trying to figure a way out of my grip. I pulled him tighter and pressed the gun so hard into his cheek that I felt the teeth against the barrel.

"Don't even think of trying to get out," I warned.

"Find them, Ted?" The other kid returned.

"Call him in here," I whispered.

"I'm in here, the kitchen. Come on in." The kid was nervous but it sounded okay. Footsteps, then the other one was in the doorway.

"What the hell!"

"Don't move. Walk into the kitchen and lay on the floor, under the table," I ordered.

He was just about to move when Heather walked in. I started to warn her when the kid spun around, grabbed her arm and pulled her tight to his chest, with one hand around her neck.

"Put the gun down or I'll snap her neck," he yelled. He was a strong kid too, probably physically capable of breaking her neck. I was about to release my grip when Heather became a blur. She slammed her foot into his instep, one hand grabbed his choking arm and pulled down while she reached up and around with the other, grasping his shirt. She yelled and bent down, pulling him over her shoulder, onto the floor. As he hit the ground, she stamped down hard on his arm then grabbed his neck with a claw grip, distributing her weight for balance and strength.

"Where'd you learn that?"

"I took Judo in college for four years." She pulled the kid up by his neck, twisting his arm around into a half nelson and locking his neck in her arm.

"I'm going to ask my friend to let you go in a minute," I said. "When she does, I want you to lay on the floor under the table. Don't try anything stupid or she'll break your neck. Okay?"

"Okay", he gargled.

"Let him go, real carefully." Heather slowly released her grip, backing away as she did. By the time he was free, Heather was far enough back to avoid any surprise blow or action on his part. The kid looked around then went down on the floor and slid under the table.

"Heather, put two chairs in back of him." She moved two kitchen chairs so they straddled his legs.

"Now you," I said to the kid I was holding. I reached over and opened the oven door. "Kneel down and stick your head in the oven, all the way in." I pushed him down and in so his head hit the back of the oven, then I put my foot on his back like Sim had done to me.

Heather moved more into the kitchen, keeping an eye on the kid on the floor. She had tied the tails of her blouse into a knot, keeping it somewhat together but low enough so you could see the ravine between her breasts.

"Who do you work for?" I asked. The kid said something but his head was too far in the oven for me to hear. "Louder, I can't hear you!" I pushed my foot.

"I'm just picking this stuff up, that's all."

"Don't lie to me, you know more than that. Who do you work for? What are you doing?"

"I don't know what you're talking about."

I reached over and cracked the gas knob just a little, enough to make it smell. The kid tried to lurch out but my foot held him in.

"Don't worry, it won't explode," I said. "But you might run out of air down there." He twisted some. "First you'll have a hard time breathing, then you'll turn blue and start to vomit. Real big retches from the pit of your stomach."

"I can't breathe. This stuff is killing me," he yelled.

"Not yet, you haven't had enough yet. You won't actually die for a couple of days. The gas will get into your blood stream, to every part of your body. You're kidneys go first so they'll give you rubber jockey shorts, then your spleen and a few other organs. Finally your brain goes, so you're one big Brussels sprout, laying there with tubes sticking out of your nose."

"I can't breathe!"

"Got the idea. Now who do you work for?"

"No one. We're in this together, partners."

"You and who else?"

"Listen I can't breathe. Let me out!"

"First talk, then breathe. Your partners?"

"Kids from school. Paul, Ken, Stan. That's all."

"What are you doing?" I asked.

"Just having fun, that's all. Hacking. Getting into banks, companies, leaving messages, small viruses that don't do any harm."

"You kids pay for all this hardware on your milk money?"

"Yeah, it's ours."

I looked over to Heather. She shook her head.

"I didn't like that answer," I said, and then I kicked him a little harder into the back of the over. "Let's try again. Who paid for this stuff?"

"I don't know. Stan. Ask Stan. Some friend of his gave it to him. Said it was for research on security systems."

Heather came over. "Who were you trying to hack?" she asked.

"What?" the kid yelled.

"What companies were you trying to break into? Who picked them?"

"Couple of insurance companies, the college, phone company. The City. But it was just for fun, test their security."

"Who picked the companies?" she repeated.

"Stan. It was his idea. He said they had the hardest systems to break into. But he was good. Got into some insurance company the first time out."

Now it was my turn again.

"Which one was that easy for him?"

"I can't remember. Christ, how do you..."

"Which one was it? Philadelphia Mutual, Reliance, Nassau?"

"Philly Mutual. That was it. Got into it the first day, like he knew the codes or something."

I relaxed my foot a little. "Okay, you're being a very good boy. Just a little more and you can get all the air you want. Did you ever see two big goons hanging out around Stan's place?"

"What? Listen I can hardly breathe in here."

"So make it quick. Two goons, big guys in suits. Maybe talking to Sue."

"Nothing like that. Just guys from school. I mean it, I'll die in here. I told you everything."

I pulled the kid out then pushed him over to the window so he could get some air. The kid under the table must have been scared to death because he didn't move during this whole thing. I kicked him on the ass.

"Okay, you're turn to play gas man."

"Hey, he told you the truth. Everything. This is all Stan's idea."

Heather whispered something in my ear.

"Do either of you guys know Robert, the kid from Long

Island? He was with you this morning."

"Yeah, some friend of Stan's. Visiting."

"What does he have to do with this?"

"Nothing...really. Doing some research from school, wanted to get into some insurance company files. We helped him out."

"So why'd he run with you? He's been hiding, did you know that?"

"He's been crashing here for about a week. Said something about a killing on Long Island, the mob, something like that. We figured he was shitting us, just hiding from his folks or something."

I was about to ask another question when Heather grabbed my arm. She asked, "What did he want from the insurance company files?"

The kids didn't say a word so I grabbed the one hanging near the window and started pulling him back toward the oven.

"We don't know, I swear. We got him into the system then gave him the terminal. He spent about an hour but he sounded like he didn't find what he was looking for."

"Which company?' Heather asked.

"What?"

"What insurance company was he interested in?"

"Oh. Reliance. That was the only one."

We let the two go but we took one of their computers so we could look through the disks Heather had. I didn't see any sense in calling in the cops at this point, at least until I found out how Robert was involved. Heather was in no condition to go back to campus, so I followed her back to her apartment. After setting up the computer in her dining room, she went to change clothes while I got coffee going on the stove.

The judo thing really surprised me. I didn't picture her as the violent type, or perhaps I just wanted to be her strong protector, not the other way around. I suppose what got to me most was the speed and force of her movements. They showed training and practice, not some casual physical education classes taken long ago in college days. I imagine martial arts are like swimming or bike riding, the skills come back quickly even after years of dormancy, but her performance in the kitchen was perfectly timed, without hesitation, almost instinctively, as Joanne's or Lydia's.

Bike riding and the smell of fresh coffee reminded me of one of my first cases. I was just out of the Marines, doing background checks on perspective employees for a large bank, trying to build up my business. I couldn't afford a car those days so I either took public transportation or peddled around town on my bike, one of those heavy single speed jobs with all of the metal. They wanted me to find out about this guy named Smithson, I can't remember his first name, who was applying for a cashier's job. His references checked out fine, but where money was concerned, this particular bank wanted a personal background check.

Smithson didn't live too far from my own place, a small rented apartment in West Philly, so I took my bike and headed out to his neighborhood. It was early in the morning, about 8 a.m., too early to go knocking on neighbors' doors, so I got a cup of coffee and donut at some diner down the block and just sat, guarding my bike that was parked outside. The coffee was good, hot and fresh, the donut was bad, hard and stale. I had to hold the damn thing in the hot coffee a full minute before it tasted like anything but cardboard. I suppose I was concentrating too much on the coffee because when I turned around the bike was gone. I jumped up, spilling hot coffee all over me, and saw some guy halfway down the block walking my bike away, not riding it.

Well, I dropped a buck down on the table and lit out of there like a guy with diarrhea a mile from a john. I raced down the street, still stinging from the coffee, screaming obscenities at the top of my lungs. Of course, people were staring at me; not only because I was yelling and running but also because I had this big dark wet mark in the middle of my pants, but all I could think about was my bike, about the only real possession that I owned in the world.

About a block from the diner I finally caught up with the guy, who had never turned around, never started running, never even got on the bike to ride it away. I grabbed onto his shoulder, spun him around and cocked my arm back about to slug his teeth in, but he just looked at me with blank eyes and a wide stupid grin. A piece of paper with his name and address was pinned to his shirt, odd for a guy that looked in his twenties.

Well, we all don't get the same brains from God, and obviously this guy was caught short on a few deliveries. He just stood there smiling saying something I really didn't understand. But I had to do something; what if the next bike belonged to someone not as soft as me. That's when I noticed that the kid's address was just a few doors down from Smithson's. I calmed down and walked the kid, and my bike, to his house.

The guy lived with his elderly parents. Now old and infirm, they had enough trouble taking care of themselves, let alone their son. You could tell a lot about them from the house. Whatever they had was neat and clean, but they certainly didn't have much, I didn't even see a television. There were a few books piled neatly on the floor; a sofa and a couple of old chairs, threadbare and worn; a small dining room table covered by a starched white table cloth with holes that were neatly sown up. Gerald was their only child, a son born late in life. They had taken care of him since he was born, since the doctors told them he could never care for himself. It would have been different now, but in those days parents just took the kid home and smothered him in love, not even thinking that anything could be done. After all, the doctor had said so.

They told me that this wasn't the first time Gerald had walked away with someone's bike. About once a month he would come home beaten up and bloody, being caught in the act by some neighborhood kids. Gerald had always wanted to ride a bike like the other kids he'd see tear down the street, laughing and yelling, but they were afraid he'd get hurt, and they didn't have the money to spare. Even if they could afford one, they said, Gerald's father was too old to teach his son how to ride.

I saw that Gerald wasn't a bad kid, he just lived in his own little sheltered world. In fact, I don't think he knew he was doing anything wrong in walking off with someone else's bike. That's why he just walked slowly down the block after taking mine, like he didn't have a care in the world. I started to like Gerald and his parents, although as I look back now I know there was a lot more they could have done for him. But they were honest, loving people who sincerely thought they were doing the best for the boy.

Maybe that's why I got involved. I came back every Sunday for about three months and taught Gerald how to ride my bike. It wasn't easy, after all Gerald was a big guy, physically not a little kid any more. I'd hold him up with one hand, pushing with the other as I ran beside him down the sidewalk. After about two weeks he was able to ride straight by himself, as long as he didn't have to stop or turn.

Then I worked on stopping for about another two weeks. I'd run beside him then yell to stop, at first grabbing onto the bike when he forgot to rotate the pedals back to brake. He finally mastered it. Turning was the hard part. Gerald didn't have much of a sense of balance or timing. When he tried to turn he'd just sit up straight as an arrow and jerk the handlebars left or right, collapsing onto the pavement with a thud.

Now that I think about it, I don't know how I ever did it. I started by showing him how I turned the bike. At first he didn't want to relinquish it, crying when he'd see me peddle away. But then he'd start laughing and yelling as I turned around and headed back toward him.

When I got close, I'd tell him to watch, and then I'd slow down as much as possible and do a nice turn in front of him. After a month of that I put him back on the bike and walked him through a few turns. Then he'd try it on his own. Well, after about three months Gerald was able to ride, by himself, around the block and down to the corner stores. The first few times his parents insisted that I'd go with him, walking or running by his side, to make sure he didn't get hurt, then I was able to convince them that he could do it on his own.

It turned out to be good for all of them. After a while, Gerald was able to pick up small amounts of groceries and bring them home balanced in a basket I attached to the back of the bike. I was getting too old myself for a bike, so one day I told Gerald it was his to keep, and then I just didn't see them for a while. Business I suppose, and other interests.

One day, about two years after giving him the bike I stopped by the house. Some new people were living there. It seems Gerald's mother died and the old man wasn't able to care for himself any more. He and Gerald went to live with a brother of his down south somewhere.

I heard from them last about another two years after that. The old man died and Gerald was put into some sort of home. His uncle, the one he had been living with, sent me a letter the old man had written to me just before he died. I cried as I read it.

Smithson, by the way, checked out fine. Gerald's folks spoke highly of him, so did the rest of the neighbors. I gave him a clean bill and got paid by the bank. He was an outstanding employee until about 1988. An article appeared in the paper about this bank vice president named Smithson who embezzled over a million dollars from the bank then disappeared into South America somewhere.

Chapter 15

"Reynold."

"Reynold."

I turned around and saw Heather standing there. She was in a thick white bathrobe, rubbing her wet hair with a terry cloth towel.

"I'm sorry I was so long, Reynold. I decided to shower before changing. I just felt so dirty from the closet. That house was filthy."

She was wearing no makeup, no shoes, just the robe and some water dripping from the ends of her hair, glistening drops that sparkled then fell to earth like stars falling from the sky. I couldn't say a word.

"Where should we go to dinner? It will help me decide what to wear?" She looked at me, sitting like a dummy, staring. "Are you okay?" she asked.

I stood up from the table and walked over to her.

"You're beautiful," I said. Then I put my arms around her and held her close, her wet hair soaking through my shirt, water dripping on my shoes.

"Reynold, I think I love you," she said hesitantly.

"I think I love you, Heather." We kissed gently; I stroked her hair as the towel fell from her hands. She smelled wonderful, a fresh almost almond scent that she later told me was from her shampoo, but it was both an intoxicant and an aphrodisiac to me then, penetrating deep into my heart and mind.

"Heather, I know I said we'd have dinner. But can it wait just a little while. There's something I have to do, important, for a case." She looked up, a little disappointed. "I'll just be away about two hours," I added. "Then we can have a nice dinner together."

"I hate for you go, you know, but if it's important, of course. Can I come with you?"

"You might get bored. I just have to talk to a man about a case."

"I'll just wait in the car, if it's okay, then we can get dinner, and maybe come back here afterward."

How could I refuse her, she looked so cute in the bathrobe and wet hair, sensual yet like a little girl pleading for an ice cream cone or trip to the fair. She dressed, a flowing yellow skirt, a white and yellow flowered blouse, then we drove out to Wallingford where Peterson lived.

Wallingford is Main Line, huge mansions on perfectly manicured lawns; big cars in every drive; no kids playing stickball on the streets or hanging out on the corner. It is a ghetto for the rich and upper class, where ground is measured in acres not feet, and where the best of everything finds a home.

Peterson's place was like the rest, a huge old stone house perched high on the lawn, far back from the street and shaded by tall trees. A semi-circular drive lead up from the street to the doorway, which was protected by white pillars, three stories high, standing on a raised platform about four steps up from grass level. A set of dark heavy-looking double doors was in the center, each decorated with a green wreath and metal bars. I looked around the place for a few minutes, and then tried the door.

"Are you Mr. Peterson?" I asked the old guy who answered the door.

He looked annoyed and said, "Who's calling?"

I handed him my card. "Ray Lindon, Interpol. A security matter, very important."

"I'm Peterson," he said. He nodded toward Heather, who was sitting in the car in the drive. "Does your associate wish to join you?"

"No. Security reasons. She must remain outside watching the door."

"Come in, if you have to," he said.

The hallway was a huge room, three stories high, with a wood and marble staircase leading up, oil paintings hanging on the walls. To the right and left were sets of closed double doors, to the back was a single door that looked like it led to a long hallway. The floor was marble, like that on the stairs, partially covered with a thick oriental-looking carpet. A huge glass chandelier hung down, the chain two stories long from the top of the hallway ceiling.

Peterson led me in to what appeared to be a library of some sort. He was a thin, old, frail man; not at all what I expected. He sat down in a dark brown leather covered chair at the far end of the room.

"How can I help you, Mr. Lindon?" While his body seemed frail and weak, his voice was strong and secure.

"May I sit down?"

He looked annoyed. "If you must." I sat down in a similar leather chair, across from him on an angle. "Now what can I do for you?"

"Mr. Peterson, I'm investigating a possible international plot to defraud your company. I'd like some information regarding..."

He sneered and interrupted. "Please cut the crap, Mr. London. I know who you are. I am quite aware of your interruptions. I have been expecting you, although I am amused by your charade."

He reached over and pushed a small button attached to the side of the table next to him. The doors opened and the two goons from the Ford, the fake FBI agents I met at Stan's apartment, came in with Heather struggling between them.

Peterson coughed. "I did not know you had an associate, Mr. London," he said. "I had been told you worked alone. But none-the-less, we have taken the liberty of asking your associate to join us."

I stood up and started to reach for my gun.

"I would advise you to remain calm, Mr. London. My associates would not hesitate to harm you or your friend over there. They are quite capable of that sort of thing, although I personally abhor violence of any type. Why don't you just sit down?"

I hesitated for a second to take a quick look at the situation. I knew what the two goons were capable of, although I wasn't sure how deeply Peterson was involved. I thought it best to sit down and see what the old man had in mind.

He looked over to the goons. "Please let Mr. London's friend have a seat. Over here," he motioned to a chair next to me, "where I can enjoy looking at such an attractive woman."

They dragged Heather over and pushed her roughly into a chair.

"Now, Mr. London," Peterson said. "Perhaps you would care to explain your presence here, under false identification, if I may add."

"Maybe you'd like to explain who these two...gentlemen are, and what they have to do with Stan, the wonder-idiot." When I mentioned Stan's name, Heather turned to me with a look of confusion on her face.

"Oh, I see you do not keep your associate well informed, Mr. London," Peterson gloated. "But it is I who ask the questions in my home, not you. Again, why have you come here? What do you want of me?"

"Just information, that's all."

"And just for information you feel you must deceive me,

illegally present yourself as a member of Interpol? Really, Mr. London. We have had quite enough of your interference in this matter."

He looked up at the two goons, who must have seen me get out of the car and tipped him off. "Take Mr. London and his friend to the basement. Make them comfortable, but secure. We will discuss this later, Mr. London."

The two goons, now with guns drawn, ordered us to stand. One of them watched Heather as the other reached into my coat and removed my 38, then they pushed us both out the double doors and down the corridor at the other end of the hallway. About halfway down they opened a door on the right and pushed us in, locking the door behind us.

We were on a small landing, with steps leading down into the dark. I waited till I heard their footsteps, and then tried the door, even though I knew it was locked. Heather meanwhile had groped around, found a light switch, and turned it on revealing that the steps lead to an unfinished basement.

It was dry and warm, used to store some old furniture and the mansion's heating system. It was obvious that no one ever cleaned down there; cobwebs were all over, thick layers of dust and dirt on the ground and other surfaces. Heather started to say something but I motioned her to remain silent as I looked around.

I didn't think the basement would be bugged with anything sophisticated, but I did imagine the house might have an intercom system. Using my hand to brush away the cobwebs, I searched the room, going clockwise along the perimeter, then through the furniture stored in the middle. I didn't find any intercom, but a few useful items that would come in handy for our escape from here, or defense if needed.

I nodded to Heather that everything was okay.

"Does this have to do with Robert?" she asked.

"No."

"But you mentioned Stan, Robert's friend."

"To be honest, I'm not really sure at this point. I came here on an entirely different case, the one that I've been working on for about a week now."

"The one you didn't want to tell me about?"

"Right. It seems that somehow Stan is connected to this case too. I've met those two hoods a few times before, at Stan's place. The connection may be through the insurance company."

"What company? The one Robert was investigating?"

"Not that one, Philly Mutual, where Peterson works. Whatever Stan and his computer whiz kids are up to has something to do with the insurance company files."

"Reynold, I think it's time you told me what's going on. I mean, I'm in this now with you, I have a right to know. Don't I?"

I explained everything to her, from the Trendles to Joanne being killed, the two goons and Police Officer Sue, the karate lessons with Master Kim.

"When I saw the papers in Stan's apartment from Philly Mutual," I told her, "I didn't want to think there was any real connection, it would just complicate matters. But now I know there is a connection because Stan and the insurance company are involved with both, that's the link. I don't know how Stan or his friends are involved in this thing, it could be just something minor, with the computers. But somehow, the two cases are involved."

She sat thinking for a minute, doodling in the dust on the floor with her finger. "Reynold, let's take this thing apart, dissect it, if you will. If we examine each aspect of the two cases maybe we can figure out the connection."

"I'd rather not involve you..."

"Not involve me?" She raised her voice. "Don't you think I'm already involved? Locked in this basement with you, threatened with guns up there." She pointed up the steps. "Don't you think that I know that Robert may somehow be involved in this, with Stan, and that man?"

"I'm only thinking of your safety. Look, I wanted you to stay home instead of coming with me but..."

"But I forced myself, that's what you want to say. That I forced myself on you."

"Not on me, just here tonight."

"Well, I'm very sorry." She turned her head, and then started sobbing.

"I thought I'm the only one who was sorry." She didn't laugh. I moved close to her, took her hand in mine. "Listen, Heather, I was glad you came with me, glad you wanted to. I'm just concerned about your safety, that's all."

"And how about your own safety?" She looked up, wiping the tears from her eyes with her free hand. "Aren't you a little concerned about that?"

"No. We can get out of here anytime we want, and I'm not at all concerned about those guys upstairs."

"What do you mean, that we can get out of here whenever we want?"

"Leave that till later. Let's talk about these cases. Dissect them for me."

"Are you sure you want me involved in them?"

"I want you every way I can get."

"Okay. I've been thinking, since you explained everything to me. I'd guess that Peterson is behind Stan all the way, that he's the one who gave Stan the money, and probably the security codes, to make it easy for him to break in."

"Why?"

"Well, whatever damage Stan and his hackers could do to

Philly Mutual would help him make the company look bad. Maybe Stan has something to do with the missing tapes, maybe not. Perhaps he's just another front in the battle that Peterson has with Green. Then again, Peterson could be behind the missing tapes himself."

"So why the goons? Why keep tabs on Stan if they are in this thing together?"

"If you were Peterson would you trust Stan?"

"No way."

"So neither does Peterson. His two friends kept their eyes on Stan to make sure he didn't double cross him, didn't turn double and take what he had to Green, or maybe didn't damage the company too much. After all, Peterson would want to make sure there was a company for him to manage when it was all over."

"Where does your brother fit in this?"

"I'm not sure of that. Of course, I don't want to believe that he's involved in any of this, or that mob killing thing that they mentioned back in the house. I'd like to think he's just an innocent friend."

"Okay, go on."

"I think we can assume that Joanne was killed, murdered, not just a robbery. The way I see it, Joanne was really expendable, a figurehead for the Paek family, one who would get the loyalty of the board members and the rank-in-file workers because of her family connection. She was really never involved with the management of the company, only taking over after her husband died. I think Peterson's main rival is Green."

"So why not kill Green?"

"It would be too obvious. Taking out Green would be a little too blunt. But by removing Joanne, Peterson would be undercutting Green's foundation. Without the Paek loyalty issue, Green would be more exposed, easier to dethrone."

"Okay." I didn't let on but I was impressed with her logic. "But why kill her now? If Peterson has the tapes, why not use them to discredit both Green and Joanne, embarrass the Board into putting Peterson in charge. Why take any type of chance with a killing at this point, when they were so close to it. Peterson could have just walked into the Board and announced that the tapes had been missing."

"Don't you see, Peterson couldn't have done that until it was made public. Green was keeping it under wraps, Peterson shouldn't have known about it. I think something happened to the plan that made Peterson feel he couldn't wait until the tapes were public."

"Explain."

"Well, it could be one of several things, or a combination. First, the tapes could have gotten out of Peterson's control. Maybe Trendle did steal them, or some one else. Maybe a third party got into the act. With no control, Peterson couldn't know what was going on, couldn't be sure he could ever use his knowledge of the tapes. If a rival company got them, he might have panicked, been afraid that the company was destroyed.

"Second, maybe something else happened, some counter-attack on Green's part, that pushed Peterson into the action. Perhaps he was running out of time himself, losing some of his own support on the board. With that failing, he'd want to act very fast, gain control while it was still possible, not wait for the tape issue to come out." She saw me staring into space. "Reynold? Are you listening to me?"

"Every word. Listen, I hate to change the subject, but there's something else I have to ask you."

"About what?"

"That judo you used today. I mean it's been years since you've been in college."

"Thanks. It hasn't been that long."

"Well, a few anyway. You reacted pretty fast, like you were just trained yesterday."

"I was."

"What?"

"I still take lessons, about once a week, on campus. We have a judo instructor that teaches classes for the Phys Ed department. When I get a chance I work out with him, usually once a week or so. There's nothing sinister about it."

"Why didn't you mention it to me?"

"What was I supposed to do? As we were lying in bed, turn to you and say 'By the way, I can throw you across the room if you get too fresh.' It's not the sort of thing that normally comes up in conversation. I'd say there were a lot of things you still don't know about me."

"I'd like to find out about all of them, about all of you."

"I think I'd like that too."

For a moment we just sat there looking at each other, forgetting that we were locked in a basement with armed hoods upstairs. I finally had to break the spell.

"I think it's time you got out of here," I told her.

"How do you propose to do that? Just walk out the door?"

"Crawl out, actually." I stood up, pulling her with me and walked over to the end of the basement. "This place has a gas heating system but it used to be coal fired. A lot of these old places were years ago. Coal was dirty, had to be delivered, so almost all of them converted over to a gas system. Do you know anything about coal?"

"Chemically and geologically, yes. Heating and plumbing, no."

"Well, a truck would pull up and slide the stuff down a chute into the bin, usually at the side or back of the house, away from the front." I pulled her into the corner. "See that over there? That's the old coal bin. That rectangle plate over there is the chute door. Leads right outside. The chute was removed but they left the door."

"Isn't it sealed?"

"No, I noticed it earlier when I was looking around."

"You don't think we can crawl through there, do you?"

"Well, I can't, just a little too wide for it. But you can."

"I'm not leaving you."

"You have to. You have to get away from here, safe, then call the police."

"But I don't want to leave you alone here. I want to be with you. Can't we both get out?"

"I looked very closely at the door. You're small enough to be able to get out. You'll get pretty dirty, but you'll be able to make it. I'd just get stuck half in and half out, wedged tight. No, you have to get out. And you have to get out now."

"Why now?"

"Well, I don't think they plan to keep us here forever. They're probably planning to move us some place else that is not associated with Peterson. If you don't leave now it might be too late."

"But what about you? I don't..."

"I've thought this all out. You have to get out. When you crawl out, run away from the side of the house. There are fewer windows there. Run west, across the neighbor's lawn until you get to the main road. Turn north, then about three blocks up there's a gas station. I remember seeing it as we drove in here. Call Bennite, the cop I told you about. Tell him where I'm at, and tell him to get here quickly."

She started to argue but I kissed her, and then pushed her up toward the coal door. I knelt down giving her a foothold with my hands, pushed hard so she could grab hold of the door, open it and start out. The last view I had was straight up her skirt, at her yellow panties, then her legs disappearing out the opening. How I could get sexually aroused at a time like that just amazed me.

Chapter 16

The more I knew of Heather the more I loved her. Her insistence not to leave me alone in the cellar endeared her to me, while surprises like her judo training kept me off guard, anticipating more surprises to come.

I wanted to know more about her, though; about her family, her teenage years, what she liked, feared, enjoyed, hated. I wanted to know what she thought of when caught off guard, about her dreams and daydreams. But most of all, I wanted her to be safe and away from that basement and the danger it presented.

These men were dangerous, more so than I let her know. I did, in fact, worry about the two goons upstairs and how far Peterson would take this thing. If he were responsible for Joanne's death, and perhaps for the Trendles', he wouldn't hesitate to add one or two more to the list. Getting Heather away from there was important, not only to save myself, but to insure her safety as well.

I don't know how long I was down there alone, deep in my thoughts. Five minutes, five hours. But I heard a key in the door and footsteps on the landing.

"No tricks London. We're coming down."

The smaller of the two hoods walked down the steps slowly, the other stood on the landing with his gun pointed down. There was no chance of hiding under the steps and surprising him, the steps were the open type and the hoods could see underneath without leaving the safety of the landing itself. So I just waited at the far corner of the cellar, the wall furthest from the coal door.

"Where's the woman?" he asked.

"Over there somewhere," I answered, pointing to the diagonal corner. "She's not feeling good."

As he scanned the room, I looked for a chance to jump him,

but the other hood had a clear shot at me.

"Where is she? I don't see her."

"I told you, you moron, she's over there somewhere. I was asleep. She must be somewhere."

The thug on the landing heard the conversation and got a little worried. "What the hell's going on down there?" he yelled. "Can't you find her? Look around for Christ sake."

The goon downstairs looked at me and cursed. "Shit. Okay, okay."

With his gun in hand, he walked slowly toward the other end of the cellar, the darker end near the heating system and coal door. I know they'd find her missing pretty soon but I wanted to give her as much time as possible to get away and get help. The guy peeked behind the boiler, then the heating system, under and around some furniture, and then he yelled back to me waving his gun, "Okay, hot shot. Where'd you hide her?"

I guess it was too much for the one on the landing. He cursed loudly then came running down the steps. "I don't believe you can't find that broad down there. What the hell are you doing?"

"I'm searching the goddamn place, that's what I'm doing," the other yelled. "Why don't you look for her down here yourself? Maybe get your head bashed in. It's dark in the corners."

"Big shitass, afraid of the dark. I got a better idea. Grab London."

He came around behind me, pointed the gun in my neck and told me to get up. Then the big one came over.

"Listen lady," he yelled. "I'll give you 10 seconds to come out of hiding or London gets it. Okay?"

Silence.

He counted to ten then waited a few seconds more. "Okay lady, it's your fault," he yelled, and then he swiped the barrel of his gun sideways into my stomach with all his strength. I doubled over in pain trying to fall, but the other hood held me up.

He yelled, "Five more seconds and he gets it again." But without counting or waiting he slammed the barrel again, this time across my face so blood started oozing from a cut near my lip. He counted to five then hit me once more in the stomach. This time the pain and my weight were too much and I fell out of the other's grip and onto the ground.

When the goon didn't hear anything he started kicking me, first around the shoulders, then in the sides, down to the legs. I protected myself from the kicks as much as possible, moving my arms to deflect his foot when I could, then the other one started kicking me as well, joining in on the fun. I was near blacking out when I heard Peterson yelling from the landing, "What's going on down there? I told you to bring them up here."

"We can't find the lady," the big one answered. "She must be hiding somewhere."

"Then why are you wasting your time with him. Look for her," Peterson said.

"We did, but we can't spot her."

"You idiots, it isn't that large down there, or that dark. If you can't see everywhere get a flashlight. I don't want London hurt here. Blood leaves too many traces."

One of the goons ran up the steps, returning a couple of minutes later with a large lantern. It gave me a minute to adjust to some of the pain and straighten up a little. With the lantern, and Peterson watching me from the landing, the two thugs methodically searched the basement. They turned over furniture, uncovered some that was draped in sheets, even opened the access door to the huge furnace.

"She's not here. She must have gotten out somehow."

That's not what Peterson wanted to hear. He cursed and came down the steps, slowly, one step at a time. "She has to be there. The door was locked, there's no other way out."

He got down to the bottom and grabbed the lantern from the hood. "Let me look. You," he pointed to one of them, "keep an eye on London. You," he said to the other, "come with me. Have your gun ready."

Peterson covered the same ground as the others but found nothing until he reached the site of the old coal chute. "Jesus, she got out there." He pointed to the chute door. "She climbed out of the old coal door."

"Then why didn't London get out too?" my guard asked.

Peterson turned toward me. "Because he's too fat, you idiot. London's just too damn fat to climb out of there. Bring him here, quickly."

The larger goon pulled me up by the collar, struggling because I refused to make it easy on him. He kicked me to get me up, and then jammed his gun hard into my back with every step.

"When did she leave?" Peterson asked. "How long ago?"

"I don't know, I was asleep."

"Hit him," Peterson commanded. The guard obeyed with a swift kidney punch.

"She could not have climbed out of here without your help, London. Now how long ago did she leave?"

"Just after we got down here, within ten minutes." I wanted him to think his time was running out, that Heather had enough time to find the police and send help.

"What did she plan to do? Go to the police? Hide?"

"I don't know." The goon hit me again.

"Showing initiative?" I moaned.

"That's okay," Peterson said. "Let's get London out of here

quickly and clean up. I want this place clean when and if the police come. Take London downtown and dispose of him."

One goon stood over me while the other picked up any sign that we had been there. There was some blood where I had been hit, and a small trickle leading over to my current spot, but they moved the furniture around to cover it. Of course, it wouldn't fool any good detective or cop that came down here. You could see that the furniture had been moved by the clean spots amid the dust where it had protected the floor; like taking a painting off the wall and seeing the unfaded rectangle of wallpaper or paint underneath, but it was obvious that they didn't care, figuring that the local police would take Peterson's word over some hysterical female who showed up covered with dirt and coal dust.

Peterson wiped my wound enough to stop the blood from leaving a trail, and then the two goons dragged me upstairs and out the back door. I tried to resist but the beating left me weak and disoriented.

You know, those TV shows always amazed me. Some guy takes a real licking, like I had, then turns around and fights off a team of bad guys. He'd have blood pouring out all over but enough energy to get off of the ground and beat the shit out of two or three guys, run after an escaping car, and save the town from death and destruction. It just doesn't work that way in real life. I took a licking but was barely ticking. I could hardly stand up or even think straight.

As we got outside I started looking around, trying to be subtle about it.

"No one's going to save you, London," one of them said. "You're a dead man. A dead fat man." The two of them laughed. They walked me around to the front of the house, making sure no cop cars were around, then over to their Ford parked behind my car in the driveway. They leaned me up against the car, then while one of them held me from falling, the other headed to the other side, I suppose to release the electronic locks this model had. Must be a bad neighborhood or something.

I didn't see any sign of cops, no other cars were in sight. I figured they'd squeeze me into the back seat and take me for a last ride. While I hadn't regained much energy, I still started to glance around for escape routes, thinking how I could overpower one of them before I got in the car. Luckily I didn't have to.

I saw something move near the corner of my eye, heard a shrill voice scream then a figure, in black, fly over the hood of the car feet first into the scumbag walking to the driver's door. I turned to see where the other goon was and saw Heather running up behind him. She jumped into the air and caught him in a headlock. Propelled by her strong legs, she jumped to his side, twisting his head and neck, and then falling to the ground bringing him down with a bang. On the ground, she pushed her weight forward, locking his head in an unnatural position; a little harder and she'd snap his neck. She held him there a couple of seconds until he passed out, then she jumped up and over to me.

"Are you all right?" she asked. "What did they do to you?"

"I'm okay, Heather. Where are the police?"

"We didn't call them, Mr. London."

I looked around and saw the dark figure emerge from the other side of the car. It was Lydia dressed in black jogging clothes, barefoot. "Lydia? Heather, what's going on? Why didn't you call the cops?"

Heather was holding me in her arms, caressing what was left of my hair. "I'm sorry Reynold, I just couldn't call them yet... because of Robert."

"How did Lydia get here?"

She kissed my forehead. "I remembered what you said about her, about her training. Instead of going for the police I got Lydia's phone number from the notebook in your car."

"They could have caught you. I told you to..."

"I called Lydia from the gas station you told me about and explained what had happened, that you were in danger. She was wonderful, Reynold. She came right over, faster than the police would have taken, and we planned to wait until someone came out of the house."

"What if they just killed me in the house then carried my body out? What would you have done then?" I didn't want to sound sarcastic. I was grateful, really grateful, for what they had done, the risk they took, but it was too much of a risk.

"You shouldn't worry too much about us, either Heather or myself," Lydia said. "You know, Heather is quite a person, Reynold. You are lucky to have her."

"Yes, I know. Listen, I don't want to cause any trouble. I'm damn glad you did what you did, and pretty proud of...of both of you. It's just that..."

"It's your time to listen, Reynold," Heather said, in control. "Lydia and I talked this over in detail before we decided not to call the police. When those men saw that I was missing, we were sure they wouldn't take a chance and kill you right here. It would've been too risky for them. If I had reached the police, they might have made it to the house in time to find your body, before Peterson had a chance to cart you away. We figured they might rough you up a little, then if they were planning on killing you, take you out alive and get far away. I knew this was their car, you described it to me, and so we planned our assault. It was just a matter of waiting."

Lydia interrupted. "Heather told me about her training and showed me what she could do. We planned for me to take out the driver because I could get over to that side faster. Heather planned to take out the one on the passenger side. We were hiding in the bushes next to the front door."

"But what if there were more than two of them? What if

Peterson was with them? Or, someone else?"

"Reynold, sometimes you're a chauvinist of the worst sort," Heather joked. "You and your manly pride. Stop asking questions and let's get out of here before someone sees us. I'll take you back in your car, Lydia will follow in hers, making sure we aren't followed."

"What about Peterson?" I asked.

"Our main concern is to take care of you right now. Anyway, we thought about him. We think he'll be scared to death when these two wake up and tell him that they'd been attacked and that you were freed. Peterson won't know what to think or who did it. He'll realize it wasn't the police. Let's just get out of here."

With their help I made it to my own car and laid gently in the back seat. Heather drove smoothly and carefully, talking most of the way about Lydia. She talked nervously, like she wanted the sound of her voice to keep me awake, alive. When we got back to the apartment, Fred appeared and helped me up to Heather's place. Lydia followed a few minutes later.

Heather took off my jacket and shirt, and then helped me into the bedroom. She took off the rest of my clothes, I showered, and then she rubbed some ointment on my legs, hips, and shoulders.

"You really should go to the hospital," she told me. "You might have some broken ribs. You should get checked out."

"It's okay. I'll be fine with your care. Just cover me up and ask Lydia to come in."

Lydia came in eating a sandwich. "How are you feeling?"

"Like a truck hit me, but otherwise okay. I can't thank you enough for today. That was wonderful."

"It was all my pleasure. In fact, I enjoyed it. Now, you

should just rest before we continue."

I looked up. "Continue what?"

Heather and Lydia looked at each other, then sheepishly to me. Lydia started to speak but Heather interrupted.

"Let me explain it to him, Lydia," she said.

"Explain what to me?" I didn't like the sound of this.

"Whether you like it or not, Lydia and I are now in on this. We've talked it over thoroughly and have decided the only way you're going to make progress on this case, and in finding my brother, is with our help."

"Your help! I don't..."

"Reynold, just calm down and listen. You've done remarkably up to this point, but we've decided, Lydia and I, that it is just too big for you to handle alone. It's time that we helped you. After all, you're trying to find my brother and the people that killed Lydia's mother."

"I can do this..."

"All by yourself? That's your pride talking, your lovable middle-aged male ego. Reynold, you've got people coming at you from all sides, and we seem to feel there's a lot you aren't telling us."

I was too tired to argue at this point even though I didn't agree with them. It wasn't my male ego talking, I thought, just my professional judgment. After all, Lydia was still a young girl, and Heather was a college professor. What did they know about detective work? I must have been frowning because Heather said, "Why don't you just get some rest. You'll feel better about it later."

"I'll rest but we'll talk about this later. Of all the dumb ideas."

Lydia looked annoyed and said, "Why? Because we're

women?"

"No, not really. It's just that..."

"It's just that this is our case as well as yours," Heather added. "You've been beaten up, you lost your gun. Things are just spread too far for you to do this alone."

"But..."

"But nothing," Heather continued. "We are part of this now, partners whether you like it or not. And if you don't like it we'll just have to do it on our own, without your help."

She motioned for Lydia to leave us alone, then closed the door and sat down on the bed beside me. "Reynold, I know you're not very happy about this, but it is something we have to do. When Lydia and I were planning what to do, back at Peterson's house, I made a decision."

I tried to speak but she said, "Just be quite and listen, please. I made a decision that may be a little presumptuous of me, but one that requires no permanent commitment from you, if you don't want to. I decided to share this danger with you, to be as much a part of you as I could, as you would allow. When this is over we can go our separate ways, if that's what you decide, but now I will do everything I can do to help you, to stand by you.

"I know we have no commitment," she continued, "we've made no promises to each other. But I also know how I feel about you. And please don't mistake my...sexual inexperience with naiveté. I'm not trying to force a commitment from you either; I'm just doing what I must at this point in time. Just as Lydia has decided. Now be quiet and let me hold you. Please."

She kissed me then fluffed the pillow under my head. I felt a little hot and dizzy, probably from the pain, so Heather sat by me and ran her fingers slowly along my neck and shoulders, carefully avoiding areas that were black and blue. My head was swimming from the events of the day; from Heather's declaration, from seeing the two of them rescue me like some old

John Wayne movie, from sorting out the facts of the case. I had this feeling that I was falling, not a frightening fall but a slow controlled descent down a long cylinder. My body spun slowly as I fell, heightening the sensation, but I wasn't afraid or worried. The bottom never seemed to get any closer, the speed never increased. I was just falling down endlessly like a man falling off the edge of the earth.

Chapter 17

The sunlight streaming through the window woke me up. The clock said 10:15 and the smell of fresh coffee told me someone else was nearby. I was in Heather's bed, covered with a light blue sheet, a light smell of almonds coming from the pillow next to mine, the pillow that still held Heather's impression from the night. For a second, I didn't remember what had happened, how I got there, but when I tried to move the pain searing through my body was reminder enough. Every inch was sore, from the back of my head to my feet. There was a wide elastic bandage around my middle and small adhesive bandages under my lip and near my right eye.

I noticed I was naked when I removed the sheet but I didn't see my clothes around. After wobbling for a minute or two, I made it to my feet and put on a pink silky robe that must have been Heather's. It smelled of almond.

Still hurting, I staggered through the living room, holding on to walls and furniture, then out to the kitchen.

"Good morning," Heather said as I entered. "That robe is just you, darling." She laughed, a beautiful laugh.

"You didn't seem to leave me any choice," I said. "Where are my clothes?"

"We had to throw them away," she said, helping me to a chair. "They were filthy, full of dirt and blood. Fred's out getting you some now."

"Fred! You asked Fred to get me clothing? From where?"

She brought me over a cup of coffee and two slices of toast, and then made a fake frown, trying to look mad. "You know, that's a very good question. We searched your office and only found a few odd shirts, and I'm stressing the word odd. I asked Fred to get them from your house...you know, where you live...

but Fred didn't know where that was. In fact, no one seems to know where you live."

"It's not important."

"Not important? You've known Fred for how many years? Ten maybe twelve. He has no idea where you live. Every paper in your desk has the office address. Even your driver's license and registration card. If I didn't think I knew you better, I'd swear that was your home. Now eat your breakfast."

The coffee was hot, with just a little too much sugar for my tastes, but the toast was excellent, a little brown on top, dripping with butter or margarine.

"I have a place, a little apartment," I told her. "Really the pits. I almost do live in the office."

"You're something, do you know that?" She wrapped her arms around me. "You have no home, no secretary." I looked at her surprised. "You didn't fool anyone with your little routine, Reynold," she said. "You disappear into the night like Zorro, except you ride into the sunset in a Toyota. Very romantic."

I pulled away from her. "Do I have to take this abuse all morning?"

"I'm afraid you have more to come. Lydia and I have a plan."

The doorbell rang. It was Fred carrying two bags from a local store. "I got some clothes for him, Dr. Goldwyn. Picked them out myself. Even got change for you." He looked over at me. "Nice nightgown, Mr. London. Fits you well."

"Shut up, Fred. Heather, I can't let you pay..."

"Oh, yes you can. Don't complain." She started pulling clothing from the bags. "Let's see what Fred picked out. Oh my. Very nice, Fred."

I'd sooner walk out in this lace nightgown than the clothes Fred picked out for me. Heather was holding a pair of light blue pleated pants, a yellow button down shirt, black leather belt, and a bright green jacket, the color of perfectly manicured lawn. Out of the other bag, Fred took a pair of gray and white argyle socks, and white shoes. White shoes!

"Fred, I'm going to kill you."

"I think it was very nice of Fred to go shopping for you, Reynold. Even if his tastes are...a little different than yours." She turned to Fred, who was handing her some money. "Thanks Fred. Please keep the change...for your time."

"Oh, that's okay Dr. Goldwyn. You take it. I'm just glad that I could help." Then he looked over to me and laughed. "Wait till the guys hear about you in that nighty."

"I'll kill you." I tried to stand up and reach for him, but the pain was still there; I just collapsed back into the chair.

"Fred," Heather said, "I think you better go now. We don't want our patient too upset, do we?"

"Oh no, Dr. Goldwyn."

After he left, I finished the coffee and toast. "Really, Heather, you don't expect me to wear this stuff."

"I would have preferred to get things from your own house, apartment, barn, or whatever you have, but I suppose you'll wear that or stay hear when Lydia and I go visit Stan."

"Visit Stan!"

"We've made up our minds. First thing on the agenda is to get the truth out of Stan. We have to find out Peterson's involvement, and Robert's."

"Now wait a..."

"Peterson will be taken care of tonight, at his home. Lydia found out that he's in the office today like nothing happened."

"Tonight. This is..."

The doorbell rang again.

"That must be Lydia," Heather said. "So I'd suggest you either shower and get dressed, or stay here. It's your choice."

She walked out of the kitchen to get the door. I heard Lydia's voice, and then some laughing.

"Well, we're leaving in five minutes," Heather yelled from the other room. "We'll be glad to help you get dressed and down to the car."

"I can get dressed myself." I stood up to get the clothes on the kitchen table but fell right down on the floor. Heather and Lydia ran in, saw me lying on the floor with Fred's clothes all around me and laughed.

"Some men just can't do anything," Lydia said.

Lydia left us alone so Heather was able to help me get dressed. Of course, good old Fred forgot to get any underwear. Then the two of them helped me down to Heather's car, ignoring my complaints and protestations.

"Ignore me all you want," I said, "but what are your plans?"

"First, we'll get a general picture of what's happening from Stan," Lydia explained. "We want more background before we confront Peterson again. Second, we'll find out about Robert's involvement and his whereabouts. If he's in no serious trouble we can call in the police."

I thought about the Feds and my license. "Well, let's hold off on that for a moment," I said.

Lydia continued. "We think Stan is the weakest link in this. This visit is just exploratory, fact gathering."

Heather drove to the campus, with me in the back seat and Lydia up front.

"And exactly how are you planning on getting information from Stan?" I asked. "His pals might be around."

"We've thought of that. Don't worry, enjoy the ride."

How could I enjoy the ride? Every time she went over a bump, pain shot through my body. And here I was, Reynold London, private detective, who was just starting to get his act together, being manhandled, if that's possible, by two women. A kid and a woman. They're telling me what to do, calling the shots, taking control. What the hell's going on today?

"Listen ladies..."

They both turned around and in unison said "Ladies?"

"Yeah, listen ladies. You've had your little fun, playing Nancy Drew. Very funny. But it's getting a little out of hand. If I were you..."

I think Heather went over a big pothole on purpose, the sadistic angel. Before I could finish, the car bounced, almost knocking me off of the seat onto the floor.

"I'm sorry, Reynold. I didn't see that one. What were you saying?"

"Don't you think you should let a professional handle this? That's all I'm saying. You can come along for the ride if you want, but..."

"Heather do you hear something?" Lydia said. "Sounds like a squeal."

"I think I do," she answered. "Sounds like time running over a closed mind, to me."

"Now I wonder where that could be coming from?"

"Very funny, girls. Very funny." I just gave up.

We got to the apartment. Lydia bent down and did some shuffling in the front seat, and then turned around and handed me a small barrel 38.

"Tuck that away somewhere where it will be safe," Heather said. "It's Fred's, if you're wondering."

Lydia shivered a little as I took the gun. "I hate guns," she said. "But Heather said you'd feel better with it, an extension of your..."

"That's fine Lydia," Heather interrupted. "Do you think you can walk?"

"After that ride I'll be lucky if I could sh...walk. Yeah, I think I can."

"Okay. We wait here until Lydia gives the sign. She'll look around for the two guys from Peterson's, although I doubt they'll be in any condition to give us real trouble. Then she'll scout out Stan's place."

"If everything is okay," Lydia continued, "I'll wave from that window up there." She pointed to the second floor window over the doorway, facing the street. "If Stan's there, I'll get into his place. You wait a couple of minutes, then knock when you get there and I'll let you in."

"This could be dangerous. You know that, don't you?"

The two women just looked at each other.

I added, "And while you're there, look for anyone just hanging around. People that just don't seem to belong." I was thinking of the real FBI.

Lydia glanced around the street then went into the building.

I took a good look at the 38. "Where did Fred get this?" I asked Heather.

"Don't know exactly. Before he left on his shopping trip, he came up to the apartment and handed it to me. Told me 'If London lost everything then he might need this. It's loaded so be careful.' Then he just chuckled and left."

It was a solid handgun, all chambers loaded with semi-jacketed hollow points, serious bullets that made a big hole on the way out. You could tell it had been cared for, cleaned and oiled regularly, probably hardly ever fired. I couldn't picture Fred taking this good care of anything. I started to holster the thing then remembered that Heather never put it on me. I just stuck it in the right pocket of my bright green jacket. It fit because of the small barrel but it would be a little obvious, weighing down that side of the jacket when I stood up.

"There's the sign," Heather announced.

I looked up and saw Lydia waving in the window. Smart girl. She was looking far across the street, not down at us, waving to some imaginary friend on the opposite sidewalk. There was so much movement over there that anyone noticing wouldn't be suspicious.

Heather turned around to me. "Are you okay? Do you think you can make it?"

"Sweetheart, I wouldn't miss this for the world."

I made it out of the car, still a little shaky, and held on to Heather as we took the elevator and then went down the corridor to Stan's place. I had no idea how Lydia got in there, but she opened the door when we knocked. Stan was sitting on the sofa with his legs crossed. When he saw me, he tried to jump up but tripped on his own feet and fell to the floor.

"You bitch! You lied to me."

Lydia ran over to him, grabbed his hand and twisted it up and over, pressing hard. Stan yelled in pain, "You're breaking it."

With the grip on his hand, Lydia pulled him off the floor and onto the sofa, adjusted her hands somewhat and stepped over the back of the sofa so she was now behind him.

He saw Heather. "Dr. Goldwyn. What's going on here?"

Heather sat down beside him. "Stan, we have to ask you a few questions. Think of it as a special final exam."

Stan motioned his other hand toward me. "What's he doing here?"

"Some time ago, Mr. London asked you a few questions.

You were a bad person and didn't answer him truthfully. Now it's my turn to ask you a few questions."

He squirmed. "I can't do a damn thing with her twisting my wrist like this. It hurts."

"Then we'll just have to get these questions over quickly, won't we? We know a lot more than Mr. London did when he saw you last. We'll know if you're lying. If you do, I'll leave the room and allow Mr. London and my friend here to handle you themselves."

I was certainly impressed, and pretty surprised at Heather's attitude. I just leaned up against the closed front door and watched.

Stan couldn't believe what was happening. He was moaning from the pain, his eyes open wide, darting back and forth between the three of us, but speaking to Heather. "What do you want? I can't believe you're doing this. You're a professor!"

"Who paid for the computers you had at the 51st street house?" she asked slowly and calmly.

"How do you...hey!"

Lydia twisted her grip harder telling him "Please answer the question."

He reached up with his other hand, trying to relieve some of the pressure. "They...some guys...came to see me about a year ago. They said they wanted...some information. Can she let up a little?"

"What were their names?" Heather pressed.

"I don't know. Big guys, real tough. Just gave me cash."

Must be Peterson's men, I thought.

"What information did they want?"

"They wanted me to break into a couple of companies and give them any reports I could find."

"That's all?"

"Well, they also wanted me to play around with some tapes, but they never gave them to me."

"What do you mean, play around?"

"They wanted me to decrypt data on a set of tapes, make some changes, and then rewrite the stuff."

"What companies did they want you to hack into?"

"Philly Mutual. That was easy because they gave me the passwords. Reliance. Couple of banks. Phone company. Can the goddamn bitch let go a little?"

"Soon Stan, real soon. What type of things did you give them?"

"Just numbers, copies of reports, memos. Whatever we found in the files. Then they told me to try to erase some of the files at Philly Mutual."

"And what did you get out of it?"

"Nothing...oh!"

"My friend didn't like that answer," Heather said.

"The hardware was mine to keep. And some stuff I got from the phone company, one of the banks."

"You transferred funds to your own account and you defrauded the phone company of equipment. Is that what you mean?"

"Yeah. Just small stuff, that's all."

That explained the FBI involvement in this.

"How much did the others know? Your friends?"

"Nothing, I didn't tell them anything. I did all of the transfers myself, they just worked on the passwords, printed out the reports."

"So what did they get out of this?"

"I paid them."

"Now how about my brother? What is his involvement?"

Stan hesitated. Lydia pushed a little harder.

"Goddamn! Let go, you're breaking it."

Heather nodded and Lydia relaxed her grip just a little.

"What about Robert?"

"He's not...really involved. He asked for help in getting some records from Reliance. Some project of his or something. He hung around with us...then got scared when he saw what we were doing. I...told him the FBI were onto us, to keep him quiet."

"So why was he hiding out? Why didn't he come back home?"

"I don't know. I thought he was just scared. He stuck with us."

"Where is he now?"

"I don't know. I swear." He looked back at Lydia, then to Heather. "He got spooked the other day, ran out with the rest of them. Haven't seen him since."

Lydia twisted some more. "I swear I haven't seen him!"

Heather looked over to me. "Do you have any questions for Stan?"

"Yeah, just a few."

"Oh shit!" Stan said.

"You said that they never gave you the tapes? "

"That's right. I was supposed to work on them but I never got them."

"Okay. Were you at the Bourse Building at all last week?"

"The Bourse? No man. What's this all about? Dr. Goldwyn?"

"She won't help you now," I told him. "Just answer the questions. Why did you send those kids after me last week?"

"I didn't want you messing around in this. Just to scare you."

"Did you ever hear the name Peterson?"

"Peterson? No. Yeah. The two guys who paid me mentioned his name once. Who is he?"

"How about Green?"

"No. I don't think so. Just a kid named Green in my math class. You mean him?"

"Lydia, do you have any questions for the young man?"

She thought for a moment then said, "I don't think so. This worm is too far removed from the head man to answer any questions I have. Anyway, I still don't trust him."

Stan jerked his head around and tried to grab Lydia with his free hand, but he wasn't fast enough. As soon as Lydia sensed his movement she bent down hard on his twisted wrist. Stan screamed in pain, and could think of nothing but bending forward trying to relieve the pressure.

"You're breaking it. Goddamn, you bitch."

"I'd advise you to talk a little nicer to the lady," I said. "She could break it very easily if she wanted to." I motioned to Heather. "Dr. Goldwyn, could I see you for a private moment over here."

She came over and I whispered, "Now I'm not trying to assert my masculine influence, but what exactly do you plan to do with him now?"

"I'm afraid we didn't plan for that. Should we call the police?"

"Glad you still need me."

She kissed me. "I'll always need you."

"About the police. Stan is a scum that belongs in jail, but I'm afraid all of the evidence is probably long gone from that house now. I think they either have to catch him in the act or track down proof from the phone company, things like that. Let's let the police handle this one on their own."

"Okay." She looked over to Stan then said, "But I want to put a good scare into him. I don't think we want Stan and his friends interfering with the rest of our investigation."

"Our investigation?" I said just a little too loud. "You really plan to go on with this?"

"We haven't done so bad so far, have we? I'd guess a little better than you did with Stan the last time."

"So what do you have in mind?"

"Just play along with me."

She walked back to the sofa and sat down next to Stan.

"Stanley," she said, "we have a slight problem. You've already lied to Mr. London once, and sent your gang after him. I'm afraid you've gotten into something far over your head. I did try to plead your case over there." She pointed to me. "But Mr. London feels you will just get in the way."

Stan stared at me, giving Heather time to wink at Lydia.

Heather looked over to me but spoke loud enough for Stan to hear. "Just make it clean, Mr. London. One shot, through the heart."

I caught on. I took the 38 from my pocket, slowly raised it and took aim at Stan's face instead of his heart.

"Hey, you can't do that." Stan was in a panic. Lydia was keeping the pressure on his wrist, which should have been almost numb by now, but he had something more permanent to worry about.

"Why can't I?" I asked.

"It's...murder...you can't. I told you everything. Jesus, Dr. Goldwyn," he pleaded to Heather. "You can't let him do this."

"Stan, I'd like to stop him but how can I? You just keep getting in the way."

"Listen, I'll leave town. Drop out of school, go back home. I'll leave today, I promise."

I lowered the gun. "On one condition."

He looked relieved. "Anything, anything."

"We have to know where you are at all times. You have to stay near a phone, answer it by the third ring or I'll come after you and kill you. Understand?"

"Okay, anything. Just let me go."

"Lydia. I think we've reached an agreement."

Lydia nodded but instead of letting him go, she took one of his fingers in her hand and bent it back till the snapping bone echoed in the room.

"Jesus, you broke my finger. Jesus." Stan withered in pain on the sofa squeezing the broken finger with his other hand.

Heather stared at Lydia, in shock at the girl's violence. She started to speak, to reproach Lydia for her action, but a cold fierce look came over the youngster's face, making her look like a different person.

Lydia bent down close to Stan, pulled his head back roughly by his hair, and then turned it so they were face to face. "I want you to really understanding something, Stan," she said. "This is not a game. That man over there would really have killed you, and he will kill you if you are not by the phone number you give us."

"My finger!" Stan cried. "You broke my finger."

"It will be all right, it's only a little bone. The pain you feel now is just a sample, a warning, of what will happen if you tell anyone about this."

She grabbed another finger, started to bend it but stopped just before the breaking point. Heather had put her hand on Lydia's shoulder, to stop her, but the girl could have easily finished the job.

"Do you see how simple it is to cause pain?" she added. "One little bend and the bone breaks. Do you know that there are over 200 bones in your puny body? Two hundred. And I can break each one of them, one by one, before Mr. London pulls the trigger and puts you out of your misery, ending your useless little life."

"I understand, I understand," he pleaded.

She let go of his finger and said, "Good."

Stanley gave us his parent's telephone number in upstate Pennsylvania before we dropped him off at the bus terminal. No one spoke during the ride, but there was a cold, distant air between Heather and Lydia. Heather was obviously still shocked by the broken finger and the vicious way Lydia behaved. I sat in the front, next to Heather, who drove, while Lydia watched Stan in the back. He just cowered near the door, staring out of the window, nursing his hand. When I could, I put my hand on Heather's lap, to calm her down, let her know everything will be okay, but I didn't say anything because I knew why Lydia had acted that way, and I think I agreed with her.

Chapter 18

"Lydia, how could you be so ruthless? Breaking his finger like that, without any reason. It's barbaric."

Heather didn't say a word until we got back to her apartment. Lydia had tried to make some conversation, polite chatter, but Heather just stared out of the window. "He told us everything we wanted to know. We even scared him with that gun nonsense. You just broke his finger."

Lydia tried to be calm but she was obviously upset with Heather's tone. "You attacked that man at Peterson's," she said to Heather. "You were pretty violent then."

Heather jumped up. "That was different. Those men were going to hurt Reynold. We were defending him."

"It was still violence, wasn't it? You still inflicted pain on another being."

"But Stan cooperated. He was..."

Lydia interrupted. "He was what? Telling us everything, being a good little boy? When Mr. London lowered the gun, Stan knew he had us. He knew we were bluffing about the whole thing."

"Reynold, will you talk to her, please?" Heather asked.

"Let's let Lydia explain," I said.

"You are a darling wonderful woman, Heather," Lydia said. "You have learned how to defend yourself, have mastered the skills and techniques of Judo. But that is not enough."

"What do you mean?"

Lydia stood up and paced around the room, picking her words carefully. "It is one thing to learn the movements. You have done that well. You have also shown that you can use those skills under pressure, that you can defend yourself, and those who you hold dear." Lydia looked over to me, and then continued. "But there is more to learn than that."

Heather, in disgust, said "But you're still a girl! What do you...?"

"Oh, don't let my age influence you. Listen to me. My mother was killed, killed violently, professionally. This isn't a game, sparring in the dojang, or for a trophy. The minute Stan knew we weren't going to kill him, he knew we were not capable of killing him, not capable of inflicting real pain. He compared us with the others involved, and realized that they were the professionals he had to fear, not us."

"I don't think..."

"You don't agree, I know. But I am sure. I am sure that Stan would have gotten off the bus at the first stop and gone right to those who hired him. Don't you see, he had to have a reminder of our strength, our determination. He had to take some of our threat with him, carry it around. He had to know that we could inflict pain, ruthlessly and quickly carry out our threat if he deceived us in any way."

Heather started to waver. "But was it necessary to break his finger like that?"

"I would have preferred breaking all his fingers, or an arm."

"Oh Lydia, really. Reynold will you say something to her?"

"I'm sorry, Heather," I said. "I think I agree with her."

"Reynold!"

"No, listen to me. I threatened him once. Then we came in together and threatened him a second time. Both times we caused him some discomfort, roused up some fear, but both times we were content to let him go. It was Lydia who showed him that he really had something to be scared about. That we were, as she said, capable of carrying out our threat."

"It's just that there's been so much violence already."

Lydia moved to the sofa, next to Heather, and took her hand. "I am sorry if I upset you. But my view of violence, of the limits we should impose in this matter, is different than yours. Remember, death has been close to me, the ultimate in violence. This isn't a game we are playing, and I'm afraid there are others, like those at Peterson's, whose limits of violence are far wider than my own. It is them we have to fear."

"I know, I know," Heather responded.

We just sat and stared at each other, afraid to break the mood. Finally Heather put her arms around the youngster and hugged her. "I'm sorry if I said anything to upset you. It's just that this is really something new to me. Maybe I have been taking it like a game, an exercise in Judo class."

"That's why I never wanted you two to get involved in this in the first place," I said. "It's serious, a dangerous matter."

Heather moved over to me. "But I am involved in it now." She looked at Lydia. "We are involved in it now, there's no way out."

"Okay, Okay," I said. "So let's see what we have. Peterson may have paid Stan and his gang of computer freaks. They were to break into some companies, including Peterson's own, and get reports, figures, that sort of that thing. Peterson didn't need information from his own company, but he wanted to put the blame for the hack on Green. He paid them to hack into rival companies for their information. The two goons were Peterson's men, probably hanging around because they didn't fully trust boy wonder.

"The FBI is after Stan for fraud, from the bank and phone company. Robert doesn't seem to be involved directly, but is after something on his own, from Reliance not Philly Mutual. We don't know where he is, but only that he's probably safe.

"Now about the tapes. Stan knows nothing about them, and I kind of believe him. But Peterson is scared enough about something to kill for it, he was ready to kill me before you two came to my rescue. If he could kill me, he could have killed the Trendles." I looked at Lydia. "And maybe even your mother.

I looked alternately at both of them. "Your mother could have been killed because she was more expendable than Green. She was getting in the way of something more important that Peterson had to worry about. Or this could be a load of shit and we have no idea what the hell's going on."

The ladies decided that the next course of action was to confront Peterson again, but this time with us in control. It was a good idea. The last thing Peterson would expect would be an attack, a direct assault by those who he last saw on the defensive. But, we decided, it wouldn't be on his home ground. If this was to work, we had to have complete control, enough to make Peterson feel that he has no choice but to cooperate to the fullest.

The plan was a simple one. Peterson never saw Lydia last night, he only knew her as Joanne's daughter, so a call from Lydia wouldn't be connected with me, or the events of the night. Lydia would call Peterson and ask him to stop by her apartment, on some pretext about the business, maybe her mother's will or some papers she found in the house after going through her mother's things. We'd make it so tempting that Peterson had to come over.

With the security in her building, we'd know for sure if Peterson came alone or not, so we could make sure he was isolated from his strong arms. Anyway, there should be no need for him to bring them along just to see a "little girl." Once there, we'd set him up, squeeze him for information. The plan looked good and we figured Lydia would call Peterson and try to get him over at night, when it would be dark.

She called his house but there was no answer, so she tried the office and got him on the line. He said he just got back from a trip, but that he could get over to Lydia's at ten that night. At about 9:30, the doorbell rang. "Who is it?" Lydia yelled without opening the door, it was too early for Peterson and she wasn't expecting anyone else.

"Detective Bennite, Philadelphia Police. Can I come in and talk to you Miss Paek?"

"Bennite? What the hell is he doing here?" I whispered. "Listen, Heather and I will hide in the bedroom. Let him in," I told Lydia, "but try to get rid of him soon. Peterson will be here any minute."

Heather and I ducked into the bedroom, leaving the door slightly open so we could hear the conversation, then Lydia let Bennite in.

"Miss Paek. I'm Detective Bennite. Remember, we talked after your mother's...about a week ago." He showed Lydia his badge and ID. "If you have a minute, I'd like to talk to you about Bob Peterson."

"About Mr. Peterson? From my mother's company?" She led Bennite to a chair so his back faced the bedroom door. "I don't know Mr. Peterson very well. How can I help you?"

"You say you don't know him very well? When was the last time you saw him?"

"Oh, at mother's funeral. Before that, about six months ago at a party the company had for employees. I went with mother."

"Were you planning on seeing him again soon?"

It seemed like an odd question to me, almost like a trap, as if Bennite somehow knew Peterson was expected. I wondered if I should try to signal Lydia somehow, but the girl was sharp enough to see the trap herself.

"Yes," she admitted. "In fact, he should be here any moment. Some old company business, some papers of my mother's. Why do you ask?"

"Well, Mr. Peterson won't be coming tonight. At 10, that's when you had your appointment?"

"Yes. But why?"

"I'm afraid Mr. Peterson is dead."

"What? Dead?"

"We found his body in his office, about two hours ago. Your name was on his appointment book, for 10 tonight."

"Oh my. Was it his heart? I thought he was a well man."

"Don't know about his health," the detective said. "But it looks like he was killed."

"Murdered? Who would kill a nice man like Mr. Peterson?"

"Was he nice to you, Miss Paek? How well did you know him?"

"Not very well at all I'm afraid. Why do you think he was murdered?"

Lydia was good, not giving much information but asking instead, leading Bennite as much as she could.

"We can't be sure until the autopsy, but he seems to have the same type of bruise that...killed your mother. Why was he coming here so late? Ten o'clock is a little past business hours."

"Oh, I found some papers among my mother's things that I thought the company should have. There were a lot of papers and I wanted to sort through them all before giving them to him. It was his idea to stop by at ten. I suppose he was anxious to get them today, not wait until tomorrow."

That's good, Lydia, I thought, making it look like the meeting was Peterson's initiative.

"How well did you know Peterson?" Bennite repeated.

"I've only seen him a few times, mother's funeral, a couple of times before that. I really didn't know him very well. Why do you ask?"

"Nothing really. I just wanted you to know that he wouldn't be over, so you wouldn't be waiting for him all night. Do you know of any enemies your mother and Peterson might have had in common? Any particular thing they were involved in together?"

"I'm sorry, no. They were both at the insurance company. As far as I know that was the only link. Do you think the same person who killed my mother killed Mr. Peterson? I thought you said that was robbery?"

Good question, Lydia. Good.

"It's too early to tell." He stood up. "Well, thank you for your time. By the way, could I take a look at those papers you had, the ones for Peterson?"

"Certainly. I'll be right back."

She came into the bedroom, being careful to open the door just enough to get in, and then she closed it behind her.

"What should I give him?" she whispered.

"Do you have any papers around at all?" I asked.

"I have the same ones I showed you. Should I give them to him?"

"Miss Paek? Is everything okay?" Bennite called from the other room.

"Yes, I'm just getting them now," she responded.

"Sure," I whispered. "Just give him a handful of the memos. Tell him to return them to the company when he's done with them."

She took a small stack of papers from her mother's desk and returned to the living room. Bennite glanced through them quietly, promising Lydia he'd send them to the company when he was done reviewing them. He thanked her and was half out the front door when he turned around.

"Oh, one more thing," he said. "Do you know a man named London? Reynold London?"

"The name sounds familiar," Lydia said. "I think my mother might have mentioned his name once. But I can't be sure. Why do you ask?"

"Oh, just police business, that's all. Don't worry about it. Well, thank you again for your time. If you find anything else that may be important, please give me a call. Goodnight."

"You did great Lydia," I said leaving the bedroom. "Very good."

She looked confused. "What do you think happened? Who would have killed Peterson?"

"I don't know. But it bothers me that he was killed like your mother was. It means that Peterson either wasn't the top guy, or that there's some other party involved in this, someone or some group that we haven't come across yet. I don't like this."

"Maybe it's Green," Heather said.

I thought for a minute. "Well I know you don't trust him. I thought he was pretty sincere, but you could be right."

"Well, then he's the next course of action," Lydia said.

"Now wait a minute. I think you two have been involved too much now. It's getting a little too dangerous, too many people have been killed."

"You're not getting rid of us that quickly, Reynold." Heather was determined. "It just means that we have to be more careful. And I think we better start with a new plan of action."

"Peterson is out, so we start with Green," Lydia suggested. "Why don't we plan the same thing for him as we did for Peterson, tomorrow night."

"I don't think that will be worthwhile," I told her. "I think we have to find a trail in another direction. We have two possibilities right now. We can work back through the computer route, try to make some sense out of the stuff on Stan's disks. Or, we can go back to the dojang, try to get a lead on anyone capable of killing your mother and Peterson in the same way. Maybe Kim will be more helpful now that two people have been killed. I don't see another choice."

"We could take a look at Peterson's place," Heather said. "Maybe there's something there that would help. Some papers or something."

I wanted to go back to Peterson's to find my gun. Reporting it stolen to the police wasn't something I cherished.

"Okay, here's what we do, if you don't mind taking a suggestion from a man," I added. "Heather, you're the computer person here. Why don't you go through those disks? Try to find a pattern, anything in common."

"And Lydia and you?" she asked.

"We'll go talk to Master Kim in the morning. I'm too sore for a lesson, but maybe it's time to take the direct route anyway. We can take a closer look at Peterson's place tomorrow night."

We made plans. In the morning, I'd pick up Lydia and we'd see Master Kim in the dojang.

Heather drove me back to her building and I checked my mail. A few bills, some angry letters from clients complaining I was ignoring their cases, the usual stuff. I was feeling much better by this time; the pain was starting to wear off. Even though I was still pretty sore in a few spots, I was able to walk by myself and drive. Wearing these clothes that Fred picked out embarrassed me, and I was getting irritated as hell without any underwear on. I needed a good shower, a change of clothes, some baby powder, and a little time to sort things out. I really didn't want to leave Heather alone that night, and I got the impression that she felt the same way, but it had been a rough couple of days and I figured the ones to come wouldn't be any better. So I drove back to my own place, after making Heather promise she wouldn't open the door to anyone, and after convincing myself I could do without her for a night.

I took a long cool shower, rubbed on some more ointment, and just lay in bed. After the time spent in that basement even my apartment should have looked good, but it didn't, and I could no longer justify its condition. I tried to picture Heather in my apartment and it turned my stomach. This place was really a dive; used furniture, stale food, sterile. Compared to Heather's apartment, or Joanne's, my place looked like something out of a horror film. No wonder I kept it a secret, perhaps as much out of embarrassment as for privacy.

I started to doze off, dreaming about Heather, picturing her beautiful face looking down at me, whispering, "I love you." It was late and I was tired, but not tired enough to miss the sound of footsteps and talking outside. Although they made a little too much noise in the hallway, they were professionals with the lock and were in the apartment quickly. I had enough time to slide off the bed, onto the floor, and pull Fred's 38 from the top of the bureau where I left it. The apartment was dark, but I could hear them come in and close the door behind them.

Chapter 19

I was naked, trapped between the bedroom wall and the bed. In my favor was surprise. They probably thought they'd catch me asleep in bed, an easy target for whatever they had in mind. Now the law is pretty clear on some things. If I thought my life was threatened I had the right to fire the minute they entered the bedroom. There was no way I could miss, I had a direct shot at the door and could get off two, maybe three shots before they could returned fire.

So I just waited. Waited for the door to open. Waited to see their outlines in the darkness. Waited to open fire. Waited and waited. I heard some whispering in the other room, then the sound of the springs on my sofa, like someone sitting down. Then silence. Two men, I assumed they were men, broke into my apartment in the middle of the night then made themselves at home on my sofa. It just didn't make any sense.

For about ten minutes I just kneeled there, with my gun aimed toward the bedroom door. My eyes were tired, and they kept going in and out of focus as I stared into the darkness, trying to concentrate on any movement of the door. I didn't hear any more noise from outside, no movement or whispering, not even the sofa springs telling me that they got up. Who the hell was out there, I wondered? Who breaks into an apartment, professionally, to take a rest? I knew I couldn't crouch there much longer, my legs were falling asleep, I kept bouncing between sleep and semi-consciousness, my eyes hurt from staring into blackness.

I thought about going for them, since they weren't coming for me, but that was tricky. Any noise I made, footsteps or the sound of the door opening enough to let me through, could trigger a reaction from them. It would be me walking through the door, my figure appearing in the dark, and maybe their fingers firing off a couple of shots before I could respond. This was some sort of game, psychological for sure, maybe deadly, definitely serious.

When I could take the position and the waiting no longer, I shifted my weight to one foot, then paused listening for any response outside. I heard nothing, so I lowered myself to the ground, lying prone, naked, on the carpeted floor, then crawled to the end of the bed. The friction on the carpet burnt my skin, where it hurt the most, but I was able to move silently around the bed and to the bedroom door. The door was open just enough so if I twisted sideways I could squeeze out without it moving.

I held the 38 in my right hand and twisted sideways, putting my head through first, looking for any movement, then my hand with the gun, then shoulder. Still silence from the room. The sofa was directly in front of the door, its side turned facing the bedroom. It was too dark to make out any figures, too silent for anyone to be moving, so I slipped out all of the way and stopped on the living room carpet. I waited there for a full minute, listening and looking for any signs of life, expecting movement and gunfire, flashes of blinding light, sudden explosive blasts filling the room. But nothing.

I started crawling again, to the right and forward, placing myself behind the sofa. By now I felt a wetness coming from my groin, where the friction from the rug wounded my genitals into bleeding. But the searing pain wasn't enough to stop my advance, until I was directly behind the sofa, near the far end table and lamp.

I shifted the 38 to my left hand then felt for the lamp cord with my right. I found it then ran my hand slowly up the wire till it held the small rotary switch attached to the cord. I kneeled slightly so I could spring up quickly, and then listened for any signs of noise or movement. I did hear something, but not what I expected, snoring. Whoever came in was sleeping, sound asleep and snoring, on my sofa.

I held my breath, concentrated on what I had to do, then in an instant rotated the switch to turn on the light and sprang up and over the sofa. I grabbed the gun now in both hands for a steady aim, prepared for a waking figure to sit up, maybe strike out with a fist or weapon.

He opened his eyes slowly, rubbed them with his fists, and then looked straight out into my bleeding genitals. "Goddamn," Fred said. "I didn't know you were into that stuff."

"What the hell are you doing here? You almost got killed."

"Would you mind moving that thing from my face. It's scary."

I didn't know if he was talking about the 38 or my organ waving in front of him, dripping blood. I put down the gun, it was his anyway, and went into the bedroom for some clothes.

"How did you find this place? And why the hell did you pick the lock to get in?" I yelled from the bedroom.

"Pick the lock? You're crazy, man. I don't know how to pick locks. Dr. Goldwyn told me to look after you, so I did just that. I followed you here when you left her place last night. Think you're the only one who can follow somebody?"

It was a little depressing knowing the Fred could follow someone better than I could.

"So how'd you get in here? I thought I heard talking."

"Oh, that was Sam. You know, the super here. I'd be damned but Sam's my cousin, on my mother's side. You know that? I knew right off this was his building when I got here. So I followed you up here then asked Sam for a little favor. He was glad to let me in. Said you were a real strange one, you were."

"Look who's talking," I said, now back in the living room with a robe on. "I thought I heard two people come in. I heard some talking before you sat down on the sofa."

"Well, that must of been me, asking myself what to do. I got tired of waiting outside, that's why I got Sam to let me in. You were asleep so I figured 'Fred, why don't you just lay down here and wait till the morning.' Couldn't think of any better way to keep an eye on you. Jesus, then you come jumping in here pointing my own gun at me with little Reynold hanging down like that. Maybe Sam's right, you are a strange one at that."

"Listen Fred, I don't want anyone to know about this place. You understand? Especially Heather, Dr. Goldwyn. Okay."

He looked around then said "Sure enough. I can see why. Even my place looks nicer than this."

"Just be sure you don't tell anyone where I live. You do and I'll..."

"No need to get hyper, Reynold. Fred won't tell a living soul. Like those two FBI guys that came looking for you today, well yesterday."

"What FBI guys?" I asked.

"Two of them. They asked me to let them into your office. I made them show me their badges and everything."

"Did you let them in?"

"Sure did. I don't want any trouble from the FBI. I heard stories about Hoover, and I don't want the FBI after me."

"Hoover died years ago, Fred." I said.

"I know that. I just didn't want any trouble."

I waited for Fred to explain about their visit but he just sat there staring around the apartment, like he couldn't believe I lived there.

"This is some place," he finally said.

"Fred, what did they do in my office?"

"How should I know? I just opened the door and let them in. Wasn't any of my business, but if I were the type to peek through keyholes, I'd guess that they looked through your desk and the one outside. Maybe went through your filing cabinets. Made a lot of noise doing it, too."

"You didn't tell them where I was, up at Dr. Goldwyn's?"

"Nope, they didn't ask. Anyway, I wouldn't tell them that. Wouldn't want to get Dr. Goldwyn in any trouble. Say man, what kind of trouble are you really in? All that shooting the other day, nearly had yourself fried in that power room. What's the FBI want you for?"

"Were they the same men you helped me lock in the storage room? The ones that got out and came after me?"

"No, sir. These were nice respectable FBI agents. Gave me no trouble, just asked for help, and got it."

"Thanks, Fred. Thanks for not telling them where I was. Did they say or ask anything else?"

"Well, that was strange. After they left your office they stopped down again. Asked me if you owned a computer. Pressed the question too, asked it a couple of times, just in different ways. Did I ever see a computer in your office? Did you ever talk about computers? Did your secretary use one? That's a good one, your secretary. I just said no, no, and no. Told them you wouldn't know a computer from the television set. Then they gave me a card, told me to call them when you came back to the office, and left."

"I appreciate all this Fred. I really do. Listen, I'm not really in any trouble with the FBI." He looked like he didn't believe me. "I'm just involved in a case that they are interested in, that's all. I'll take care of them in the morning. Now I'm exhausted. I just have to get some sleep. Stay here if you want, just let me sleep until the alarm goes off in the morning. Okay?"

"Sure. If you don't mind I'll just sleep right out here. Your place is a mess but this sofa's pretty comfortable."

He laid down, swinging his legs so his feet rested on the arm of the sofa, his head on a pillow at the other end. "Goodnight, Reynold. See you in the morning."

The alarm woke me up with a fright. I showered and dressed, found Fred nowhere in the apartment but a pot of fresh coffee on the stove. I was stiff, but moveable, no longer constrained by the pain of the day before. I took some pills for the soreness, and then called Lydia as I ate breakfast. She was home and ready to go to Master Kim's.

Heather was wide-awake, reading those disks on the computer, she told me. Her voice sounded calm and sexy over the phone. We arranged to meet at her place later that day.

When I got to Lydia's she was waiting downstairs, looking more like a little girl than the street-wise sophisticate of the past days. Looking at her, dressed all in pink, complete with pink Reebok sneakers, it was hard to imagine her using the force and power I'd seen, having the maturity to handle herself so well. You could easily mistake her for a high school cheerleader with nothing more serious on her mind than dating the team captain.

She was very quiet on the ride up, so quiet that I felt ill at ease. Something seemed to be bothering her, although she said everything was all right when I asked. We got to the dojang about 10:30. The door was closed but through the window we could see Master Kim sitting at his desk, going through some papers. The training hall was empty, the lights out.

"Please come in," Master Kim said when we knocked. "It is good to see you, Reynold. And you too Lydia. How can I help you?"

"Master Kim, it's about the same thing we discussed before. Only now two people have been killed the same way."

He looked surprised. "Two people? Joanne and who else?"

"A man in Joanne's company, a man called Peterson. He

was killed in his office the same way Joanne was killed, but the police are calling it murder, not robbery."

"How can I help you?"

Lydia said, "We want to find the man who did this, Master Kim. I have to, for my mother's sake. I have to find him."

"Why do you have to find him, Lydia?" Kim asked.

"For revenge. To honor my mother. You should understand that," she answered.

"Ah, yes I should, shouldn't I? But why do you come to me?"

"Master Kim," I said. "We've come to you seeking answers. Two other people, a husband and a wife, were killed with butterfly knives. Killed quickly and cleanly, one straight through the neck."

"Butterfly knives, as you call them, Reynold, can be used by anyone. There is no martial art involved with them."

"But Master Kim..."

"Let me think a minute," he interrupted. "Let me think."

He sat there at his desk, looking down at his hands. At first he had no expression, but then he looked up at Lydia and frowned. Then he looked down again at his hands. For three minutes we sat there quietly, politely, doing as Kim requested, giving him time to think. It seemed much longer but I kept an eye on the clock over his desk.

Finally, he said, "Yesterday I looked into this matter a little more. I think the technique used to kill Joanne was learned in Korea."

"Can you explain that?" I asked.

"I spent some time talking to masters back home, in Korea, about it. We came to the conclusion that it may have been a little known technique that was mastered years ago, during the war."

"The war?"

"When many Americans were in our country. There was a group of Americans who became masters in our martial arts, blending the techniques they learned in the Special Forces with our own. It is possible that the killer learned the technique from one of those soldiers. Some stayed in Korea after the war."

"Thank you, Master Kim," I said.

He paused a moment before speaking, then spoke very slowly, very deliberately, looking directly at neither of us, but right between our chairs, straight ahead at the closed door.

"The blow that killed your mother, and the other man it now seems, was executed by a master. He, or she, is very dangerous."

"Sounds like stuff from the Kung Fu movies," I said.

"Believe me, Reynold, this person is no actor. Now it is almost time for my morning lesson. I'm afraid I have to change and prepare for class. If you will excuse me. But I will be happy to discuss this more with you later."

We rose. Lydia told him to let me know if he heard anything else. In the car, on the way back down town, I thought over what Kim had told us.

I dropped her off at her apartment and shot over to Heather's. I wanted to see how she was making out with the computer disks, do a little paperwork of my own, then relax a little before we sneaked back to search Peterson's place later that night. I circled the block a few times, looking for suspicious cars, a police or FBI stakeout in particular. After the visit from the FBI, I wouldn't have been surprised if they were waiting for me. Instead of parking in the lot, I parked about two blocks down, and then slipped into the building by the back entrance. I was sure no one saw me.

I wanted to check in at the office first. I found Fred sleeping in the utility room and sent him upstairs to look around, to warn me if he saw anyone hovering around. He was happy to help. Five minutes went by, then ten, fifteen. Fred never returned. After about 30 minutes I assume he just forgot to come back, or just fell asleep in the office as he often did on warm summer days, so I took the service elevator up the floor above mine, and then walked down one flight using the steps. The hallway looked clear but still a little cautious, I slipped off my shoes and tiptoed to my office.

The door was open. Fred must have checked the place out, left the door open on his way out, and forgot to come back downstairs to tell me everything was okay. I dropped my shoes and went into the office, but when I turned the light on I saw Fred sitting, not sleeping, on the sofa, looking behind me.

"Fred, you were supposed...."

Someone grabbed my arm, bent it roughly behind my back in a half nelson, and then pushed my head down, slamming me right into the filing cabinet. A hand went into my jacket, feeling under the arm for a holster, and then two arms frisked me, starting at the feet. He found Fred's 38 in my pocket, then continued up the shoulders.

"Okay, let him go," I heard. I turned around to see the two beefy faces of the FBI agents who so nicely talked to me at Bennite's.

I started to say, "Listen you" but one of the agents got wild and started pushing me, yelling, "You jackass, you cost us six months of work."

The other yelled at him to stop, finally grabbing him by the arms and pulling him away from me.

"But that ass blew the whole case, the whole case just like that."

"I know, but calm down," the other said. "We won't accomplish anything by pushing him around."

"Push him around. Push him around?" his voice getting louder. "I could kill him." He started after me again but luckily for him, his partner held him back.

"London, you better sit down there," the calmer one said, pointing to my chair behind the desk. He turned to his partner. "Why don't you sit down outside while I explain this to London."

"I want to be hear what you tell that turd ass."

"I think it would be better if you calm down outside." The angry one glared at me, cursed under his breath, and then went out, dragging Fred with him. "I'll take this turkey outside," he said. "I want to talk with him."

The calm agent turned to me, sat down on the sofa, and then laughed. "My partner gets a little over excited."

"Well, if he can't control himself, maybe he needs another line of work," I said.

"London, before I go nuts on you too, why don't you wise up and shut up. You are an ass, do you know that?"

"Sticks and stones."

"We've been watching Stan and his friends for six, seven months now. Keeping track of their activities, even tapped his phone. We had a camera crew just across from the 51st Street house."

"Did I photograph well? I hope you got my good side."

"Then one day the team saw this funny looking man walk back and forth past the house. Ten minutes later Stan's gang ran out, and the guy walked right in the front door. A woman, a real nice looking one, joined him a little later, then two of the gang. We don't know what went on in the house. Stan's friends left the house, and the man and woman walked out carrying a computer. That night we had some interesting pictures to look at. Seems we knew the man."

"Anyone I know?"

"Well, it's a funny thing. Here's how we figure it. The guy is the big boss. He's in charge of the whole operation. He met with two of his gang, and then he walked out with a computer and a lot of incriminating evidence. When we nail the gang, the boss will get ten to fifteen, easily. Fraud, bank robbery, conspiracy. Maybe even life with a touch of murder thrown in. Sounds right?"

"Sounds like fiction to me. Sell it to Hollywood."

"London, we got enough pictures of you, enough contacts with Stan and his band of merry men, to make a pretty convincing case. When we find that computer you took we'll have all the proof we need. Of course, I'll give you a chance to tell your side of the story. Right here, right now. Unless you want to call your attorney."

The way I figured it, they had nothing on me, just a few pictures showing me in the house, carrying out one of the computers used in the crime. They could place me in Stan's apartment; maybe they even found some of the computer printouts in my office. They could try to link me with Trendle's murder, and his wife's, maybe even prove that I was one of the last people to see Joanne alive. They had nothing, but just in case, I thought I should test the waters.

"What do you want to know?"

"Who's the boss? Who did Stan take orders from? Did you find anything out while screwing us around?"

"You won't like the answer," I told him.

"Try me."

"I think a guy named Peterson who worked for Philadelphia Mutual."

"What do you mean worked for?"

"They found him dead yesterday. Check with Bennite. I think it's his case."

"Christ. So you're trying to lay the blame on a dead guy. That's a lot of cooperation."

"Hey, I'm telling the truth. Check with Stan."

"We would but we can't find him. Seems he just left town suddenly."

"Did you check his parents?"

"Called them first. They haven't seem him for weeks."

That little bastard was supposed to stay by the phone. Maybe Lydia should have broken his whole hand.

"So," the agent continued, "you can't prove any of this. Can you?"

"Look, I know it seems a little strange, but I'm telling you everything. I could wrap this thing up for you, too, if you just give me a little time."

"You want us to give you time? Let you wrap it up for us? London, what are you talking about? This is a federal case, for God's sake, not one of your pitiful get-me-proof divorce cases."

"One week, that's all I need."

"You're crazy, do you know that? Crazy. By rights I should pull you in now, throw you in Bennite's jail, then into a Federal pen by the morning. And you want a week."

"I could get the boss, the evidence. Even solve a couple of murders to make Bennite happy."

"Now you're solving murders, too. Like who killed that guy Peterson, I assume?"

"Or you could arrest me and have the case laughed out of court. What are you going to prove? That I'm an idiot of a private detective? That'll really help your career. Can't do any worse for mine. That you staked out Stan and his friends for six months and just let me walk right in there and screw it up for you? That you had some poor policewoman running around undressed to do your work for you? That you let Stan just waltz out of town? Some feds you are."

"Listen London..."

"No, I think it's time you listen to me. You can go ahead and threaten me with those pictures. We both know that's a load of crap. You just want to scare me, scare me into telling you everything. Well, I don't know a goddamn thing yet, not a goddamn thing that makes any sense. I got a few pieces, some chunks, that's all. Someone threw up and I'm sifting through to find the meat. It all looks like vomit right now, but I know there's meat somewhere. It seems I got a hell of a lot closer than you did, even with your wiretaps and stakeout teams, and I'll get even closer yet. Just lay off of me for a week. Just seven days and I'll give you everything. All the credit. That's all I ask."

Chapter 20

"He's one mean mother," Fred said.

The agents left, not very happily, and only after warning me what would happen if I didn't contact them within a week. I knew these guys weren't your typical FBI. In my few other dealings with the Bureau, its agents proved to be a competent lot, trustworthy, loyal, and all that. I don't know where these two clowns came from, but I was sure they'd be transferred to some swamp in Florida when this was all over.

Some of the parts to this puzzle were slowly coming together. To be honest, I was far from understanding anything, but at least I could make a few good assumptions about some of it. I kept a lot of my thoughts to myself, mostly because I didn't want Lydia to go off on some mission of revenge, or Heather to get too deeply involved. There was still a lot I needed, but I figured I was bound to start getting some real evidence soon.

I forgave Fred for getting trapped in my office, for letting it slip that I was in the building. I mean, he was scared blue when he came back in my office. I asked him what the agent said, but Fred just shook his head and mumbled.

The first thing I did was check on Heather. So far her name hadn't come in to this, with either Bennite or the FBI, and I wanted it to stay that way. I owed Fred one for that. She was hard at work on the computer, with numbers flying by on the screen. It looked like junk to me, but I hoped it made some sense to her.

When she spoke, I could detect an underlying excitement, a spring about to let go.

"Most of this stuff is client information, about policies," she explained, pointing to the screen. She hit a few buttons, the screen changed. "This is the financial status of the company, Philly Mutual. Sales, expenses, debts, that sort of thing. But I think I found something on the printouts you gave me."

She held up one of the computer sheets I found in Stan's place. "This looks like security codes to me. I'd say the left column is employee numbers, the right their access codes into the system. I can't tell what company they're from, though."

"If they're from Philly Mutual then he got them directly from Peterson," I said. "How could he have gotten them from some other company? Shouldn't they be secret or something?"

"They should be, but some companies aren't too good with that. Tell me again about the other papers you saw."

I explained how the room was littered with them, that most looked crumpled and dirty, like trash.

She shook her head like I said something that made sense then said, "Now I know how he got them. From the trash."

"What do you mean?"

"They got them from the trash. Probably went through the cans or dumpster outside of the company. I've heard stories about people doing that but I never knew for sure."

"You mean the company threw out all of these papers? Even ones with passwords?"

"You'd be surprised what you could find in the trash. Remember seeing stories in the tabloids about things found in celebrities' trashcans? Out in Hollywood? Well, the same goes for companies. Sometimes they're not very careful about what they throw away. Even old passwords that aren't used anymore can be helpful in breaking current ones. This stuff should have been shredded."

I could just picture Stan knee deep in somebody's garbage. That's where he belonged.

"Anything else?"

She smiled. "Everything else on the disks is much of the

same. Except this one." She held up a single computer disk, looking like a proud new mother showing off the baby.

"Looks like all the rest to me," I said.

"Well, let me show you." She put the disk into a slot in the computer, and then pressed a couple of keys. "This is different," she said, "because it's the project Robert is working on. Each file has his name listed in its properties box. It was one that you found in Stan's apartment, not at the 51st Street house. Here look at this." She pressed some keys then pointed to the screen. "It's an inventory of jewelry and other items, mostly from the estate of a Nellie Watson."

The screen was headed Police Inventory - Nassau County, and showed a list of jewels and other personal effects.

She pressed a key and the list kept rolling on the screen, listing more jewels, bank deposit books, items of clothing, and finally at least three screens full of insurance policies for Nellie Watson and someone named Henry Kothe.

Heather explained. "It seems Nellie Watson was killed in 1926, that's probably the killing Robert was interested in, not a present day one. I called the University library. They looked up Nellie Watson for me and delivered copies of some old newspaper clippings just a few minutes ago. Let me get my notes."

She reached for a yellow tablet and thick manila folder on the floor. This was the first time I saw this view of Heather; excited, almost effervescent, moving and speaking so fast she could hardly catch her breath.

"It seems that Nellie was the ex-wife of Sliding Billy Watson, a big burlesque performer at the beginning of the century. She owned a roadhouse, a place called the 300 Club, on Merrick Road, in Freeport. A waiter they had fired killed her and her partner, Henry Kothe, one night. Here's the folder."

As she talked, I paged through printouts of old newspapers, reading headlines like "Fired Point Blank into Woman's Face," "Turned 3 Bullets Into Man's Body" and "Waiter Mum on Reason for Commission of Crime -- Was Not Drunk Says Police."

"The police inventoried all of her effects found at the Club, the ones listed on that report before. They probably went to her estate. But here's the interesting part. Sliding Billy was a pretty rich man at one time. From the news stories it seems there was more property that Nellie had that wasn't in the police report. I think Robert is looking for that stuff. He needed the insurance company reports to see what was found, and what their own investigations showed."

"From all those years ago? How does Reliance have that stuff on the computer?"

"Usually they wouldn't have anything this old in their database. This case should have been closed a long time ago. The only thing I can imagine is that there's something still current about this case, or it's in their files for historical reasons, because of Sliding Billy. I really don't know, but from what Stan said, and from what Robert told me about his interests lately, I think this is the case he was working on. It's the only thing on the disks relating to a specific person or incident."

"I don't want to burst your bubble," I told her, "but why would your brother be interested in this?"

"Well, here's what I think. I think he started doing a research paper or something on the history of burlesque. He ran across this Watson story and he just got involved in it. I think Robert's looking for some kind of hidden treasure, stuff that Nellie had that never made it to the police inventory. I made some calls to an old friend up in Freeport, where the murder took place." She looked at my face. "Just on old family friend," she quickly added. "The 300 Club is now a gas station, but the

Watson house is still standing, owned by two young women. Maybe Nellie's things are buried somewhere in or around the house. Maybe that's what Robert was trying to find out."

"You're talking about a murder that happened 70 years ago, for Christ's sake. Don't you think the family got the stuff long ago, or some other owner of the house? Maybe there's no other stuff to begin with. I mean this is a long shot."

"It's a long shot to you, but it's the only one I have. I'd guess Robert is in Freeport, looking around that house. And that's where I'm going."

"Heather, if you want to go up there I want to go with you. Only can it wait a day? I'm still in the middle of this other mess."

"Of course. I'm not running up there today, and there's no way you're going to stop me from helping you. In fact, Lydia and I already planned..."

"Lydia and you already made plans? Look what happened the last time..."

"Well, what did happen? First we saved you from being killed, taken for a ride, isn't that the expression? Then we finally got some truth out of Stan. Not bad, I'd say."

I forgot about Stan. "Speaking of Stan, where the hell is he?"

"I assume he's sitting by the phone at his mother's house."

I forgot to tell her about the feds. "Not according to the FBI," I said.

"What do they have to do with this?"

"I just had a nice visit with the local G-men, downstairs in my office. They weren't up here, were they?"

"Don't you imagine that would be the first thing I'd tell you? Really, Reynold."

"Well, they're looking for that computer there, and those

disks. You know, you'd serve a couple of years for withholding evidence if they found them here. Anyway, they tried reaching Stan at his house. No luck."

"We better try. Here," she handed me the phone. "Give him a call."

Stan answered on the second ring.

"Hello" he whispered.

"Stan? Is that you, old buddy?"

"Yeah, it's me. What do you want? You know that bitch really broke my finger."

"I hear people have been looking for you but you've been a bad boy, not staying near the phone."

"I've been here, just like you told me. My mom said that someone called before I got here, though. I stopped first to see the doctor about my finger."

"It ain't going to fall off, boy. It's just broken, that's all."

"Well, what do you want?"

"Just calling to see if you're there. That's all. By the way, do you know that Peterson is dead?"

"Peterson, dead? When did that happen?"

"Couple of nights ago. Killed with a karate chop. You think you might be next in line?"

"What are you talking about?"

"I don't mean to scare you Stanley, but maybe whoever killed Peterson is after you too. You were taking orders from him."

"I just gave him some computer stuff, that's all. Printed some reports, took some stuff to the transfer shop, that's all."

I whispered to Heather, "What's a transfer shop?" but she shook her head and shrugged her shoulders.

"What's a transfer shop?" I asked Stan.

"A conversion shop. A place that transfers data from one media to another. You know, to different size disks, from tape to disk, that sort of thing."

"Do they also transfer stuff from disk to tape?"

"Well I suppose. But these days it's usually the other way around. People are taking their old tape records and moving them onto disk. But they could transfer records from disk onto tape if you wanted them to."

"What did they do with the stuff you brought over?"

"Hell do I know. I just dropped it off, that's all."

"One more question. Did you ever see any tapes, storage tapes, from Peterson or anybody involved in this thing?"

"I told you before, never. I just dealt with disks, that's all."

"Okay, Stanley, you're doing good. Stay at home, but have someone else answer the phone for you. Your mom or dad. Don't talk to anyone but me, or Dr. Goldwyn. Got that?"

"Got it."

Now it was my turn to question Heather. "Okay now," I said. "Tell me about this plan."

She explained what she and Lydia wanted to do next. I hate to admit it but it sounded okay to me. Then I filled her in on our discussion with Kim, and how I thought we might be looking for someone trained by an American in Korea.

She told me about her mom and dad. How her father died about eight years ago, leaving her mother alone to take care of Robert. Her father was a doctor, one of those old fashioned family doctors serving a small Long Island town. He made house calls, was friends with his patients, just a regular guy that was part of the community. Her mom didn't have to work. Instead, she stayed home and took care of the kids, volunteered for the local charities, did all the proper things. But then Dr. Goldwyn died and his wife was alone.

They used to share everything, Heather explained. Her mom and dad would talk for hours, exchanging their experiences of the day, their thoughts. They did everything together, as much as a doctor's schedule would allow. And even though Mrs. Goldwyn had her own bevy of friends, and her own activities, the husband and wife were as close as any couple they knew.

When her father died, Heather was concerned that her mother would go into a deep depression, feel abandoned by her husband. She thought that the closeness the two shared would magnify her mother's loss. But it wasn't that way.

"Mother was amazing," Heather said. "Robert and I went back right away, trying to support her, to help her fight depression and anxiety. But she was amazing. Sure she cried. She couldn't sleep for weeks, but she never once seemed morose.

"One morning I came down and she was making breakfast for Robert and I. Instead of us taking care of her, she was taking care of us. At first, I was worried. I was concerned she might have been holding in the real pain, afraid to acknowledge the truth, but that wasn't it. In fact, about two weeks after father died, mom came up to my room and said she wanted to have a heart to heart talk.

"You know what she said? I'll never forget it. She told me that she missed my father terribly; that at first she wondered how she'd ever get on without him. But after a while, she said, she started to thank the Lord for the time He had given them together. She was thankful for how close they had been, for the time they had shared, saying that those memories would sustain her. She told me that the closeness she shared with my father was a bond that would never go away, not even in the face of death, and that as long as she always thought of that closeness, she'd be okay."

About two days after their heart to heart talk, her mother told Heather to get on with her own life. To go back to work and stop treating her mother like a child who needed a babysitter.

"I think that's why I won't let you do this alone," Heather told me. "I don't know what's in store for us, and as I said before, I'm not asking for any commitment. It's just that I want to feel that closeness that my mother felt with dad. I want to fill my heart with memories and experiences. With you."

Chapter 21

It's hard to explain how I felt about this closeness stuff. Don't get me wrong; I loved the idea of being with her, sharing the rest of my life with her. But remember, I was an old horse that's never been ridden, as they say. Maybe that's why I started thinking about Nancy again and how close we had come to getting married, if it wasn't for the frogman.

I met Nancy through a case; one of those dirty divorce jobs where I was paid to prove this lady was cheating on her old man. I got the case through a friend of mine, Ed, an ex-Marine who took a job for the City after he quit the corps. It was for his best friend, a guy named Dan Coppersmith. It seems that Dan knew for sure his wife was cheating on him. Little things, like his wife staying out all night "with the girls", strange excuses, small lies he caught her in. They had been married about 12 years, and I got the impression he just wanted out of the marriage anyway. So one day I meet Dan where his wife worked and he pointed her out to me in the crowd. She wasn't what you'd call a beautiful woman. She was plain, maybe a few pounds overweight, but she dressed well and carried her head with pride. A man could do a lot worse.

It only took me one night to get the proof he wanted. I followed her after work to this hotel, saw her get a key from the desk, and go up to a room on the third floor. That's where I met Nancy.

I was standing at the end of the hallway, watching their room, when Nancy got out of the elevator. She walked down the hall to the room right next to the one I was watching. As she got closer to me I started messing with some flowers on a table, trying to look like I belonged there. Anyway, she put her key in the door but it wouldn't turn, the lock must have been jammed, so she called me over.

"Can you come over here?" she commanded. She must have thought I worked there.

Well, I wanted to blend in so I answered "Yes Ma'am" and walked over.

She pushed the key in my face. "This key doesn't work."

I put it in the lock and started turning it left, then right, pushing harder and harder. She was standing there, tapping her feet and making noises like she was in some hurry.

"Can't you do anything?" she said. "Why do they hire people like you? If you can't open the door get someone who can. I don't have all day, you know."

She was really getting on my nerves, but she was a looker, I'll say that for her. She was wearing the most expensive clothes I had ever seen, and talked with her little nose stuck in the air at just the right angle.

"I'm doing the best I can ma'am. Just be a little patient."

"Patient?" she said. "I'm not paying these rates to be patient. I'm paying for that room in there. That room that I can't get into because you can't even get the key to work."

"Listen, ma'am..."

"Don't ma'am me, bellboy. Just open the door immediately or I'll have you fired."

She started to raise her voice pretty loud, being real obnoxious, like she was better than everybody else because she was paying for the goddamn room. So I really started to push that key now, until it started to bend, then it finally twisted off and broke in the lock.

"Now look what you've done. I insist that you get me in this room immediately."

"Okay lady, you want to get in the room? I'll get you in." I slammed my shoulder against the door as hard as I could but the door didn't budge.

"What do you think you're doing? Get a key, you idiot."

I banged again into the door. "You said you wanted to get in immediately, so that's what I'm doing." I rammed the door a third time.

"You're crazy. Insane," she screamed. "You can't get in that way, you'll break the door. I won't pay for it if that's what you think."

"I'm just doing what you wanted ma'am, that's all." One, two, three more bangs and the door swung open, wood splintering on the inside.

"You're a sick man. You know that, don't you?" she said. "I can't believe you did that."

"That's what you wanted, wasn't it, lady. To get in." I stepped inside the doorway. "Well you're in now. Happy?" I handed her the broken stub of the key.

I turned to leave when I saw that her room had one of those connecting doorways with the one next door, the one with the lady I was supposed to watch. This would be perfect, I thought. If I could listen in at the door, maybe even peek through the keyhole or something, maybe even open the door just a little, I could really get the dirt I need for this case. It would be great.

"Listen lady," I said. "I'm sorry. Why don't you let me clean this mess up? It'll only take a few minutes. Can you wait in the lobby?"

"I'm not leaving you alone in my room, you idiot. I want you out of here now. I can't believe..."

"Shhhh. Be quiet. Do you hear that?" I didn't hear a thing.

"Hear what? What are you talking about?"

"Do you smell that? Smells like gas coming in from the next room." I didn't smell a thing.

No Waiting To Die

"Gas? There's no gas in these rooms. You're insane. That's it. You're insane."

"No lady, I'm telling you. I hear these strange noises and I smell gas, or something dangerous, coming from the next room. You better let me check it out." I closed the door.

"If you think..."

"Please lady, this could be dangerous." I walked over to the connecting door and started sniffing around it.

She stood there with her hands on her hips. "Will you please get out of here? Now. Or do I have to call the manager or the police?"

"Don't move!" I said forcefully. "Quiet. I think there's some poison gas coming from the room next door. Be very still. For your own sake."

She seemed to believe me because she stopped talking and just stood there, staring at me. I put my ear up against the door and listened. I could just hear muffled noises, no words. I looked in the keyhole but couldn't see anything.

"I'd better open this door just to check things out. But be very quiet. Please."

I slowly turned the lock, the doorknob, and then quietly opened the door so I could see the corresponding door from the other room. Nancy was quiet and had moved closer to me; I assume to hear for herself if there were any noises. I was able to hear clearly now what was going on in the other room. I heard Ed's voice and Dan's wife. My pal and his best friend's lady. They were screaming about God and I could hear the bedsprings squeak under their pressure.

"What..." Nancy started to say.

"I'll explain about it in a minute lady. Please, just let me listen."

"Listen?" she whispered. "Are you some sort of pervert?"

I noticed that she wasn't yelling now, but whispering so the couple next door wouldn't be disturbed. I took that as a good sign.

"I'm a detective. Please be quite just a minute more then I'll explain everything."

I kept my ear to the door, trying to listen, when I felt Nancy crouch down beside me and put her own ear to the door. "Oh my" she said.

The noise from the room was reaching a crescendo. The voices and moans increased in tempo with the bedsprings, and the joining wall started to vibrate. Nancy started repeating "Oh my" over and over, pressing her ear harder against the door, and moving her body back until it came in contact with mine. Her own body started moving in rhythm with the beat from next door, her breathing increased. Then a scream and it was over. Silence, no voices, no bedsprings, no walls shaking. I started to back away when Nancy turned around to face me, her eyes wide open, her lips moist.

We looked into each other's eyes. I was thinking that this broad must be nuts or something, but she threw her body against mine, knocking me to the floor, then jumped on top of me.

I didn't get out of there until the next morning. I never heard the lady leave next door, and I just didn't give a damn. When I did get out, I called my friend Ed.

"Did you find out if she was cheating?" he asked.

"Sure did. Followed her to some hotel last night."

"Good," he said. "Did you see the guy?"

"No. Never got a look at him, but she's cheating alright."

"Great work, Reynold. I knew you could do it. Just give Dan the report and he'll be able to divorce her."

He seemed a little too anxious, a little too happy that I caught them cheating together. But then I remembered how much

Dan wanted out of the marriage. So I made the call. Not to the husband, but to the wife. We met at the bar of that same hotel. I told her who I was, that her husband had hired me to follow her, and that I knew she was having an affair.

"An affair? Last night was the first time. I feel so dirty, so ashamed."

"Sure lady."

"Don't you see? My husband has wanted a divorce for a long time now. But I won't give him one. Then last week, a friend of the family started showing an interest in me, being real nice. I don't know how it happened, it just did," she cried.

Well I knew how it happened and I told her what I thought. I told her that her husband and my buddy Ed planned the whole thing, setting up both of us as dummies. Seduce the wife, use it for evidence, dump the wife as cheaply as possible. Only I didn't like being taken for a fool.

I gave Dan the bill and insisted he pay me before I turned in the final report. I suppose he had talked to Ed, so like an idiot he paid up. Only he wasn't happy to find out that my report showed his wife as a loving, loyal woman who just went out that night to meet a new friend named Nancy.

Chapter 22

That night we put their plan into action. I drove Heather and Lydia out to Peterson's place for a closer look. The house was dark except for the light over the front door, no cars in the driveway. I knocked and rang the bell but no one answered, so I let us in with my lock-picking talents. The house was hot inside, as if the air conditioner had been turned off for some time, and the air was stale. We listened carefully and heard no signs of life before turning on our flashlights and starting a search of the house.

I took the library, Heather and Lydia started in the living room. We were looking for papers, files, and any documents that might shed some light on Peterson's involvement with Joanne or Stan.

The library was the room where I met Peterson the last time I was in the house. It was a large room, the walls lined with books, a big dark wood desk in one corner. Without making a sound, I slid open one drawer at a time and thumbed through the papers there. The top drawer was mostly blank stationary and pens, a roll of stamps, calendar, and ruler. The two large drawers on the bottom of either side were for files. Both contained what looked like business papers about the insurance company. Three of the smaller side drawers were just as mundane, but the last one was quite interesting.

On top was Peterson's address book. I didn't recognize most of the names, except for Joanne's and Green's.

Underneath the address book was a small green ledger, accounts of some sort. Then underneath that was a manila folder marked CONFIDENTIAL. I was just starting to look through it when someone turned on the lights in the entrance way and I heard Heather scream and a man's voice yelling.

I didn't want to give myself away yet so I pushed the drawer closed, tiptoed to the hallway door, and peeked out. It was Peterson and one of goons. I knew Peterson was supposed to be dead but he was going through their handbags while his pal held them off with a gun.

"What are you two doing here?" Peterson asked.

"You're dead," Heather said. "We were told you were dead." She looked at Lydia and said "Didn't Bennite tell you Peterson was killed?"

"This isn't Mr. Peterson," Lydia said. "I know Peterson. I've never seen this man before."

"Quite right, ladies. I have not yet had the pleasure of meeting this young woman. Now, why don't you tell me why you're here?" He looked at Heather. "I'm quite surprised that you returned here."

"If you're not Peterson, who are you?" Heather asked.

"My name is Edward Cartmonde, and I've lived with Peterson for about a year now. You and London just assumed you were meeting Peterson that night, so I did nothing to change that assumption. Assumptions can be quite dangerous. Now what were you looking for?"

Heather and Lydia gave each other quick glances, and then stared at Peterson, rather the man we thought was Peterson. I was about to take a chance, to draw their attention, when Lydia spoke.

"I have a paper here in my pocket. It will explain everything." She motioned with her head down toward her right pocket. "I'll get it for you."

"Don't move," Cartmonde said. He looked over to his friend with the gun. "John, get the paper."

He moved closer to her, very slowly, holding the gun with his right hand. When he got close enough he put his left hand into the pocket of her jeans.

Lydia looked up and to the right. The movement caught John's attention and he momentarily moved his eyes in that direction giving Lydia the time she needed. She spun to the left, swinging her right leg up and kicking the gun out of his hand. Then she hopped forward on her left leg, keeping the right one up, kicking him three times quickly in the stomach, pushing him further back with each kick. Cartmonde started to move for the gun, now on the floor near the door, but Heather headed him off and grabbed the gun before he got close to it.

"Hold it right there!" she yelled.

John was already on the floor holding his midsection in pain. Peterson stopped short.

"Good work, girls," I said. "I was right there if you needed a man."

Cartmonde turned his heard toward me. "London, I should have known you'd be here."

I pulled John off of the floor, and then we pushed them both into the library and onto chairs. Heather held the gun.

"Okay, now what is this all about?"

What happened next is hard to explain. Cartmonde was opening his mouth to talk when the room filled with an ear-splitting shriek. I saw Heather go flying across the room and fall on the floor, her gun sliding into the corner. I turned around but heard another yell, then felt something hard slam against my chest knocking me down and out.

When I opened my eyes I saw blackness. I had trouble breathing and my chest felt like a car had just run me over. I could tell that I was laying on my side, against a stone wall, but I couldn't see or hear anything else.

"Heather? Lydia?" I whispered. "Are you there?"

I heard a moan, then a hacking cough, a wet cough like someone clearing blood out of their throat.

"Heather? Lydia? Is that you?"

"Reynold". It was Heather. Her voice was coming from straight ahead, about 10 feet into the darkness.

"Are you okay? Heather, are you okay?"

She coughed again.

"Heather!"

"I'll be okay," she said. "I just have to rest. Please don't make me talk, just let me rest. But talk to me, please."

"I'm sorry this happened, Heather. I love you and I didn't want anything to happen to you. I love you so much. I just want to take care of you. I'll try to get over there."

I started to move but realized my hands and feet were tied.

"I think I'll wait just a bit, Heather. I'm a little tied up now."

She gave a small, weak, laugh.

"Lydia? Are you here? Can you hear me?"

"I don't think she's here Reynold," Heather responded.

"Don't talk, Heather. Just listen. A lot has happened this past week. We've said a lot to each other and I think you know how I feel about you. A couple of times you've talked about commitment, giving me an out if I wanted it. Well, I don't want an out."

"Oh, Reynold..."

"Just rest, Heather. There are some things I have to say. I really don't deserve someone like you. You have to know that. You deserve much more than me. But if you want me, I'm yours as long as you want. When we get out of this you can have all the time you want to make up your mind, really think about it."

She coughed.

"And we will get out of this. I promise. I won't get this close to having you and let you off that easily."

I paused a minute, listening carefully for her breathing. It was heavy and labored, punctuated with small moans and sighs. She sounded in pain, struggling to hide the true extent from me. She didn't say anything and I knew it was because of the pain that talking gave her. I knew she probably needed rest but I didn't want her to black out, fearing she'd never return.

"Heather, you've probably figured this out by now. Cartmonde must have a partner or employee who is a karate master who must have attacked us in the living room. The real Peterson was killed in his office. He..."

Someone turned on the lights and I had to shut my eyes against the glare. I heard footsteps, some pushing and crying. As I opened my eyelids slowly I saw Heather laying on the floor opposite me, tied hand and foot, bleeding from the mouth. We were in the basement again.

I heard more noise, someone falling to the ground. Then the room went dark before I could see into the light.

"Lydia? Is that you?"

"Mr. London? It's me." Her voice was weak and tentative.

"What happened? Why did they just bring you down here?"

"It is Green, my mother's friend."

"Green? What do you mean?"

"Green is the mastermind behind this entire thing. He was upstairs, I saw him."

"Are you okay?"

"They broke my arm."

"What did they do to you? Those..."

"I'm okay, Mr. London. I'm okay now. How's Heather?"

"She's hurt but holding on. Tell me what happened upstairs."

"They broke my arm. Green is a martial arts expert, he's

probably the one who killed my mother."

Just then the door opened and Green walked down. "Nice to see you again, Reynolds."

"What is this all about?"

"I've worked many years for the company, always under the shadow of the Paek family. They wouldn't have had a dime if it weren't for me. I set everything up for them when I came back to the States from Korea. Then they treated me just like another employee."

"You learned martial arts in Korea? Did Joanne know that?"

"She never did, until her last day on Earth. I was in an elite unit in Korea, and I met an old marine who taught martial arts. I studied under him all the years I was there, in secret, using the money I earned from the Paek family to pay for lessons."

"And the lessons they paid for were responsible for Joanne's death."

"Ironic, isn't it," he said.

"Then what's all this about tapes and computer data? Where did the Trendles fit in this? Why did you get me involved?"

"That's a lot more than you need to know." He walked back up the steps and turned off the lights.

"Bastard."

"Reynold, you're language," Heather said. She was trying to be humorous but I could hear the pain in her voice, and it hurt me.

"Quiet Heather. Just rest." I turned my head in Lydia's direction, even though it was too dark to see a thing. "Lydia, can you talk?"

"Yes. I'm okay. Now what are we going to do?"

"I don't know Lydia. I really don't know."

This was worse than I ever thought it could be. Maybe I

should have married Nancy and gone in the shoe business or something like that. Maybe I should have insisted on doing this alone.

This time they were playing it real safe. We were tied up, laying in separate areas of the basement, and the lights were off. There were no windows so the room was pitch black, not even a trace of moonlight.

I always liked the dark when I was a kid. I wasn't afraid of it like other kids were, and would even close the curtains to block out any moonlight at night. I'd sit in bed staring into the darkness playing this game with my ears. Without sight, I'd concentrate all my energy into hearing, straining to hear night sounds from outside, or the small creaking sounds made by the house itself. Once I picked up a sound, I turned my head slightly in its direction, trying to picture in my mind what was making it. I tried to imagine what it was like to be blind, to have to rely on the other senses for contact with the outside world. After awhile I would just fall asleep.

I would have liked to do that here, in the basement. Instead, I struggled to keep awake, to hide the wheezing sound coming from my chest every time I spoke. I talked to both Heather and Lydia, to keep their spirits up, to make sure Heather had something to concentrate on, to live for. It must have been hours. I would talk about a minute or two, then shut up a minute to listen to Heather's breathing. During one of those pauses I heard some scraping noise from the far side of the basement, near the coal door. The noise got louder and louder, until I was sure I heard the chute door open, and the rustling of fabric as someone came in through the door, not escaping out of it. A small pinpoint of light scanned across the floor, alternately lighting Heather, then me, then Lydia.

"Who's there? Who are you?" I said. I could sense someone close to me now. I saw the beam of light then felt hands free the ropes from my hands and feet.

"Free Lydia," a voice whispered. "I'll take care of the other woman."

I crawled over toward Lydia, feeling the floor for obstacles with my hands. When I reached her, I groped around until I felt her bonds, and then painfully worked them loose with my own sore hands.

"Wait here," the voice said. "I'll see if they are gone."

I heard the sound of soft steps on the stairs, and then I saw a crack of light as the door opened and a dark figure, crouching down, slid out of the door, then closed it so the light disappeared.

"Heather, are you okay?" I said.

"I'll be alright. I just need some help. How's Lydia?"

"Don't worry Heather. I'm okay."

The door opened, this time wide, and the lights went on. The bright light hurt my eyes but I had to see who was there. I shaded my eyes with my hand and squinted. It was just a blur but a small figure came down the steps. As the figure got closer I could make out more detail until I saw Master Kim walk over to Lydia and help her up.

"We must get out of here quickly," he said. "Reynold, can you help that woman up the stairs?"

I had a lot of questions but it was no time to get answers. Somehow we managed to get up the basement steps and into the hallway. I leaned Heather against the wall, went into the library, and got the confidential folder from the desk drawer. Then we got into Kim's car and drove away.

Chapter 23

I didn't want the police involved. Not yet. They had hurt Heather and I wanted to get even for that.

Suddenly I realized how patronizing I must have sounded when I told Lydia not to think about seeking justice for her mother's death. But now I know how she felt. I guess I didn't understand before how strong a force revenge could be.

Right or wrong, I wanted to take care of this myself, to get the satisfaction of hurting Green and the others, as they had hurt Heather. One part of my mind knew that the police should be called; that we had enough evidence to warrant an investigation; that this was getting too dangerous for me to handle with a couple of amateurs. But none of that mattered. I wanted to see Green writhe in pain as Heather did, to see Cartmonde feel his arm being broken, slowly and deliberately.

That's all I could think about. This compelling hatred boiled in my head, intensifying with each painful breath, with each glance at the woman I loved.

I didn't know how Kim got there and I was too concerned about Heather and Lydia to even care. He wanted to take us to the nearest hospital and to call the police. It took some arguing but I finally convinced him of the need to keep this thing quiet, so he drove us to a small hospital in Northeast Philadelphia where he knew the emergency staff.

"They have been good in treating injuries from tournaments and fights. They won't ask many questions," he explained.

The emergency room was quiet and empty when we got there. Only one doctor was on duty. He spoke to Kim for a moment then looked quickly at all three of us, deciding to treat Heather first. The rest of us just sat in the lobby and waited.

With some time to think, I grew suspicious of Kim's sudden appearance for our rescue, thankful but suspicious.

"How did you find us, Master Kim? Why were you there?" I asked him.

"After we talked, I was very worried about Lydia. I know she is headstrong and just might seek revenge. Last night, I went to Joanne's apartment to look for Lydia, but as I got out of the elevator, two men were coming out of her door. I followed them to that large house, found my way in through that trapdoor, and found you."

"We're glad you came, Master Kim. I don't know what would have happened if you hadn't showed up."

Just then, the doctor walked up. "Your friend took a real beating," he said, "but she'll be okay. She has three broken ribs; one might have punctured a lung. A very small fracture in the sternum. She'll be fine but she needs a lot of rest and care."

"Can I see her?" I asked.

"Not yet. She's having some tests done, and then they'll wrap up her ribs. I'll let you know." He turned to Lydia, "Now let's take a look at you, young lady."

They walked back into the treatment area. Kim waited until they were gone then said "Please tell me what this is all about."

I told him the whole story, from Warren's death to Green's attack last night. I explained how Green was stationed in Korea and learned the martial arts. He interrupted a few times to ask questions, or for some clarification. From time to time he'd nod his head, signifying he understood where some point fit in, where something made sense. It took a while to tell the whole story and before I knew it the doctor returned.

"Mr. London. You're next."

I stood up asking about Lydia.

"Oh, she's fine. A remarkable girl, that one. Broken arm,

lots of small bruises, contusions. She should have been in a lot more pain. Most girls her age would have come here in hysterics with all that damage. I hardly knew she had been hurt until I examined her. Remarkable"

"Yeah, she knocked me over the first time we met, too."

Luckily I wasn't in bad shape. X-rays showed only one broken rib but I had a lot of sore muscles. They taped me up, gave me some pills, and sent me away with Lydia in her cast. Heather had to stay a few days. I hated leaving her but I had some important things to take care of and I wanted to give her good news when I visited her again.

We dropped off Lydia at her place, and then Kim joined me at the office. He sat on my sofa paging through a magazine while I read the confidential file I took from Peterson's house. It filled in some of the holes.

Finally, Kim broke the silence. "Okay, Reynold, what do we do next?"

"We, Master Kim?"

"This is my fight now too, Reynold.

"I appreciate your help. You're right. I don't think I could do much in this condition. Especially with what I just found out."

"In those papers?" he asked.

"Yes. They don't explain everything that's been going on but they clear up a few points. Among other things, there are records of payments. About twenty thousand to Stan, that's a lot of money for a kid like that. They must have paid him to break into Philly Mutual, do enough damage to the company to discredit Joanne.

"I'm still a little fuzzy on the details, but it looks like Green was behind this whole thing from the start. He planned everything to discredit Joanne and put the blame on Peterson. He never intended the tapes to get into the wrong hands, but wanted them changed slightly to cover up his own embezzlements. He was writing false policies and collecting on the insurance himself. I still have no clue about the Trendles or where the tapes are."

Kim stood up and paced around the room. Finally, he said "I think we now have to make some sense in all of this. I have to go back to those men and get our questions answered."

"Not without me, you don't. You can't do this alone either, you know."

"But your rib. How can you..."

"I can and I will." I stood up, masking the pain, "Now let's get out of here."

"Rest first, Reynold. We all need rest."

I slept on the sofa, Kim on the floor. I had a hard time falling asleep. My mind raced with thoughts and pictures, my teeth ground together until my jaw hurt like hell. Hatred and revenge are dangerous states. I could feel myself being taken over, my judgment being clouded, and losing control. Kim was wise to make us wait. In this mental state I'd really be no good to anyone.

In the morning, we drove back out to Peterson's house. My car was still in the driveway, along with the Ford and a fancy Chrysler. I was calmer then, but no less resolved for revenge. I was angered not only by their actions of last night but also by their unbelievable gall. With all that went on, with all of the damage they had done, they were still in the house, like nothing had happened. Didn't they think we'd go to the police? To the FBI? Kim parked a block away and we walked back toward the house. I hid behind some bushes while he crept up to the place and took a look around. He was back in five minutes.

"There are five of them in the house. One young man does not look happy. I think he's being guarded so he cannot escape.

He and one other, his guard, are in the kitchen in the back of the house. The others are in this room filled with books."

"That's the library," I explained.

"Yes, the library. They are talking and yelling. I think they are trying to make plans. One man is doing most of the talking." That must be Green.

"We have to get answers from these men, but there are too many of them for us. Let's wait and see."

We both sat behind the bushes waiting. Kim was a patient man and a remarkable one. For two hours he sat with his legs crossed watching the house. He eyes were alert at all times, his head slowly scanning back and forth across the area. I couldn't sit in one position more than five minutes. I'd shift my weight, move my legs, moaning each time. I thought it was a waste sitting there and told him we should storm the place.

"Why don't I go in the front, you the kitchen," I explained. "You take out the man in the kitchen, and the kid if you have to. Then we'll meet and go into the library together. We can get the drop on them and find out what we need to."

He laughed. "Sounds like a movie I saw on television, Reynold. I could take out the man in the kitchen, but you'd have to take care of who answers the door. If that was Green, you'd have to shoot to stop him, and he might not give you that chance. If one of us were delayed the other would be facing him alone. Green is a formidable man. It would be a real contest between us. Even with your gun, you'd have a difficult time subduing him. No, I think we should wait and see. I don't think they will be together for long. Patience, Reynold. Patience."

It was easy for him to say. Nothing seemed to bother him, but I was going nuts out there. I was sweating to death, being bitten alive by bugs. My legs were getting numb from crouching behind this stupid bush. Then my goddamn hay fever started acting up and I didn't have a handkerchief or tissue. I checked every pocket but not one thing to blow my nose into.

I had everything else with me. On the way over I stopped by my apartment and got this old 45 automatic I kept for emergencies. I hated the gun; it was too heavy and not very accurate, tended to jam if fired rapidly. One full clip was in the gun, three others weighed down my jacket pockets. I also took a knife, a front-loading switchblade that I rarely carried.

But I didn't bring one tissue, not even a piece of lousy paper. God, did I have to blow my nose. In the old days I'd just use my sleeve, or my shirttails, but it didn't seem right. I mean picture this. Big time detective Reynold London and Master Kim staking out the dangerous Peterson mansion. Kim was alert, scanning the horizon, his senses on edge ready to react. London was pulling out his shirttails and blowing his nose, then tucking it back into his pants.

When Kim was concentrating on the house, I looked around the bushes for some wide, soft, leaves. I finally found some that were useable then blew my nose, relieving the pressure on my sinuses. I was burying them under a pile of dry leaves when Kim pulled on my shoulder.

"Look," he whispered. "They're coming out. Two men are leaving."

Sure enough, two guys got into the Chrysler and drove away. We watched as their car went out of the driveway, turned left, and down the street out of sight. One was Cartmonde, the other one of the fake FBI agents. That left only Green and the two in the kitchen.

"Now it's time," he said. "Just the three of them. Let's go."

Keeping low, Kim went around the bushes and ran up to the side of the house. I waited until he signaled, and then I followed the same way, just a little slower.

"Now we use your plan," he said. "But you go around to the kitchen, get in and take care of the man there. I'll take care of

Green in the library. Get there as fast as you can."

"How are you going to get into the front?"

"Don't worry about that. Take care of the kitchen. Look at your watch." He looked down at his. "Don't make any noise for five minutes, then do what you have to. Now go."

I followed the contour of the house, ducking below ground-floor windows until I got to the back. The kitchen was in a newer addition built onto the back of the house, so it stuck out beyond the original building. I hugged the wall till I got close, but far enough way so I wouldn't be easily seen, and hid behind a chimney. From there I could see into the kitchen through a large window. One of the goons was standing with his back toward the window and Stanley was sitting at the table. It looked like his hands were tied.

Carefully, but as quickly as possible, I left the sanctuary of the chimney and made my way up directly under the kitchen window. It had been only four minutes so I kneeled down below the window trying to hear what was happening inside. While waiting I made a hasty plan for taking care of the goon inside. It wasn't very sophisticated but it would be fast and effective.

I looked at my watch. It was now just over five minutes. I crawled backwards and stood up so I was at the junction of the house and the kitchen addition, just out of sight from the window. In my left hand I had some small stones that I had picked up, the 45 in my right.

I held my breath then tossed the stones onto the window. The goon spun around to look, his gun extended in his right hand. I swivelled out with the 45 raised, aimed fast and shot through the window, hitting his arm and splattering him with glass so he dropped the gun and doubled over in pain.

"Duck down, Stan. Get your head down," I yelled. Then I ran over to the door and blasted three 45's into the handle and lock. I kicked the door open, and ran in. The goon was moaning, blood dripping from his arm and where some small pieces of glass must have flown into his face and chest.

"You okay, Stan?"

"Jesus, London. They were going to kill me."

"How did you get here?" I asked him.

"One of them came to my house and told me everything was cool, that we were back in business. But he brought me here instead and tied me up. He said they were going to kill me so they couldn't be traced."

I picked up the hood's gun and put it in my pocket, then I pulled him up by the hair and pushed him toward the library, Stanley following mumbling about being killed.

I had no idea what to expect in the library. If all went well, Kim had somehow gotten into the house and disabled Green, if he could.

We got to the hallway and I noticed that the main door was still closed and locked from the inside. The library doors were open so I pushed the bleeding hood in and, just in case Kim was in trouble, holding the 45 out with both hands and scanning the room ready to fire.

One of the windows was shattered with glass all over. Kim stood, facing Green, both staring at each other.

"It's over, Green," I said. "Just sit down and let us call the police."

"Nothing is over," he sneered. "Do you think you two can really take care of me?"

Kim and Green were in striking stances facing each other. Their muscles were tight, poised to react instantly to movement from the other.

Kim shook his head. "You are a disgrace, Green. You are a disgrace to your masters in Korea. Why did you do these things?

No Waiting To Die

Why?"

"Why do you think? Money." Green looked down at his hands as if he was thinking of something to say, but it was just an attempt to distract his opponent. Suddenly he propelled his body into the air, twisted himself to the right and extended his leg viciously out toward Kim's face. Kim leaned back and ducked down. He raised his left arm up, deflecting the kick, then slid to the right out of Green's way.

As Green landed and turned around, Kim slid closer then jumped into a side kick, aiming at Green' chest. Green saw the kick coming, turned and blocked Kim's foot so he was caught just lightly on the shoulder. Kim punched out with his right hand. Green blocked that and caught Kim on the chest with a sharp left.

The two masters parried, alternately attacking and defending with quick strong movements that made their clothes snap in the air. Kim was good but Green seemed to have a slight edge, his added years of experience having their effect on the younger master. Each was able to score on the other; blows that weren't fully blocked, a defense just slightly off in timing. I could see them both tiring, distancing themselves for a second of rest, and then charging again with full force.

Green propelled his body into the air, spun entirely around and whipped his leg toward Kim's head. Kim shot back, raising his arm in defense then striking out with a kick of his own, but the defense and counterattack were just slightly off the mark. Green's foot connected sharply on Kim's defending arm, pushed it out of the way making final contact on the side of Kim's head. The blow stunned him, knocked him down to the ground. Green knelt down and grabbed Kim's right hand. He twisted it up and around snapping the wrist, then raised his own arm back into the air, his hand straight and rigid like a human knife. He held his hand in that position and I could see his muscles tightening, ready to release a powerful decisive blow to Kim's neck.

I finally had a clear shot at Green and planted one right in his chest, so he fell down with a thud.

"Did you kill Trendle and his wife?" I asked him. "Do you have the tapes?"

"Yes I have them." He coughed up blood.

It was difficult for Green to speak.

"I got the money together just to keep Joanne in the dark. I had no plans to leave the money anywhere; after all, I had the tapes all along. I planned to leave the money in the elevator and have one of my associates pick it up. I would then tell Joanne that they took the money but did not return the tapes."

"So what happened?"

He laughed, a sick painful laugh. "I delivered the cash in a large case. The same type as Trendle's sample case. My man was supposed to pick up the case, but when he got into the elevator, Trendle was there and there were two cases on the ground. My man picked up the wrong one."

He stopped talking and coughed again. I could tell he could hardly breathe, that each word was painful to him. But he knew he was dying and wanted to tell it all.

"After my man realized that he had the wrong case, he located Trendle and tried to get the case back again. Only Trendle resisted and my man killed him. My man panicked and ran out without the case, anyway."

"Why did you kill Mrs. Trendle?"

"We were worried that Trendle called his wife in the few minutes he was out of sight. There were papers in the case, along with the money, that might have identified me. We killed the woman, and then told Joanne to go to her house and look for the tape. We were hoping she would have been caught by the police and arrested for the murder."

"Why did you kill Peterson, after all? And what does this

guy Cartmonde have to do with anything?"

"Peterson was getting suspicious of me and Cartmonde. We fixed Peterson and Cartmonde up about a year ago so we had someone on the inside. Cartmonde kept tabs on Peterson, and he had access to all of Peterson's papers in the house. But Peterson was starting to suspect something was going on, and we figured it was time to get rid of him."

"So why did you get me involved? Why have me look for the tapes when you had them all along?"

"You were just to be a diversion, proof to Joanne that I had no idea where the tapes were. We figured a loser like you would just spin his wheels, going after Peterson and taking the pressure off of me."

Chapter 24

It took weeks to clean this case up. Bennite was mad as hell and threatened to take my license for withholding evidence, interfering with a police investigation, and breaking a few other laws he dug up for the occasion, but the two Feds saved my skin. I called them in after Green died. They met us at the house and I told them the whole story. They weren't interested in Philly Mutual, just the phone operation and Stan's access into bank records, so they took credit for breaking the whole case.

With information from Stan, Bennite was able to find Cartmonde, and they rounded up a few other of Green's accomplices, so he got a share of the credit.

We found the tapes in Green's office and returned them to the Philadelphia Mutual board. One of the other executives was named interim president until the board decided what to do, but I was given a nice reward for my efforts. It wasn't a quarter million, but enough to furnish my apartment.

Lydia recuperated quickly, cared for by a great aunt, on her father's side, who flew in from Korea. She was an old woman who loved her young charge, and she told Lydia stories about the old days. About a week later I went to Lydia's place. Her arm was still in a cast but she looked healthy and happy.

"Thank you, Mr. London," she said as she kissed me.

"Thank me for what?"

"For taking care of everything, and for saving the company from men like Green."

We talked about other things, plans that Heather and I had made. Then I asked her about her own plans.

"Well, I certainly don't have to worry about money," she said. "My share of the company will see to that. So I am going home to Korea."

There was one last thing I had to do before closing these cases, find Robert. Heather had received even more information about Nellie Watson and she was convinced Robert was in Freeport. Kim's doctor put his arm in a cast and taped me up a little. "A temporary patch," he said. Actually, the worst part was the poison ivy around my nose from those goddamn leaves. Fred drove me up to Freeport, Long Island, to look around. Sure enough, a gas station stood at the site of the old 300 Club but we found Sliding Billy's old house on Elm Street. Two young women were sharing the house and had gone to great expense restoring it. They already knew that the house once belonged to Sliding Billy and his wife. They said a college student had stopped by a week ago while he was doing research for a paper. He stayed a few days, looked around, and then left.

So we drove out to see Heather's mom, Jean. She knew who I was the minute she opened the door; it seems her daughter talked a lot about me over the phone. Jean couldn't have been happier since Robert had come home the day before.

"I've been trying to reach Heather but she doesn't answer the phone," she explained.

Well, Robert was safe, and that was important, I suppose. But I needed something else. I took Robert out for little walk, got some closing details about Stan and the 51st Street operation. He told me that he didn't find anything in Freeport and just got bored with the idea of buried treasure.

"Why didn't you call your sister? She was worried to death about you. You just left your stuff and took off."

"Hey, I wanted to, really. But after what went down with Stan and all, I was just scared."

"Too scared just to give her a call?"

"It was just a few days, that's all."

Kids. I belted him good. Jean later told me his swelling went away in a few days.

For some time, both Heather and I were in bandages. She called it our bondage period. Then late one hot August night, when all of our limbs were free from plaster and gauze, we were sitting on her balcony watching the stars. We were sitting on a webbed lounge chair; I sat against the back of the chair, she was in my arms, between my legs. Her hair was smooth and silky, smelling slightly of almonds, and she was wearing jeans and a blue off-the-shoulder top that felt soft and fluffy against my bare arms. With all the talking we'd done, we never talked about us. About the commitment that she was so willing to give but never asked for in return.

I whispered, "I love you" in her ear and held her tighter. She squirmed a little and said, "I love you" in return. I kissed her head, her neck, then caressed her bare smooth shoulders with my lips. She moaned and pressed her body more against mine.

"Reynold, I love you. I need you," she said.

I caressed her arms, making long slow strokes up and down against her skin. She purred, took my hand in hers and held it against her lips. I lightly touched her shoulder with the fingertips of my other hand, barely touching her skin, so the sensation of contact built a feeling of suspense and anticipation, prolonging the pleasure.

I slid my fingertips over her shoulder, then down beneath her top and onto the round soft skin of her breasts. My fingers made slow circles around her contour, moving closer with each pass toward her nipple.

She turned around and kissed me, then stood up, bringing me off the chair with her.

The sky was dark except for the stars, it was quiet and the air was still. We couldn't hear the sound of cars on the streets below, just the rustling of our clothes as they fell to the ground. She was beautiful naked. Long slender legs, small waist, her hair like a halo around her smiling face.

Hints of sweat glistened on her skin, the salt tingling my tongue as I wiped it from her breasts. I stroked her gently as I ran my lips over her body, as her hands found their way between my legs, feeling me as I grew in excitement, as our pleasure increased.

"Heather, I love you. I want you. But if you're not ready, I can wait," I told her.

"I don't want to wait any longer," she said. "I saw a doctor in the hospital. He gave me pills. Now give me you."

We walked into her bedroom and laid down side by side so almost our whole bodies touched. The dampness on our skins only heightened the pleasure as I let my hand travel down her body, over her shoulder, down the valley of her waist, around the sensual skin of her hip, onto her thigh.

This time she didn't shudder when my fingers found the wetness between her legs, when they explored slowly and carefully into her center. Instead, she held onto me, slowly, tenderly stroking me, her fingers tightening slightly with each cycle.

The pleasure was intoxicating and addicting. I found myself losing control, circling the inside of her with my fingers, further and further.

Then she removed her hand and pulled slightly away.

"I'm sorry Heather. Am I rushing you?"

"Stop saying that," she whispered.

She rolled me over on my back, and straddled me with her legs. She grabbed my wet member with both hands, and sat down, moaning as she did, until I was buried deep inside of her.

Coming Soon
to Bookstores Near You!

TYPE A

A Brooke Castle Adventure

From TYPE A
A Brooke Castle Adventure

I started driving to work and something stuck me in the rear end. Something hard and sharp. I pulled over and felt around but couldn't feel anything. I drove another block, was stuck again right between the cheeks and pulled over.

This time I felt it. I must have pulled off the price tag in my new panties but not the plastic thing that holds it. You know want I mean --- a piece of plastic with two things on the end so you have to cut it to get it out. I forgot to cut it.

Now there was no way I could work all day with this thing sticking me in the behind. I didn't want to yank it out and ruin new $2.99 panties, so I tried to wiggle it back and forth hoping it would break. That's not easy to do when it's behind your back, down your butt, and you're sitting in the car with a steering wheel in your chest.

I slid over to the passenger seat and looked in the glove compartment for a knife or scissors, but couldn't find anything. So I wrote "put scissors in glove compartment" on my list, and went back to bending the thing back and forth.

I was having no luck at all, and then I heard a knock on the window. Here I was sitting in the passenger seat, parked on Ventnor Avenue with my hand down my panties, and Officer Walker was looking in the window.

"Is everything okay, Brooke?" Now he's on a first name basis.

"Everything's fine. It's just a tag I can't get out."

He flashed a great smile and looked at my hand down my pants.

"New panties. Plastic tag. You know how it is," I said. Did that sound as stupid as I thought it did?

"Yeah, I know," he laughed. "Sure you're okay?"

"I'm fine. Thanks."

"Nice earrings, by the way."

He started to walk away and I realized I wasn't okay. I was getting late for work and I knew the thing would drive me crazy until I got there, so I beeped the horn a few times to get his attention.

"What can I do for you?" he said.

"Can I speak to your partner, the policewoman?"

"She's not my partner. She was just riding with me for training the other night."

"Whatever. Can I speak with her?"

"Sure. But she's not on duty today. You can call her at the station tomorrow."

"That's okay. Thanks anyway."

"Okay."

Now I was desperate. So I beeped the horn once more to get him back to the car.

"Brooke?"

"Do you have a scissors?"

"I have a small one on my Swiss Army knife. Why?"

"Listen, this may seem a little strange, but I desperately need you to cut something for me."

"Let me see," and he opened the door and sat in the driver's seat -- my clean seat, without any paper or seat cushion! I wasn't really prepared for that, now I'd have to clean the whole thing.

"I can't get this tag out of my pants and it's driving me crazy. Could you cut it off?"

"You want me to cut the tag out of the panties?"

"That's right. One snip, and no looking further than you have to."

"Okay with me."

I thought about it.

"Here's the plan. First, you clean your hands and the scissors with that spray stuff I have in the back seat. Then you get the scissors ready. I'll pull the tag up as far as I can and then you cut it in half. But do not cut the panties. They're brand new, from Wal-Mart." He didn't have to know that last part.

Officer Walker sprayed his hands and this tiny little scissors that folded out from a pocketknife.

"That's the scissors you have? What kind of scissors is that?"

"It's the only kind I happen to have."

"It's so small."

"It's always worked before."

"You'll have to be practically down my pants to cut anything."

"I thought that was the general idea. Anyway, it's the sharpness not the size that counts."

"I bet you say that to all of the girls."

"Listen, do you want it cut or not?"

Not much on foreplay, is he?

I pulled the top of the panties out and up as far as I could, and tucked the back of my scrubs as far down over my ass as I could. No sense tempting the poor man, yet anyway.

"Okay. Now!"

He wasn't as quick as he could have been. He reached over and tried to cut the plastic.

"Hold still, Brooke. You keep moving."

"I'm trying to hold still. Do you think it's easy doing this?"

"You're moving it."

"Your thing is just too little."

"My thing is fine."

He tried again, and then finally, "Listen, this is the only way I can do this."

He slid one hand down my back and grabbed my hand holding the tag. Then he bent over so his nose was almost in my panties and snipped off the tag.

"All done."

"Great. I hope it was as good for you as it was for me. And you can move your hands now."

"Do you want me to pick out the two pieces of the tag?"

"That's alright. I can do that. I really appreciate your help."

"Anytime. Now drive carefully."

"Thanks. And by the way, I think now that you had your nose and hands down my panties, I should know your first name."

"Luke."

"As in Cool Hand Luke?"

"Except I can promise you, my hands are always warm."

It took me about 15 minutes to calm down, cool off, and find the pieces of the tag after he left. Can't blame that hot spell on estrogen, though. Then I started laughing hysterically. Luke Walker must have gotten a lot of grief after Star Wars came out.